DAC CROSSLEY

Escape from the Alamo

ISBN: 1-4538-3631-4
ISBN-13: 9781453836316

ACKNOWLEDGEMENTS

When I was a small child of six years, my mother introduced me to the Alamo. Mom held my hand while she pushed open the huge wooden door. There, inside the gloom, she told me the story of the Alamo battle. The line in the sand, the death of Travis and Bowie, and the triumph of Santa Anna, who then lost it all at San Jacinto. Mother was a historian, and more importantly, a teller of tales. This one's for you, Mom. I Remember the Alamo!

I beg the indulgence of my fellow Texans for the liberties I've taken with some of our heroes and the sequence of events in the years of the Republic of Texas. It is, after all, only a work of fiction.

I'm eternally grateful to my writer friends—Paige, Pat, Jim and Genie—who kept the momentum going when it lagged. The ever-patient Lizz Bernstein remedied my grammar and syntax. The remaining flaws are mine.

Chapter 1

Davy Crockett yanked open the heavy door and peered into the dark chapel. He waited until his eyes adjusted to the murky interior before slipping inside. Stars were visible overhead; the chapel's roof had fallen in long ago. A sputtering torch added its smoky traces to the faded adobe blocks. He stepped cautiously, feeling his way along the wall. The munitions were stored in here someplace. He wouldn't want to stumble into them in the dark. Outside the chapel, bonfires kept the darkness at bay. Inside, away from the tensions and fears tormenting the troops of the Texians, he hoped to catch a few moments of sleep before dawn, before the battle that was sure to follow.

He settled down on a wooden shipping crate and carefully propped his long rifle against the adobe wall. "There, now, Betsy, rest yourself until first light. You'll have a chance to speak then, for sure. 'Course, you may need to learn Spanish." With a soft chuckle, he stroked the time-worn wooden stock, then rubbed his hand up and down along the pitted barrel. "We've seen many a shoot, Betsy. Likely this one will be a rough one. We got ourselves into a pickle this time."

He leaned his head back against the wall and closed his eyes, letting out a soft, throaty sigh. What was I thinking? he asked himself. Davy, you dang fool, you had to come down here to this ugly little town, bringing along a bunch of Tennessee dirty-shirts. You could be back up on the Brazos or at San Felipe, palavering with old Sam Houston. Hell, you could be helping out with the Texian Congress, speechifying and maybe dancing a reel or two. Not squatting in this pisshole with this bunch of fools.

He jerked fully alert when a loud moan broke the silence. The wail rose higher, then tapered off, and then faded away. Poor Bowie, Davy thought, settling himself back again. Old Jim must be outa his mind with that fever by now. No more knife waving for him, not for a while. At least he wasn't arguing with Billy Boy Travis about splitting the command. I shoulda skedaddled when those two roosters started pecking at each other, he chided himself. That was trouble in the making right there. 'Course, once Bowie got sick, Travis took over everything. It's his shindig now.

His ruminations came to a halt when the big door creaked open part way and a slim form slipped inside, moccasins soundless on the stone floor.

"Davy? Colonel Crockett?" The whisper drifted through the darkness.

"Over here, Possum." Davy recognized the rail-thin shadow, the hesitant movement of his young admirer, George Hanks, whom he'd nicknamed Possum.

The slender figure materialized out of the darkness, stopping abruptly when another loud wail pierced the stillness.

"That's Colonel Bowie. Sit yourself down, Possum."

Possum squatted on his heels beside his Tennessee idol. Both hands clutched his long rifle as he leaned forward slightly, using his weapon as a prop.

"He's purty sick, ain't he?" said Possum.

"Sick enough."

Possum stirred uneasily and squinted at Davy out of the corners of his eyes.

"How we gonna handle this?"

Davy knew exactly what he meant. "I reckon we got ourselves into a little do-si-do here, come dawn. We Tennesseans gotta defend the long barracks. Gonna be quite a shooting party."

Possum sat quietly for a moment, then shifted again so that he was facing Davy.

"Look here, Colonel. I heard some of the boys talking, saying mebbe it's time for us to skedaddle. Pull back a bit."

"I fear that time is long past." Davy bit his lip.

"You seen all those Mexicans out there? Thousands of soldiers. And those damn trumpets blaring all night. They're gonna attack us, ain't they?"

"I reckon. I don't know if that racket is supposed to scare us or work up them Mexican soldiers into a fighting rage."

"We could slip the wall before it gets light. Just injun our way right through them Mexicans. That's what the boys is saying. One of the old injun fighters told me he done it before. We could slip away, couldn't we?" Possum shifted his feet uneasily.

Davy thought for a moment. "I guess we could. Anybody who wants to light out, go ahead. I wouldn't blame nobody. We had our chance when Colonel Travis drew that line with his sword, asking us to step across if we'd stay with him. All of us stepped over. Colonel Bowie had to be carried across, remember?"

"Shit, everybody watching, we had to cross over, didn't we?"

"Guess so."

Possum lapsed into silence. A pre-dawn stillness filled the chapel. For the moment, Bowie was quiet. Somewhere in the darkness, a cricket began to chirp.

"Look, Davy. We ain't really soldiers, are we? Most of the boys is injun fighters, that's all. I ain't no soldier myself, not at all. My Pap fought in the Creek Wars like you done. I was too young for fighting. I'm just a woodsman, you know? A hunter, like. Besides, Colonel Travis ain't following orders, is he? We heard he's supposed to pull stakes hisself? Ain't that right?"

Davy sighed. "No, he didn't follow orders. General Sam, he wrote to Travis, told him he oughta blow up the Alamo and fall back to the Guadalupe River."

"Well, how come he didn't?"

Davy struggled to stand erect, leaning on the long rifle to pull himself to his feet. "Reckon he hoped somebody would come and help us. Or maybe Santa Anna would just pass us by. Travis and Colonel Bowie couldn't decide on who was in command here." He sighed again. "I guess the situation just drifted along 'til it got outa hand. William Barrett Travis was mostly worried about his honor and his reputation. For a South Carolina lawyer, he's come a long way."

Possum gained his feet and rested his hand on his friend's shoulder.

"Colonel? Are we gonna get out of this fracas with a whole skin? Alive?"

Crockett laughed, made a fist and tapped Possum on the cheek. "Why sure, old son, we're gonna be fine. That Mexican army is mostly conscripts. Likely they'll bolt when we start slinging lead. We're forted up here pretty good. Watch, I'll bet they make one attack and then decide to pass us by. The worst that could happen—well, if we get caught, we might spend a few months down in Mexico, courtesy of Santa Anna. Now, you know, he'd dearly love to capture Davy Crockett. Be a real feather in his cap. We'd summer in Old Mexico. That wouldn't be so bad, would it?"

The chapel door burst open.

"Colonel Crockett!" The boy's voice crackled with excitement. "Colonel Travis wants you. The Mexican army is getting ready to attack!"

"C'mon, Betsy." With his long rifle cradled in his arm, Davy led his friend out into the morning light, then stopped and looked back at the chapel. The first blush of dawn peeked through the arched facade atop the structure. The white adobe blocks seemed to glow in an unnatural light. The Alamo, he thought. I'll remember this place.

He reached out and grasped the boy's shoulder, spinning him around. "Son, what day is this?"

"It's Tuesday, sir."

"No, no, what *day* is it?"

The boy screwed up his face, pondering. "I think it's March 6, sir. In the year of our Lord 1836."

"Mark it down, Possum," said Davy Crockett. "Mark it down."

PART ONE

Chapter 2

He was splashing along behind Davy Crockett, wading up a shallow creek, slipping on the rocks and laughing. Suddenly, Davy tripped and fell face down in the stream. Possum giggled out loud and woke himself up. One eye popped open. He tried to focus on his surroundings. The dream dissolved into a white mist as his mind cleared. Still laughing softly, thinking of Davy, he blinked his eyes and tried to focus them. Green, a green thatch filled his field of vision, green stalks and brown stems. Right there in front of him, blocking his vision, sat an enormous bug. When it twitched its legs he concentrated on it. A large grasshopper, a giant one, biggest he had ever seen, seemed to be watching him.

Grains of sand coated the tip of Possum's tongue; he tried to spit them away, but his mouth was too parched. He smacked his lips and licked them, trying to clear away the sand. Only one of his eyes seemed to be working. The other was pressed against the dirt.

He realized where he was. Lying flat on his stomach in a meadow, his head turned to one side. The stems of grass pressing against his cheek smelled fresh, a meadow in the morning, like Tennessee. And it wasn't a giant grasshopper, after all. He was seeing eye to eye with a little bitty grasshopper, a baby one, so close it almost touched his face. Possum laughed out loud. That's why it seemed so large; it was right in front of him. As he studied it, the grasshopper stepped forward and crawled onto his nose. He pursed his lips and blew a breath towards the little bug. It waved its long antennae, testing the wind, and suddenly vanished from sight, leaping away from him, leaving an itch on his nose.

What am I doing here? Possum couldn't remember where he was. He frowned, searching his memory. How'd I get here? Where's Davy? Possum put his palms flat on the grassy sod and started to raise his body. A wave of pain washed over him, a searing stab in his abdomen. With a groan, he collapsed back to the ground. None of this made any sense. He sought images from his memory. What had happened? The memories would not come. Nashville? Was he in Nashville? With Davy? No, that's not right. Not Nashville. Where was he?

Possum blinked again. Now, a large brown lump appeared right in front of his face. He squinted and concentrated on it and realized it was a huge brown moccasin, covering a giant-sized foot.

"You hurt, son?" The gruff voice was flat, the question matter of fact.

"I don't know," Possum mumbled, twisting his head to stare upwards at a big man. He licked his lips free of grit and tried again. "I guess I am. What happened?"

"Well, let's check you over." The big man dropped on one knee and rolled Possum over. Possum gritted his teeth to suppress a cry; his left side stabbed with pain. Possum grabbed his waist, pressing his hand against the wound.

Wound? What wound? He couldn't remember being wounded. He found himself in the grip of a giant bear covered in buckskins and sporting a grizzly beard. With one arm stuck under Possum's shoulders, the giant was probing him gently.

"Son, you got an old wound here. Looks like you mighta aggravated it a little. Don't see much fresh blood, but it's seeping a bit. Whatcha doing lying here on the ground?"

"I don't remember." Possum brushed the big man's probing fingers away.

"What do they call you, son?"

"Possum," he said through gritted teeth.

"I'm Wallace. Let's get your legs under you." The huge man grasped Possum under the arms and stood him erect. Possum shifted his weight, one foot to the other, steadying himself against the pain pinching his left side. He took a deep breath, trying to keep from doubling over. When he straightened himself up he only reached the big man's chin.

"Wallace?" asked Poss.

"That's me, Big Foot Wallace, scout extra-ordinaire. What's your story, son?"

Possum shook his head, eyes down, confused. His legs started to buckle. He grabbed Wallace's belt to steady himself.

Wallace snapped his fingers and pointed towards a large black horse cropping grass nearby. "Say, ain't that Colonel Lamar's bad horse? The Arkansas Devil? Was you trying to ride that sonofabitch?"

"Ooh!" Possum exclaimed. "Yes, I was. I wanted to go with Sam Houston to fight Santa Anna. Wanted to fight the damn Mexicans. I couldn't march because it hurt too much. The colonel told me to take his horse. It wouldn't do nothing right, just circled and bucked. I guess I got throwed."

"I guess you did," chortled Wallace. "Son, you are lucky to be alive. Lamar must not like you very much." He carefully released Possum and nodded when he was able to stand by himself.

"I just kinda insisted. I just wanted to go with Houston's army, to fight Mexicans."

Big Foot Wallace turned his head and spit a brown stream of tobacco juice. "Army? Hell, son, it ain't no army. It's a goddamn mob old Sam tried to train. Sam wanted to herd 'em over closer to Loosiana. See, he wanted to get more Americans involved, mebbe get the Unitey States to come to his aid. But the boys was itching to fight." He spat again. "Couldn't hold 'em any longer, what with Lamar on his big white horse, parading back and forth, waving his sword. Old Sam just made a speech and turned 'em loose."

"What about the Mexicans?" Possum shaded his eyes, trying to see across the meadow. He could see people gathered in a grove of live oak trees. "The Mexican army? They still fighting us?" He glanced around at the ground, seeking his weapon. Abruptly his legs gave out. Wallace grabbed him by the shoulders again and steadied him.

"You done missed it." Wallace laughed and wiped his mouth on his sleeve. "Them Texas boys stormed across the prairie and just flat ran those Mexican soldiers outa their pants and coats. Shouting the whole time. 'Remember the Alamo! Remember Goliad!' Couldn't stop 'em."

"Remember the Alamo?" A thought stirred in Possum's mind. Images tried to coalesce, lingering fragments of memory, but they eluded him. "Did the Mexicans surrender?" he asked.

"Most of 'em never got a chance! Houston couldn't hold the boys. He took a bullet hisself. I guess them boys are still killing ever Mexican they can catch. Old Sam yelling his head off—'Take prisoners' is what he shouted."

"General Houston shot? Is he gonna be all right?"

"He got a right bad leg wound. Mebbe a cannonball took him down, I don't know. General Sam did hisself proud. Two horses was shot right out from under him. Come on, let's go find him. He done sent me out here looking for wounded Texians. Weren't many of you boys got hurt. C'mon, I need to report."

Wallace put a big arm around Possum's shoulders and guided him slowly across the fields. "C'mon, son, you can make it." Possum found he could keep his legs moving, although the wound freshened with every step. Wound? What wound? Bayonet wound? Why did he have a bayonet wound? He shook his head, confused.

Sudden dizziness overwhelmed him. He faltered, panting, clutching his side and swaying on his feet. Wallace grabbed him and held him steady. Possum looked up at Wallace's face and noticed him chewing on his lower lip.

"Were you in the fight yourself? You get hurt?"

"Naw, I ain't hurt none. Didn't get into much scrapping, myself. See, I been trailing behind Santy Anna's army. Me and Deaf Smith. Both of us been burning down the bridges across the rivers. Sam wanted Santy Anna's army trapped, away from General Filosola and them other Mexican armies. Guess old Sam got what he wanted, didn't he? We burned the bridge over Vince's Bayou. Trouble is, son, I ain't seen Deaf Smith since then. That old buzzard is Sam Houston's favorite scout, and he ain't got the sense God gave a horny toad." Wallace sighed deeply. "I was hoping to find him back here. Well, let's make tracks."

A wave of nausea washed over Possum. His legs twisted and he slumped towards the ground. He could feel sweat breaking out on his body. He was dizzy, his head whirling.

Wallace grabbed him again. "Whoa there, son. Lemme carry you."

Possum pushed Wallace's arms away. "No, no," he gasped. "Just let me be for a minute." He dropped into a sitting position on the meadow, both arms clasped across his abdomen, legs folded under himself.

Wallace squatted on his heels, staring into Possum's face. "Stay here," he muttered. He glanced over his shoulder at the grove of live oak trees. "The army's gathered over there. I'll try to find a stretcher. The boys can carry you to camp."

"Just leave me be for a little while. Mebbe you oughta go look for your partner. Likely he needs you." Possum took a deep breath. "I can make it to the camp on my own. You go on, now."

Wallace stood erect and scanned the horizon. "Goddamn Smith. Mebbe he's found his way back to them oak trees. Houston's laid up there. I'll take a look-see and then come back."

Possum raised his head and watched Wallace's huge back retreat towards the trees. The pain was easing, now that he was sitting quietly, holding himself still. He tried to organize his thoughts, reaching back for memories. How did he get here?

The Mexicans. A memory surfaced, an image sprang into his mind; an old adobe structure. Possum gasped. The Alamo! His skin crawled. He remembered it now. He squeezed his eyes shut and concentrated. He was back, immersed in the battle. He felt the cold wind blowing in his face, the sun at his back. He smelled the acrid stench of gun smoke mixed with burning wood. He hugged himself and gasped. He remembered the frantic Mexican soldiers, screaming, forced back by the Texians' gunfire time and again. Yes, that's right; he'd dropped a flintlock rifle too hot to hold, and another one was handed to him. He fired that rifle and another, but the Mexicans still came at him, surging through the gun smoke, climbing over the bodies of dead and wounded. He was crouched at the end of the long barracks, next to the Alamo chapel. That's right. The memories surged to the surface of his mind. His fingers twitched as he recalled firing, loading, firing, loading, bodies falling, but still they came. Right over the wall in front of him they surged, a shrieking press of bodies, forcing him back, smothering him.

Possum yelled, a wavering cry, and opened his eyes. He looked about himself, taking in the meadow in the afternoon sunlight. The memories evaporated. Nothing more came to him, no more recollections, no matter how hard he concentrated. Was it a dream, then? Was it real? Where the hell was Davy Crockett, if it was just a dream?

Possum looked towards the Texian camp. Shadows were getting long; over his shoulder the sun settled among the live oaks. The yellow-orange orb suddenly brought forth another memory. He twisted around and stared into the sun, pulling at the dreamlike image.

A campfire. He remembered looking across a campfire, where Mrs. Dickinson's white face, brushed by the firelight, loomed out of the darkness. Lieutenant Dickinson's wife, she was. That's right; she had been there in the Alamo, he was sure. Did she get away? She must have. The image of her dark hair and those flashing black eyes, reflecting the firelight, rose to his mind. She was speaking urgently, looking from face to face around the swirling flames. Her voice came back to him.

"Remember! There were no surrenders," she hissed. "None! All fought to the death. Everybody. They are all heroes. All of them." She had slowly scanned the group huddled around the fire, settling finally on Possum. "You, young man. I don't know who you are. I don't know how you got here. But if you were in the Alamo, you died there. Remember that, sir. Remember it."

Possum squeezed his eyes shut, concentrating on that memory, trying to bring it back, like recalling a fragment of a dream. He saw Mrs. Dickinson's eyes, searching him out, gleaming in the firelight, boring into him. What did she mean, he had died there? Then the woman's face was replaced by Joe's black shiny face, visible where it reflected firelight. Joe—Travis's slave, wasn't he?—was tending the small fire, watching him. Was Travis there, too? No, Possum said to himself. Travis was killed. Shot through the forehead. How did he know that? He recalled Mrs. Dickinson's daughter, little Angelina, her white dress dirty, clinging to her mother near the flames, shrinking away from Joe.

Possum opened his eyes and concentrated on the setting sun. The memory of the campfire vanished.

A shout erupted from the live oak grove, followed by a prolonged set of cheers and whoops. What was happening over there? Possum got a knee under himself, then a leg, and managed to rise. He staggered a few steps toward the trees before his consciousness dissolved into a gray field of sparkles. He felt someone grasp his arm, just as a cloud of darkness descended over him.

Chapter 3

Possum's eyes flew open, startling him out of a dreamless sleep. His head pounded a steady beat. Nausea built in his throat; he fought it back with a cough. Lying on the bare ground, flat on his back, he gazed straight up through the arms of a big oak tree, its branches outlined against the dusk of the evening sky. He turned toward his right and saw another man stretched out on the ground next to him, not moving, a Negro.

Possum eased his body into a sitting position. Could that be Joe, Travis's slave? No, he decided, that's wrong. It wasn't a Negro after all. It was a swarthy man, his eyes closed, a bloody bandage covering his chest. Possum's side throbbed; he held it close and lay back down.

Joe, black Joe, more servant than slave. Something about Joe's gentle hands...Holding his side, Possum concentrated on Joe's image, forcing memories to surface in his mind. He closed his eyes, sifting through images that erupted, jumbled memories. Yes, he had it now. He recalled Joe's strong hands holding him ever so carefully, helping him to sit on the back of Mrs. Dickinson's carriage as it jolted along a rutted road, each bump sending waves of pain through his body. Joe leaning towards him, whispering urgently. Relating how he'd rescued Possum while the boy was unconscious, knocked senseless and stabbed with a bayonet.

Bayonet? Cautiously, Possum caressed the left side of his stomach, grimacing at the tenderness. Bayonet wound? Yes, that's what it is. He'd caught a bayonet.

Joe's soft murmur had spoken to him of the last moments at the Alamo. Mexicans killing everyone except women, jabbing with their bayonets, over and over. Joe had watched it all, and he shared with Possum what he'd witnessed, relieved to share his distress, to have someone to tell about the slaughter. He remembered Joe holding him, tears slipping down his ebony face, the two of them side by side on the back of Susanna Dickinson's carriage as she urged it into the night.

Possum forced himself to remember what he'd endured himself during the battle. The press of the shouting Mexicans, so many of them. Somebody behind him, passing him a loaded musket, its barrel already hot. Was it Davy Crockett behind him, yelling to him? Davy shouting words of encouragement, ringing out over the clamor?

It was all coming back now, clear in his mind, memories popping to the surface, over and over. Possum shuddered, his eyes squeezed shut, images competing for position in his consciousness.

He saw Joe hunkered down beside a campfire, speaking softly with Mrs. Dickinson. How quickly the Alamo fell, they'd agreed. Poor Travis killed right off, drilled through the forehead after firing his double-barreled shotgun. The Mexican soldiers out of control, swarming into the compound, screeching their fury, jabbing bayonets into the living and dead. Lieutenant Dickinson struck down at last, soon after he'd said goodbye to his wife. The Mexican soldiers' blood ran hot; they stabbed and stabbed and stabbed again, raging, killing over and over.

Possum concentrated on Joe's image. Using it for guidance, he tried to recall the rest of Joe's story, all the details, how the battle for the Alamo ended. Davy Crockett surrendered, Joe said, along with the few others who'd lived through the Mexican assault. Santa Anna lined them all up and had them shot, executed. Joe had seen it all, every bit of it. Santa Anna singled him out and demanded that he identify the Texian leaders. Joe took the Mexican general to view the remains of Jim Bowie, still in his blood-stained cot, shot and bayoneted repeatedly. The body of Travis, placed in one of the chapel rooms, covered with a serape, looking peaceful in death.

Santa Anna assigned Joe to assist Mrs. Dickinson, to help her carry a message to General Sam Houston. Submit or meet the same fate, Santa Anna ordered. The woman and her daughter were placed on an open carriage, handed food and blankets. Stern-faced and proud, she drove her carriage away from the Alamo, east towards Gonzales Village. Joe had managed to lift Possum, unconscious, onto the back of the carriage and conceal him under a robe. That's what Joe told him.

The memories overwhelmed him. A wave of grief swept over Possum, racking his shoulders, a weight pressing down on his chest. He struggled to sit up, then wrapped his arms about himself. He rocked back and forth, moaning Davy's name to himself. Was Davy really gone, murdered? And all of his Tennessee comrades butchered, along with the other Texians. That's what Joe said. Where was Joe now?

In Possum's mind, Joe's face was dislodged by Susanna Dickinson's visage, ruddy in the firelight, distorted by anger, blossoming large, threatening him. Was he to be forever haunted by her specter? That contorted face, scowling at him, anger streaming from all her pores? Again she spoke to him, leaning across the campfire, once more hissing her demands, insisting that he listen. All fought to the death, she told him over and over. All the men were heroes. Every single one of them had died fighting.

Possum was beginning to grasp what it was that Susanna Dickinson wanted him to understand. He could never reveal to anyone that he had escaped the massacre at the Alamo. No one must ever know. He had heard it told over and over again, from the soldiers in the Texian army, how the brave defenders of the Alamo fought to the last man, refusing to surrender to the army of Santa Anna. How they sacrificed themselves to gain freedom for Texas, freedom from the oppression of Mexico. Possum's escape gave the lie to that bold gesture.

What should he do? He couldn't go back to Tennessee; they would surely know of the Alamo battle by now. Where in the world could he go? What should he do? It was a secret that threatened to ruin him. Was there no escape?

Possum stared into the distance, taking in the campfires springing to life, the Texians continually milling about. Had those rag-tag Texians actually defeated the Mexican army, those hordes of vicious soldiers who attacked the Alamo? Was this the end of the war, here at San Jacinto? Was Santa Anna conquered? Big Foot Wallace had said so. Was it true?

Possum slumped back against the oak tree. He wiped his face with his hands, now mindless of the pain in his side. Why was he in this place? How did he manage to get here, to San Jacinto? He couldn't remember. Panic seized him; he attempted to rise to his feet. He was too weak; he fell back against the oak tree, shuddering.

"Easy there." Possum turned towards the voice. He recognized General Sam Houston himself, leaning beside him against the same oak tree. Houston's left foot was swathed in bandages and stretched out in front of him.

"Feeling better, soldier? Wound not too bad? Hungry? Here, have an ear of corn. This is what we'll be doing from now on—growing corn."

"San Jacinto corn," a man standing beside Possum said, grabbing for an ear. Other soldiers scrabbled for souvenir ears of corn, mementoes of Sam Houston and the battle of San Jacinto.

In the fading sunlight, Houston's face shone flour white, dripping with sweat. His wound must be a bad one, Possum realized. Was the General dying? Houston's officers were gathered close, watching him. One put his hand on Possum's shoulder, holding him back, away from Houston.

"Now boys, I'll be fine." Houston searched from face to face. "Where's Wallace? He must keep a close guard on Santa Anna."

"He's alive? Santy Anna is still alive?" asked Possum.

"Alive and kicking," laughed a tall officer, his face covered by a slouch hat, his hands on the butts of two pistols stuck in his belt. "Mebbe not for long."

"Now Lamar, you let him be," commanded Houston, rousing himself to point at the man. "I charge you—Santa Anna is the security of the Republic of Texas. Keep him alive. He must send messages to the other Mexican troops in Texas. He must order them to go back to Mexico. General Filosola's army must be notified of Santa Anna's official surrender. Urréa's soldiers must be notified, too. All those Mexican armies must return below the Rio Grande, and at once. Santa Anna is our guarantee that they will do so." Houston slumped back against the tree. "Big Foot? Where is that rascal? I want Wallace and his men to guard Santa Anna. They must protect him from my own army."

Possum looked up at Captain Lamar, the tall officer. "Sir? What day is today?"

"Why, soldier, it's the twenty-first of April." Lamar laughed loudly. "San Jacinto Day. We'll all celebrate this date. You can mark it down, old son."

Possum settled back and closed his eyes. That's what Davy had said about the Alamo. Mark it down.

Davy Crockett dead? No, Joe must be wrong. Davy can't be dead, he can't be. What had Davy said to Possum, there in the Alamo? Santa Anna would like to capture Crockett, take him back to Mexico. Yes, Davy must be alive, maybe a prisoner but still alive. Joe must be mistaken.

I'll go back to San Antonio, back to the Alamo, Possum decided. He nodded, accepting the idea. That's my best course. I'll find Davy, track him down in whatever prison holds him, even in Mexico. I'll find him. He'll know what we should do.

This renewed sense of purpose encouraged Possum. Unknowing, he'd made his way to this battlefield and had given himself over to the fight against the villainous General Santa Anna. That battle was over. Finding and freeing Davy Crockett, that was his new objective. He'd find his way back to San Antonio. Someone there must know something about Davy.

Holding tight to his wound, Possum slumped over and surrendered himself to the sleep of exhaustion, oblivious to the turmoil surrounding him.

Chapter 4

When Possum woke again, he found himself enveloped in darkness. Someone was crying out, sobbing in pain. Possum realized he'd been moved away from the oak tree; he'd been placed on a low cot. His probing fingers found the ground a few inches below him. He raised himself on his elbows and searched about, peering into the gloom. A few campfires burned low. He realized that he was still on the battlefield of San Jacinto. He saw the shapes of other men lying on cots near him, indistinct in the shadows, moaning in their sleep. Suddenly weak, he laid back down and stared into the murkiness, fighting his way in and out of a dream state, still wrestling with his memories of the Alamo battle, testing them, trying to put them in order. Disjointed images surfaced again, fighting men, yelling Texians and the ever-pressing Mexican troops. He let his mind drift, and for a moment the smell of the black gunpowder surged through his nostrils. The shouts of the Mexican soldiers rang in his ears. The feel of a long rifle, heavy in his hands, blistering hot, as he fired it into a mob of oncoming soldiers. He remembered being pushed back, the Mexican bodies surging against his.

He shivered with a sudden chill and tried to huddle under a thin blanket he found draped across his legs. Possum's body tensed, and his wounded side responded with a jolt of pain. He couldn't recall when he'd received that injury. Someone told him it was a wound from the triangular bayonet of a Brown Bess musket, the weapon the Mexican soldiers carried. He thought he remembered a surgeon changing his bandages. Possum shifted onto his right side. After a moment, the pain subsided.

The cot and the blanket covering him both smelled musty. Likely, these were spoils captured from the Mexican army. He realized that he was surrounded by other wounded soldiers, both Texians and Mexicans, judging from the prayers and curses he heard. The babble of moans, the whimpers, and especially those sudden cries of pain or fear, chased sleep away.

He tried to focus on his surroundings. The only illumination came from the low campfires and a distant bonfire, blazing near an improvised stockade. He could see groups of Mexican prisoners huddled inside that enclosure. Even the sentries were resting tonight, leaning on their long rifles, tired of taunting the prisoners. Both armies were exhausted, physically and emotionally, after the long day of recovery from the short battle. Only the wounded were stirring. What had Davy said? Misery don't take sides.

A pang in his abdomen informed him of the need to empty his bladder. Carefully, he elbowed himself to a sitting position and eased his legs over the edge of his cot. Cold air seeped down-slope towards the bayou, carrying with it a wisp of fog, little trails of moisture making their way through the encampment. With a shiver, Possum tugged the little blanket across his shoulders.

He could see the shape of a cot right beside his own, barely illuminated by the campfires. As his vision cleared, he realized that a man sat on it, silent and immobile, watching him. Possum squinted but could not recognize him. Well, no surprise there; he didn't know most of the soldiers in this motley army.

His bladder tugged at him again, and he struggled to gain his feet, only to settle back down once more. His legs trembled and his head whirled. But his bladder insisted. He gathered himself for another try.

"Here, *Señor*, use this, if you will."

Possum looked up to see his fellow sufferer from the nearby cot holding out a walking stick.

"Thankee," said Possum, his voice weak and gravelly. He forced himself onto his feet, using the stick for a brace. "Thankee kindly," he repeated, clearing his throat, his voice stronger now.

"*De nada*. For nothing." His companion slowly lay back on his cot.

Leaning on the walking stick, Possum groped his way to a tree a dozen or so feet away from the group of wounded soldiers. He managed to undo the pantaloons he was wearing and relieved himself against the tree trunk. How did I come into possession of these broadcloth trousers? he wondered. Were they part of a Mexican army uniform? And the loose shirt he had on, where did he get it? At the Alamo he wore his old buckskins, not tattered cotton garments like these.

When he maneuvered back to his cot, he was able to walk more steadily. He ran his hand along the shaft of the walking stick; it seemed to be ornately carved, but, in the darkness, he could make out no details. His fellow patient was sitting up again, and Possum returned the stick to him. The two men sat looking at each other through the gloom.

"Where you been hit?" Possum asked. "Catch a bad 'un?"

"I have been shot through the shoulder. As a wound it is not bad. The bullet passed through. I am alive, and that may be bad enough. Even though your General Houston is generous with his captives, as I have been told."

"You—you—" Possum struggled for words. He tried again to clear his throat.

"I am Joaquín Torreón, Captain of Lancers in the Army of the Republic of Mexico." The shadowy figure offered a slight bow, from his sitting position on his cot. "And you are?"

"You're a Mexican!"

"Obviously. As are most of the wounded you hear crying out their agonies. None of us knows his future here tonight."

"Lancers, huh?" A memory came back to Possum, a recollection of Joe the slave, hearing him talk about the Lancers, telling the story. "Lancers," Possum repeated. "When some of the boys broke out of the Alamo and run for it, afoot, you Lancers rode them down. Killed 'em all. Speared 'em. Huh!"

Possum gathered himself together, agitated now. Another memory asserted itself. The Texians running through the brush behind the Alamo chapel, this way and that, the horsemen pursuing them with those deadly lances. Had Possum seen it, not realizing what was happening? Or was it Joe, telling him the story? No, he had seen it for himself.

"I was not at the Alamo, my friend. You are mistaken." Torreón spoke softly, in flat tones.

"You're a liar." Possum's anger rose; he raised his voice, strong and loud. "You damn sure were at the Alamo. You and your men rode down them boys. They were afoot. They never had a chance. You speared 'em. I seen it all. God damn you!"

Torreón leaned forward and spoke in a soft but urgent tone. "Listen to me! That is all in the past. We had our day and now you have had yours." A match flared, revealing the captain's finely-chiseled features as he applied the flame to the end of a cigarillo. "Furthermore," he continued, exhaling smoke, "you may have things to explain yourself." He waited, glaring at Possum, his cigarillo now a red burning dot in the night. Possum's throat suddenly constricted; his breath came with difficulty. He stared, wide-eyed, at the Mexican. He'd let something slip.

"That is right, *Señor.* Think carefully. I have heard today, many times, how the Texian heroes at the Alamo fought to the last man. There were no surrenders. And no attempts to escape were made. All died fighting, so I have heard." Torreón drew deeply on his cigarillo, turned his head and blew a long puff of smoke away.

"So you see, my friend, the Lancers could not have run down any Texians fleeing from the Alamo. There were none to chase. And," he continued, "how would you know what happened. Were you there?"

"I heard about it," Possum said with a scowl. "And I ain't your friend," he added, now in a lower tone of voice.

"No," said Torreón. "I think it is you who do not speak the truth. My Lancers did their work well. And you did not hear it from them. No," he continued, leaning towards Possum, "I think you were a witness. I think you were at the Alamo battle and managed to escape. Are you a survivor of the battle of San Antonio? Do your fellow Texian soldiers know this?"

Possum leaned back on his cot, speechless.

"I thought not. Now, would you like a cigarillo? It will be morning soon."

Possum turned on his side, his back away from Torreón, hands clutching his wound. Susanna Dickinson's angry face erupted from his memory, frowning at him. The lancer captain was right; he could not accuse the man without revealing his own past. He had lost everything. His friends from Tennessee and Arkansas, and maybe even Davy Crockett. He was alone, with no outfit, no equipment, no weapons, not even his own clothes, in this strange place.

Who am I? What has brought me here? The thoughts raced through his brain, obscuring his memories, confusing him. The world suddenly seemed strange, dark and unfamiliar. He felt lost, alone, his identity seeping away from him. He had nothing. He had only his name to cling to. Possum, Possum he said to himself, concentrating on his name, silently reinforcing his sense of self. All else was lost, gone, as though it had never been.

He could not, would not, stay here. No, his duty was clear. He must rescue Davy Crockett from whatever prison he might be in. Or find him, wherever he might be hiding. Davy will know what to do.

I'll go back to the Alamo. I'll pick up Davy's trail. Marching with the Tennesseans, on the road to San Antonio, he'd trusted Davy to direct everything, to keep the little company moving in the right direction. Possum had helped break trail for the company, right through Arkansas, scouting ahead, always at Davy's orders. But could he find the way himself, alone?

Possum began thinking of plans, schemes to escape this encampment. He imagined himself slipping away in the night, finding a good horse—not that black devil!—and making for San Antonio. After he found Davy, maybe they could return to Tennessee, far away from this miserable Texas. Or find a new home for themselves, maybe in Arkansas. Or Florida. Pap had been to Florida with Andy Jackson to fight the Creek Indians. Pap hadn't liked Florida. Too many skeeters.

He huddled under his blanket, legs drawn up, facing away from Torreón and the firelight. His night vision had improved enough so that he could make out other images in the darkness. He became aware of another man perched on a cot a dozen feet away, watching him. A chill ran down Possum's spine. Had that man overheard his conversation with the Mexican captain?

The shadowy figure rose silently and slunk, stooped over, to kneel at Possum's side. A sudden flare-up from the campfire illuminated the man's face. Yellow teeth protruded past thin lips surrounded by a scraggly blond beard. A hint of foul breath caused Possum to flinch away. The man offered Possum an ingratiating smile and laid a hand on Possum's shoulder. "How do?" he whispered.

Possum shook off the hand. He twisted on the cot and turned over facing away from the stranger, facing Torreón. Possum saw that Torreón was awake and watching him, too. He closed his eyes and pretended to sleep.

Chapter 5

A twittering of birds dragged Possum out of a dreamless sleep. He swung his legs over the side of his low cot, cautiously protecting his wounded side with his forearm. Early morning sunlight splashed across the quiet meadow that only yesterday had been a battlefield. Possum stared, yawning, at the blend of wildflowers, yellow, pink, blue, and deep red blooms that studded the meadow. Had they been there yesterday? He glanced up into the branches of the big live oak tree sheltering him, now occupied by a quarreling cluster of blackbirds.

This peaceful daybreak sight took Possum back to Tennessee, to his father's farm in the springtime. The recently-turned earth in the fields, dew rising as the sun struck the sod. Pap urging Sally the mule into another dawdling pace, preparing the ground for corn seed. Pap, a silent, morose father, spoke more to Sally than to anyone else.

Pap wanted to grow only corn. He believed that the popular new cotton crops destroyed the soil. Corn found only a meager market, however, and families needed more to support them. A meat hunter, Pap supplied his family with deer, coon, squirrel, quail, whatever he could bring down. Possum happily assisted Pap with his hunting. As a teenage boy, Possum found hunting much more attractive than walking behind a mule. A wry smile crossed Possum's lips when he recalled slipping away from Pap and Sally the mule to follow a deer trail, an escape that had earned him a caning.

Betty Mae, Pap's new wife, grew vegetables in the garden that Mama used to keep, plants that added to their meals. Pap brought Betty Mae home from Lawrenceburg Town and told Possum she was his new mother. A plump girl in a shapeless dress, Betty Mae spoke very little, answering Pap's questions and never talking to Possum. He couldn't bring himself to call her "Mother." After the childbirth fever took Mama, he'd watched Pap bury his grief in the hard work of farming. Possum tried to help Pap raise baby sister, but she was always sickly and soon died, also. Pap may have found comfort in Betty Mae, but he frowned all the time and moved slowly, like an old man.

Would Pap be able to plant his corn this year, all by himself? Possum wondered if he should go back to Tennessee. But no, he couldn't do that; they would already know about the Alamo. They'd think he'd died there. How could he explain himself if he went back? I'll go back to Tennessee after I've rescued Davy, he decided. Davy Crockett will explain; he'll tell them how I come to be alive. Davy will make it right.

Possum had been right there on that day in the Lawrenceburg Town square when Davy Crockett conceded his failed attempt at reelection to Congress. "You can all go to hell," he shouted, "and I will go to Texas." Possum cheered loudly, along with the throng of well-wishers. Going to Texas! It was an adventure enormously attractive to a twenty-year-old farm boy. Possum collected his flintlock musket, borrowed a spavined horse from an unsuspecting neighbor, and trailed after his hero.

A hand shaking his shoulder jarred Possum out of his reverie. He stared out over the army camp; it was now broad daylight, and men were stirring, walking here and there, talking loudly and laughing.

"Let me look at that wound, soldier." The soft, slightly accented tones came from a slim man standing over him. "Let's see if we can get you on your feet. I'm Doctor Labadie. Let me help you pull off that shirt."

Possum raised his arms and the doctor slipped the cotton shirt over Possum's head, then off of his arms.

The doctor said, "I don't recall seeing you earlier."

Possum didn't recall seeing the funny-talking doctor, either. But then he didn't remember much from the past few weeks. "Where you hail from?" he asked with a wince from the doctor's attentions.

"Canada. I'm French Canadian. I came down here to help you Texians gain your independence. Your army needs doctors even more than soldiers."

Doctor Labadie cast aside the old bandages and leaned close to Possum's wound, sniffing at it. He pressed his fingers around the swollen flesh, taking note of the places that made Possum flinch. "I have seen such wounds," he said. "I believe a bayonet from a Brown Bess musket did this damage. Its triangular blade leaves a distinctive gash." The doctor frowned at Possum. "You didn't receive this wound on the San Jacinto battlefield. It is perhaps three or four weeks old."

Possum didn't try to explain. He shuffled his feet, waiting for the doctor to continue.

"Well, however you got it, the wound appears to be healing properly. Are you able to eat? Solid food?"

Possum nodded, shifting his feet again when Doctor Labadie's fingers probed another sore place. Yes, now that the doctor mentioned food, he did feel hungry. He licked his lips.

"How about defecation? Do you defecate normally, without pain?" He looked up at Possum's face and noted the blank stare. "That is, sir, can you shite?"

"Can he ever," came a shout from behind Possum. "I can smell him from here."

"That's good," said Doctor Labadie. "I'm going to bind up that wound as tightly as I can. I'll wrap this bandage all the way around your body. That should help you move with less pain."

"I guess bandages ain't gonna help them greasers too much." The same sneering voice came from behind Possum.

Turning around and around as the doctor wrapped him in a long bandage, he caught a glimpse of a man sitting on a nearby cot. Was he the man who yelled just now? He looked to be the man who approached his cot last night. As he turned again, Possum recognized the man by the smirk on his face. Yes, that was last night's visitor.

Possum continued to revolve as the doctor wrapped the bandage around and around his abdomen. When he faced toward Torreón's cot, he noticed that it was empty. The Mexican Captain had disappeared. Most of last night's wounded had vanished, as well.

"I want you to walk around camp today. The exercise will help you regain your strength. We've set up a few canvas tents where you wounded soldiers will be sheltered from the weather. You should find yourself a place in one of them." The doctor was loading his medical supplies into a carpetbag, already looking across Possum's cot towards his next patient. "This camp is unhealthy. Corpses of Mexican soldiers are decomposing in the marshes, unburied, ignored by the army. I hope we can vacate this battlefield soon."

Doctor Labadie moved quickly to the next cot. Gathering his pantaloons together, Possum turned to watch.

"My arm hurts something fierce, Doctor," whimpered the man. A small, thin figure, he perched on the edge of his cot, offering his left arm to the doctor. Possum noted the man's pallid complexion, thin beard, and watery blue eyes. Wisps of stringy blond hair clung to his forehead. A smirk exposed protruding yellow teeth. He waved his arm towards Dr. Labadie. Possum noticed that the forearm was wrapped with a cloth, maybe torn from a shirt.

The doctor removed the makeshift bandage and scrutinized the slash on the man's arm. His patient cried out when the doctor probed it.

"There are soldiers out there with worse wounds who are still ready to fight," said Labadie. "This does not look bad. It is not a deep cut, and no muscles or tendons look to be severed." He stared at the soldier, a thin smile on his lips. "I will bandage it for you. Then you must return to duty."

"No, I ain't able just yet. It hurts too much. Careful there with them bandages." When the doctor finished, the man added, more softly this time, "Doc, you got any of that Mexican laudanum? I could use a bit. Then I could go back to soldiering tomorrow."

The doctor frowned. "Laudanum is for the seriously wounded, those in real pain. Think of General Houston, performing his duties despite a terrible wound. Look at this man here." He pointed towards Possum. "He asks for no palliatives. Nor should you." He snapped shut his bag and stalked away.

"Talks funny, don't he? My name's Grady Bleeker. I'm from down Louisian'. I come across the Sabine River to see what all the fuss was about. Thought I might move to this Texas." He sighed deeply. "I ain't sure no more. If you gotta fight Mexicans all the time, maybe it ain't worth it. Fighting red'uns is bad enough. Now, what's your story?"

Possum sat back on his cot and studied Bleeker carefully. More likely he was running from something in his past. Bleeker would make a sorry excuse for a soldier. But then, most members of the Texas army didn't look or act like soldiers either. Possum found them dirty and ill-mannered, dressed in ragged garments of all sorts.

"I'm from Tennessee," Possum said at last. "The Elk River country, near Lawrenceburg town. That's in southern Tennessee, damn near in Alabama."

Bleeker scrambled off of his cot and slouched across to sit down beside Possum. He extended his hand and Possum hesitated for a moment before shaking it.

"I'm called Possum."

"That ain't no name." Bleeker laughed, his head back, mouth open. Bleeker's breath reeked, the same foul odor Possum had detected last night. He could see gaps left by missing teeth.

"Hanks. George Hanks." Possum surprised himself, blurting out his name so suddenly. He tried it again. "George Hanks." He released Bleeker's hand.

"I heared you the first time," said Bleeker. "George—Possum—how'd you feel about skedaddling back to Louisian' with me? We could take Lynch's Ferry right across to dry land. Then it's just the Trinity and the Sabine in our way. I got friends who'd help us cross both of them rivers. We'd be in Nawleans in no time."

Possum frowned down at his feet. "Mebbe," he said. "I ain't got no outfit right now. That doctor says I ain't up to traveling neither."

"Think on it. You ain't gonna be too popular in Texas. I heared you talking with that Mexican captain. Was you, I'd light out pretty quick." Grinning, Bleeker elbowed Possum in his ribs. Possum flinched away from him, alarmed. As he feared, Bleeker must have eavesdropped on his exchange with Torreón. The man could make lots of trouble if he had a mind to.

"See, I'm a slaver. These Texians are all riled up right now. We heared about all them families leaving their homesteads, running from the Mexican army. Now, there's sure to be slaves in the mix, some separated from their masters. We could catch 'em up, take them back to Louisian' and sell 'em."

Possum kept staring down at his feet, wiggling them restlessly. He didn't cotton to slavery; Pap had talked against it. Possum shook his head, no.

"Think on it. Niggers are worth more across the Sabine. Hell, we might get a little money together, even buy a few here in Texas. You ain't one of them nigger lovers, are you?"

Was this a challenge? Possum responded softly, "I never held no slaves."

"Hey, they got breakfast over there." Bleeker leapt up from the cot and scurried away. Possum watched him go, scampering along like a squirrel after acorns. He didn't look all that sick. Possum shifted uneasily on his cot. That made two people, Torreón and Bleeker, who knew his secret, that he'd escaped from the Alamo battle. And, of course, Joe the slave and Mrs. Dickinson, but neither of them were likely to reveal his history. Possum had no intention of accepting Bleeker's invitation. Talk of slavery made Possum uneasy. Pap had been against slavery and had railed against his neighbors who converted their lands to cotton production.

What to do? Possum hoped the strange little man would leave him alone, but that wasn't likely. Bleeker was the persistent type, and he knew Possum's secret about the Alamo. That gives him power over me, Possum realized. Grady Bleeker was a problem, and Possum didn't know what to do about him. What would Davy do?

Possum smiled. Davy would talk Bleeker to death.

Torreón was less of a worry, since he wanted to conceal the fact that he'd headed a troop of Lancers at the Alamo battle. He couldn't expose Possum, for fear that Possum would expose him.

Possum straightened up abruptly when a new thought occurred to him. How desperate was Torreón to protect himself? Might he try to silence Bleeker? Or me? He turned to look at Torreón's cot again. There was nothing left on or around it, no indication that Torreón had been there.

He gained his feet and tested his wounded side. The doctor was right; the tight bandage allowed him to move without much pain. He took a few tentative steps, looking around. He noticed three new tents lined up in the live oak grove. Dr. Labadie had said those were for the wounded. I should find a cot in one of them, he thought.

When he took a deep breath, Possum realized the camp smelled of death, the odor of decomposing corpses, just as the doctor had said. How could anyone eat hot food? He gritted his teeth and began a slow walk towards the base of the big oak tree where he'd seen Sam Houston yesterday. Sure enough, a few ears of corn still lay at the base of the tree. Stooping, ignoring the discomfort, he picked up an ear of corn and began to nibble on it.

Chapter 6

Possum watched a party of Mexican soldiers straggle out of the Army camp, heads down, bedraggled, marching in loose ranks, weaponless, but each wearing a knapsack. They made their way carefully along the edge of the bayou, marching away toward the south. Were they headed for San Antonio, he wondered? Is that the trace I need to follow, when I search for Davy?

"That's the last of 'em." The voice came from behind Possum. Big Foot Wallace stopped beside him and proffered a plug of tobacco. Pulling out his little belt knife, Possum cut off a chaw and returned the plug.

Wallace ejected a brown stream of spittle; a trace of it didn't quite clear his beard. "Gave the Mexicans their parole, he did." Wallace gestured with his chin towards the trees. "Tom Rusk is doing everything he can to get this army organized. He's gonna march south and look for the rest of the Mexican army."

Possum nodded. He'd listened to Thomas Rusk, who'd replaced the ailing Sam Houston, disagree stridently with Davis Burnet, president of the Republic of Texas. Possum stood in ranks as Rusk bellowed commands to the undisciplined Texian soldiers, often with little effect.

Wallace turned his head to spit another stream of tobacco juice. "Some of them Texian soldiers want to get paid right now," he said. "That ain't likely. Some of them want to go home and start planting. Some others want to go south and fight more Mexicans."

"I seen Texians packing up and leaving camp."

"Don't blame 'em none. It's time for getting crops in the ground. Them farmers is getting anxious."

Possum winced, thinking about Pap, back in Tennessee. Pap would need help with the farm this year.

"Well, looky there. Here comes Deaf Smith." Wallace gestured with his knife. "Looks like the old horny toad done found his way back."

Possum squinted into the sunlight and made out the figure of a horseman. He came from the direction of Vince's ferry across the bayou, walking his mount slowly, holding a long rifle across his chest. He wore dirty buckskins. A slouch hat was pulled low over his face. He stopped his horse in front of them and stared down.

"About time." Wallace took hold of the horse's bridle, steadying the animal while Smith dismounted. "Your family doing okay?" Wallace asked.

"Yep. I rode on over to San Antonio and helped them get settled in, back on the farm. It's quiet in San Antonio right now. The Alamo battle is still on everybody's mind. Things is a bit uneasy."

"Glad to hear it's quiet."

"I thought I better come back and see if General Sam needs any help with these so-called soldiers. Like you, you old buffalo." Smith showed a playful grin to Wallace.

Wallace pointed his knife toward Possum. "Here's one of them soldiers. He got wounded; taken a Mexican bayonet."

"How do," said Possum.

"He can't hear you. He's deaf, sure enough. Deaf as a rock but he can read your lips if you look straight at him. He can feel the wind of a whisper behind him, and he can smell an Indian a half league away."

Possum tried again. This time, he faced Smith and looked him right in the eye. "How do?"

Smith nodded at Possum and returned his attention to Wallace.

"Road to San Antonio's done got crowded. All those folks who skedaddled ahead of Santa Anna's army—they're scrambling back now, ready to start farming again. Rivers are all up with this goddamn rain. The Brazos and Colorado are flooded well over their banks. They finally got a ferry running at Gonzales Town, carrying folks across the Colorado."

"People gotta get their crops in the ground." Wallace offered the plug of tobacco to Smith who shook his head no.

"Looks like you got shed of the last of the Mexican army. I seen them take off down the trail." Smith rubbed his horse's neck.

"Tom Rusk gave 'em their parole. They took the walking wounded along," said Wallace.

"Weren't many left, were there? What happened? You boys been throwing 'em in the bayou?"

"A few Mexican soldiers got hauled downriver in that old steamboat. The boat what took General Sam to the coast. Seems our boys are taking some other prisoners home, to help with the plowing and planting."

Smith nodded. "Likely a good idea. Probably they'll make good Texians outa them prisoners. I doubt they got much of a life to go back to, down in Mexico. Most of them were conscripts anyway, just peons shoved into uniform. The ones with good teeth."

An understanding dawned on Possum. Maybe that's what happened to Torreón. "What about the officers?"

"General Sam kept most of the officers as hostages. You curious about your captain friend?" asked Wallace.

"He ain't my friend."

"Well, a goddamn smarty from Groce's Plantation rode in and asked for somebody to tutor his children in the Spanish language. Your friend volunteered right promptly."

Possum wanted to change the subject away from Torreón. He waved his hand to attract Smith's attention, and looked at each man in turn. "Does this mean the war's really over?"

"What do you think?" Wallace addressed Smith.

"For now, anyway." Smith turned to face Possum. "I carried Santa Anna's command down to General Filosola's army, telling them to go back to Mexico. They palavered about it. You know, Santa Anna being a captive and all, was it a legal order? Filosola himself took charge and started marching south." Smith turned back to Wallace. "They left a pile of equipment behind. Might be worth looking into, if you track down towards Velasco."

"Guess he didn't have much choice about pulling out, did he?" said Wallace.

"No, he didn't. An army of a thousand, supply lines long, all this rain we been getting. Pulling back to Mexico was Filosola's only option. I 'spect he'll be back, one day."

"What about that other Mexican army? General Urrea?"

Smith grabbed his horse's reins and heaved himself back into the saddle. "Urrea? I think he was the best of the Mexican generals. He's still in Goliad. 'Spect he'll take off for Matamoros also."

"So it's done?" asked Possum.

"It's like this, old son." Wallace angled toward Smith so he could follow the conversation. "It's like you get into a shooting scrape with a bunch of Indians. You shoot down their chief. So, they withdraw and argue among themselves about who's chief now. Mebbe they won't settle it. Mebbe half of them will ride off, leaving the others to fight if they want to. Mebbe they pick a new chief and come back to fight some more. You gotta wait and see."

"That's about right," said Smith. "The Mexicans gotta reorganize their government now. They might decide to come right back to Texas. We'll have skirmishes; you can count on it. Comanches, Wacos, Apaches, they're the real problem right now. Running right across the Balcones hills, nobody to stop 'em."

"Any of the Mexicans still in San Antonio?" asked Possum.

"San Antonio's a Mexican town," said Wallace. "They're all Texians now. A bunch of them aren't happy about that."

Smith nodded. He shook the horse's reins and patted its neck.

"I mean to go there. To San Antonio." Possum hadn't intended to blurt that out. He caught his breath; a thrill ran down his spine. Always, before now, somebody else had guided him, made decisions for him. First it was Pap. Even when he skipped out on his chores and slipped away into the woods to hunt, he knew that Pap was there, planning ahead for the next day, waiting with instructions for his son. When he left Tennessee for Texas, it was Davy Crockett who was the leader. Possum simply followed Davy, took orders, did what Davy said. Now he was alone, with no one to tell him what to do.

"Son? Looks like you got something in your craw."

Possum looked up to see Wallace eyeing him closely. Deaf Smith, a puzzled expression on his face, watched Possum's lips.

"Just thinking, deciding what to do next."

Smith stroked his chin, studying Possum, who shuffled his feet nervously. "Soldier," said Smith, "Texas is gonna need men of courage like yourself. There's certain to be more trouble with Mexicans along the border. And there's the Indians. Fighting men are gonna be in demand."

The comment startled Possum. He'd never considered himself a fighting man. He'd never fought in an Indian war, like Pap had. At the Alamo, he'd fired the rifles handed to him, but he didn't know whether he'd actually hit any of the Mexicans. Possum squared his shoulders and accepted the title: Fighting Man. It sounded good.

"God's truth," said Wallace, nodding. "You're a good soldier, and Texas is gonna need you. Maybe you oughta join up with one of them Ranger companies they're organizing."

Smith leaned forward in his saddle, frowning. "It ain't no business of mine, but you got folks to look out for? A place you need to be? A farm to go back to, maybe?" He continued to scrutinize Possum's face.

Possum thought briefly of Pap following Sally the mule. Some day, somehow, he would go back to Tennessee, but not just now. He couldn't.

"Nope," he said softly. "Just considering what I oughta do."

"San Antonio's a good place for a fighting man to be." Smith turned his horse toward the camp, then held it back. "Likely, that's where the pot will come to a boil," he offered over his shoulder. With a nod toward Wallace, he galloped off toward the camp in the oak trees.

"Mr. Wallace?" Hesitantly, Possum pushed himself into Wallace's attention. "Here's my problem. I ain't got no outfit. This here, what you see of me, is all I got in the world." He stood with his arms wide open. "Just these scabby clothes and a small knife. I used to wear deerskins I'd tanned myself. I had a good flintlock long rifle. And a Bowie knife I bargained for in Arkansas, on the way to Texas. I done lost everything I had."

Wallace arched a stream of tobacco juice to one side. He wiped his lip with the back of his forefinger, studying Possum.

"I didn't get in on it when the boys split up whatever they'd captured. I was wounded. Ain't the army supposed to help its soldiers? With weapons, at least?" asked Possum.

Wallace thrust his chin towards the army camp. "Come on, son. Let's see what we can do."

Following in Wallace's wake, head down, Possum wondered if he'd done the right thing. He didn't know who to ask, other than Big Foot Wallace. Had he said too much, been too forward? He couldn't travel to San Antonio, or Tennessee or any place at all without weapons.

Wallace slowed his lumbering pace when he reached the encampment. He stopped beside the tall officer Possum remembered as Captain Lamar. Lamar was in animated conversation with Tom Rusk, an equally tall, burly man, wearing a black frock coat. His deep-set eyes sparked in anger. Both men turned towards Wallace.

"What is it, Mr. Wallace?"

"General Rusk, this man here is a soldier who's lost his outfit. He's a good man, and I'd like to set him up anew, from Mexican gear we done captured."

Rusk nodded and waved Wallace away. He resumed berating Lamar, who responded in a sarcastic tone of voice. Possum felt Wallace's tug on his sleeve, pulling him away from the two feuding officers.

Two soldiers guarded the spoils of war, a heap of boxes, bundles and loose equipment under protection of a canvas shelter stretched between two small trees. The nose of a small cannon protruded from under the canvas. Both guards rose to stand beside the mound of plunder, frowning at Wallace as he approached. Possum stayed behind him.

"It's all right, boys," said Wallace, pushing them aside and stirring the contents. "Here's a Mexican musket, a Brown Bess flintlock. It might suit you, soldier."

Possum accepted the weapon with a frown, hefting it, examining the lock.

"I know, I know, it ain't like the long rifles you Tennessee boys is used to. But it's reliable enough. It fires a 75 caliber ball, too big for the American flintlocks." Wallace handed him a box fitted with a leather strap. "These here are the Mexican cartridges. Ball and powder in a paper case. Watch me." Wallace selected a cartridge and held it up for inspection. "See, the Mexicans would half-cock the hammer. Then, they'd bite off the end of the cartridge. You needed good teeth to be in the Mexican infantry." Wallace ripped the end from the cartridge with his teeth, then poured powder into the pan and uncocked the lock. "It's got a good frizzen," he said. "It'll hold the powder good when you release the hammer. Now," he continued, "you can ram the rest of the cartridge right into the barrel. It holds the powder and ball, and the package makes the wadding." Wallace loaded the musket and handed it to Possum. "Give it a try," Wallace said.

Possum sighted on a tree at the edge of camp, far away from anyone. When he pulled the trigger, the hammer snapped forward and the powder in the pan burst into flame. A half-second later the musket fired. Possum felt a mild jolt against his shoulder.

Wallace waved an arm at the Texians whose attention had been attracted by the rifle shot, reassuring them that all was under control. The two guards waved as well, laughing at the others.

"I hit the damn tree right where I was aiming."

"Yes, you took a little bitty chip out of the trunk."

"There's not much kick to this little flintlock." Possum half-cocked the rifle and cleaned the powder remnants from the pan, rubbing it with his thumb.

"That Mexican gunpowder ain't much. I'll get you a passel of Dupont powder. The army's got a-plenty. And some more balls and buckshot. If you get into a shooting scrape, you'd better add more gunpowder and two-three rounds of buckshot on top of the ball. Hold on there," he added when Possum started away. "You oughta have a good knife and a pistol or two. Take this here haversack. You think some of these clothes might fit your skinny carcass?"

"These oughta do. Thankee."

Wallace took hold of Possum's elbow and led him away from the dump. "Son," he whispered, "they captured about twelve thousand dollars in gold and silver. That ain't counting what the boys squirreled away before the officers got ahold of any of it. I kinda liberated a few dollars myself." He opened Possum's haversack and slipped a generous handful of coins into it. "Watch out for them card games," Wallace said with a wink.

"I seen you testing that musket." Possum recognized the oily voice. Grady Bleeker had slipped up behind him. "Looks like you might be heading out soon, now that you got some weapons and all."

Possum didn't reply. He'd stuck two pistols in his newly-acquired Mexican belt, along with a big butcher knife in a cloth scabbard. He'd discarded his torn cotton garments for a broadcloth shirt and button-front canvas britches, all courtesy of the Mexican infantry. He adjusted the shoulder strap supporting a canvas bag of powder and shot.

"Some of us boys is gonna go hunting in the brush. Know what I mean?" Grinning, Bleeker winked. He raised an elbow to jab at Possum. Stepping back to avoid the elbow, Possum glanced across Bleeker's shoulder and saw a pair of men watching them, scowls on their faces. "Seems like a good time to pick up a few strays. Before their masters find them. Why don't you join up with me and my cousins? We'd be pleased." Bleeker stuck a small ivory toothpick between his yellowed teeth.

"I'll think on it." Possum shouldered his pack, and holding his flintlock across his chest, walked away towards the big oak tree.

"Don't wait too long," Bleeker called after him. "Folks might get the wrong idea. We got secrets, you and me. 'Course, I ain't the kind to go blabbing everything I know."

That implied threat stopped Possum in his tracks. He turned back to see Bleeker sneering at him, his two companions watching, stone-faced, their muskets grounded. Had Bleeker revealed to those two that Possum was an Alamo survivor? He had to leave soon, before Bleeker tried raising the stakes. His secret was no longer safe in this army camp. Perhaps his life wasn't either.

Chapter 7

When blasts of gunfire shattered the midnight stillness, Possum made up his mind to quit the Texian army immediately. He pushed his way out of his tent and mingled with other soldiers who were running this way and that, yelling and confused. A pall of gun smoke drifted down the slope towards the bayou. The combatants, whoever they were, must have taken their quarrel outside of the camp.

Possum had noted distasteful changes beginning to develop in the makeup of the Texian army. As soon as the farmer-soldiers drifted away, new recruits from the United States replaced them. Ruffians, in Possum's opinion, brawlers or scoundrels with whiskey jugs who were looking for another war, anxious for a fight with the remnants of the Mexican army.

Grady Bleeker moved among the newcomers, laughing and poking at them, sampling their whiskey, making friends. Big Foot Wallace expressed his disgust with streams of brown spittle aimed in their direction. Thomas Rusk harangued the new troops endlessly over their poor military discipline. Captain Lamar loudly proclaimed his desire to march south and invade Mexico, to Rusk's outspoken displeasure. With so much unrest sweeping the camp, Possum was ready to abandon the Texian army. Tonight's gunplay convinced him that the time was ripe to head for San Antonio.

Possum had assembled a supply of equipment for his journey, starting with the firearms Wallace had given him and supplemented with items he'd scrounged here and there. He'd studied the corral of horses and mules, watching to see which ones were personally cared for. At last he settled on a big dark lop-eared Mexican army mule with a calm disposition, one that nobody else appeared to want. Possum offered the animal an ear of corn each evening, striking up an acquaintance.

In the early hours just before dawn, Possum saddled the mule and tied his equipment to it. The army camp had fallen silent after the midnight gunplay. The remaining campfires burned low. Throwing his blanket coat across his shoulders and clutching the Brown Bess flintlock across his chest, he coaxed the mule out of the corral. As quietly as he could, he led the animal away from the army camp, urging it through the woods in a northerly direction. Wallace had given him directions to the Harrisburg road. The rays of a last-quarter moon slipped through the trees, shedding enough light for Possum to watch his back trail. He stopped occasionally and listened intently. Aside from a night bird, and the calls of frogs down in the bayou, he heard no noises. No sentry challenged him.

Possum stumbled when he reached the Harrisburg road, a mucky, rutted trace leading in an east-west direction, barely visible in the gloom. He shook the mud from his moccasins and swung into the saddle. The mule offered no objection when Possum turned its head to the west and urged it forward, keeping it to a walk. Soon, the animal's easy pace lulled Possum into a doze, his head sinking to his chest.

He came alert when the mule stopped abruptly, pitching Possum forward. The sun was well up in the sky, beating down on his back. He glanced about, surveying his surroundings. The muddy road ran straight between groves of trees, oaks and tall pines, crowding the trace on both sides. Only the chattering of birds broke the silence.

Shaking the reins and digging in his heels had no effect on the mule. Possum dismounted and stroked the animal's neck and flanks. Its stiff-legged stance reminded him of Pap's mule Sally, when she decided she would go no further. He looked about, peering into the brush, seeking a place to rest himself and the mule.

When a puff of breeze struck his face, Possum detected the odor of smoke. He squatted, peering into the brush, until he made out a thin gray wisp rising among the pine trees. Was it a campfire? He tugged again at the reins, urging the animal forward once more, but the mule resisted. She's had enough for now, Possum decided. He was unaccustomed to the saddle and needed a rest himself.

Sniffing the morning air again, Possum recognized the smell of cooking, something frying. "Hello, the camp," he called, softly and hesitantly. He heard no response and called again, louder. "Hello."

"Come into the fire and show yourself." The invitation came in a low, flat voice. A cautious guard standing watch?

"Man coming in," called Possum. He grabbed the reins and turned the mule's head; it followed him willingly into the copse of trees. He looped the mule's reins to a convenient bit of brush and eased slowly toward the curl of smoke, holding his musket to his chest.

"They's some parched corn coffee left in the pot. Might kill you, though."

"The Mexicans already tried." Possum stopped beside a circle of stones which surrounded a low-burning campfire. He scanned the woods and soon spotted a figure hiding behind a tree trunk and peering out cautiously, a long rifle held at the ready.

"Was you at San Jacinto?"

"I was."

"You by yourself?"

"Just me and the mule."

The figure who emerged from behind the tree looked Possum up and down. A small, wiry man, with a shapeless hat covering his hair and a cotton shirt tucked into pants, he kept his rifle turned in Possum's direction. At last, the man turned the rifle away.

"I guess you're all right. Can't be too careful on these roads, you know. Folks was friendly and helpful when we was all running away from Santa Anna and the Mexicans. Now that we're headed back home, things ain't always so friendly." He gestured with his rifle to a tin coffee pot perched on a flat rock beside the fire. "Help yourself."

Possum squatted beside the fire and poured a splash of coffee into a tin cup. "Me and the mule just need to rest a bit."

"You're lucky you got a mule. We'uns are pulling a cart by ourselves. Make yourself easy."

The corn coffee tasted bitter but it was hot. Possum hunkered down beside the little fire and sipped slowly, relaxing. He was on his way, at last, glad to be away from the worry and turmoil of the army camp. Tension drained away from his shoulders.

The sound of children's laughter jerked him alert. Possum stared into the faces of two young boys, a white child and a Negro, who ran up to squat across the campfire, giggling at him. When Possum threatened to get up, they raced away laughing, one after the other, down a slope and away from the campsite.

"You boys simmer down now. Here, mister, have a piece of corn pone." A tall Negro woman leaned down and handed Possum a tin plate. His gaze started with her scuffed leather boots, black full skirt and blouse as it moved up to a stern face scowling down at him. Her face was the color of coffee with cream, lined by her frown. A red bandana covered most of her black hair. Possum gaped up at her; she made a striking figure.

He struggled to his feet. "Thankee," he said, accepting the plate. The woman was near his own height. For a moment they studied each other's faces. Suddenly embarrassed, Possum looked down, away from her stare. He hadn't been close to a woman, or even seen one, for so long now, not since San Antonio. He'd never, ever been that close to a negro woman.

"We're gonna get back on the road."

Possum wanted to say something to the woman. He didn't know what; an unaccustomed feeling swept over him. "Ma'am," he began.

"Oh, those boys! I'll get them. You boys!" she shouted. "Come here right now."

Over her shoulder she spoke to Possum. "My name's Miller. Cassandra Miller."

Possum chewed on the corn pone, and washed it down with a sip of the bitter coffee, now cold. When he reached over to set down the cup, his wounded side cramped. He grabbed it, grimacing. Riding that mule must have aggravated it.

"You hurt, mister?" A tiny woman approached him. She wore men's clothes, many sizes too large for her, pants and shirt-sleeves rolled up. Brown locks of hair straggled from beneath her floppy-brimmed hat.

"I'm all right." Possum spoke through clenched teeth.

"Lessee." The woman grabbed Possum's shirt and lifted it before he could stop her. "A little seepage through that bandage there. How'd you get wounded?" she asked.

"He was at San Jacinto." The wiry man stopped beside her and dropped the pack he was toting.

"I'm Bertha Kinney. This here's my husband, Willie."

"William Kinney," said the man, extending his hand. "They calls me Willie sometimes."

"Possum. Possum Hanks." He accepted the handshake.

"Want me to take a gander at that wound?" Bertha still held Possum's shirt. He gently removed her fingers and arranged his clothing.

"I guess it's all right."

"Gunshot?" she persisted.

"Mexican bayonet."

Cassandra shoved past. "We need to get on the road." She had corralled the boys and led each by a hand, striding purposefully to a heap of baggage. Each lad picked up his own little haversack and slung the strap across his shoulder.

Bertha said, "We'uns got a nice little farm, a ways up on the Brazos. Me and Willie. We pulled out ahead of the Mexicans, like everybody else. Now, we hope it's safe to go back."

Eyebrows raised, Possum glanced toward Cassandra, the question unspoken. She lifted her head, chin thrust forward. "I am a free woman. I'm not a slave. You hear me?"

He nodded, shuffling, uneasy. Her confrontational manner intimidated him. He didn't have much experience with Negroes or with slavery. Pap had said it was wrong. Davy did not seem to care for the idea, either. Grady Bleeker flashed into his mind. No, Possum decided, he didn't want anything to do with slavery, not if he could help it.

"Sandra got separated from her folks," offered Willie, smiling broadly. "We's all headed back to the Brazos river. She's been a big help to us."

Cassandra kept her flinty gaze fixed on Possum.

"Maybe you oughta change that bandage," Bertha persisted. "I could help you."

"It ain't much bother." Possum stuffed his shirt into his trousers. "I'll be all right." He turned to the side, preparing to go.

Bertha stepped in front of him, holding him up. "Mister Possum, maybe you'd like to travel with us." Hands on hips, Bertha smiled up at him.

"Now, now, Mother, this gentleman will want to be on his way." Willie nudged her but Bertha stood firm. She pointed toward Possum's mule.

"We only got a hand cart. We been taking turns pulling it." Bertha's intentions were clear enough.

Possum glanced at Bertha, Cassandra and Willie in turn. They stood silent, waiting. He rubbed his chin, considering. He wanted to reach San Antonio as soon as he could, to look for Davy or try to cut his trail. But then, Pap had taught him to help his neighbors, and these folks could use his help. He knew what Davy would do. Davy Crockett would pitch in, wouldn't he? Of course.

He smiled at Bertha. "I guess this ole mule could pull your cart. If we asked her right."

Possum half-cocked the musket and cleaned the pan and touchhole. Then he primed and loaded it with small shot, following the ritual for the Brown Bess. It was good to be hunting squirrels again. Today he'd missed the first animal he'd shot at.

Now, with four other squirrels hanging from his belt, he felt a happiness he hadn't known for weeks.

As he slipped through the stands of hackberry trees and live oaks, shafts of sunlight all around him, Possum's spirits soared. He stopped beside the bayou and studied his reflection in the still, black water. A fish jumped, splashing, making a circle of ripples. Possum squatted on his heels and took a slow, deep breath. The woods smelled of decomposing leaves and pine needles, a restful scent, like the Tennessee hills. He thought back to the battlefield with its odor of death and offal, an unclean aroma, so unnatural to him. He felt as though the trees were cleansing him, purifying his aching body. How long could he linger here?

Willie Kinney had asked him to kill a squirrel or two for the pot. Possum jumped at the chance. Kinney had offered to let him use his own long rifle for the hunt, but Possum declined it. He wanted to familiarize himself with the Brown Bess.

Possum tossed a pebble into the bayou and watched the reflections disappear in the ripples. Something didn't add up. Willie claimed that he wasn't much of a shot, not a very good hunter. This didn't ring true, if Willie was indeed a farmer on the Brazos as he claimed. On the frontier, every man was a hunter, or he wouldn't survive. Perhaps Willie simply didn't want to leave his family alone with a stranger. On the other hand, maybe they just wanted to take the mule. At this moment they could be fleeing down the Harrisburg road. He frowned at that thought. Perhaps he'd better get on back to the road.

Possum started through the woods at a fast trot, but stumbled. A sudden weakness overcame him. He leaned against a hackberry tree, fighting off a wave of dizziness. His head whirled. Was it the bayonet wound, coming back to plague him? Sweat surged from his face; he wiped his forehead with his arm, staggering backwards. He wrapped an arm around the tree to steady himself. When his knees buckled he slid down to sit beside it.

After a moment's rest, his head ceased whirling. He pulled up his shirt and studied the bandage. He couldn't see any fresh blood. He probed around the edges; tender it was, but no worse than in the morning.

As he rose to his feet, he heard the soft clop of horses' hooves out on the muddy Harrisburg Road. A familiar, whining voice echoed across the grove of trees. Grady Bleeker was on the road, headed west, bound in his direction.

Possum peered out from the shelter of the underbrush, careful not to expose himself. He saw Bleeker haranguing his two companions from the army camp. As they rode past at a fast walk, Bleeker mentioned gunfire. Had they heard Possum squirrel-hunting? His hand tightened on the Brown Bess musket. He'd hoped that Bleeker would return to Louisiana and out of his life. If the man stayed in Texas, Bleeker was likely to cause trouble sooner or later.

He watched the trio disappear around a bend in the road, Bleeker riding in the middle and urging the others onward. Possum realized they'd soon overtake the Kinney family. He struggled to his feet, tucked the Brown Bess into his elbow and hurried after them.

Chapter 8

When he hurried around a bend in the road, Possum caught a glimpse of Grady Bleeker and his friends. They faced the other way, sitting astride their mounts, blocking the road between him and the Kinney family. Willie stood beside their cart, facing the horsemen, his musket held across his chest, his jaw set firmly. Bertha stood just behind him, worry written across her face. On the far side of the cart, away from Bleeker's gang, Cassandra stood straight as a ramrod, holding the mule's reins. She spied Possum in the road behind Bleeker and quickly looked away, her eyes shifting downward.

She's warning me, Possum realized. She doesn't want to give me away by staring at me. He took his cue from her and slipped into concealment among the roadside trees. Slowly and noiselessly, he made his way forward through the woods, approaching the horsemen, stopping when he could hear their voices clearly.

"We're soldiers of the Republic of Texas," Bleeker was proclaiming. "We been deputized to round up all the runaway slaves and see that they're returned to their lawful masters."

"Slavery ain't legal here, you know that. There's no slaves here. Not in Mexico." Willie shifted his feet nervously. His flintlock's muzzle twitched in Bleeker's general direction, wavering in Willie's uncertain hands.

Bleeker laughed. "This ain't Mexico no more. It's the Republic of Texas. You remember them so-called indentured servants? They're slaves now. We're catching them up." He gestured with his chin toward Cassandra. She glowered back.

"I ain't heard nothing about slavery coming back," Bertha chimed in. Looking daggers at Bleeker, hands on her hips, she pushed herself forward past Willie. He took a hand off of his musket and grasped her sleeve, urging her back beside him.

"Well, Ma'am, it is." Bleeker smiled disarmingly, head nodding politely. "The Republic of Texas is gonna be a slave country. And we soldiers is gonna help see to it that it is. It's our duty."

"The future of slavery ain't been decided yet." Bertha shook her finger at Bleeker. Willie nodded vigorously, his head bobbing up and down.

"All right, that's enough of this jimmer-jammer." One of Bleeker's companions, a bulky swarthy man, stood up in his stirrups and beckoned to Cassandra. "Come here, gal, we're taking you along with us."

"I am not going anyplace with you." Cassandra lifted her head and lowered her brow at the men, her eyes flashing danger.

"Well, look at her. Guess she needs gentling." The speaker grabbed his crotch, chuckling maliciously. His companions joined in the laughter.

"She's ours. You can't take her." Bertha scurried back around the cart to stand at Cassandra's side.

"Now, now, don't get upset." Bleeker waved his hand, a disarming gesture. "We'll just take her on down to Harrisburg. You can claim her when you get there."

His heavy-set companion urged his mount forward, a wide grin on his face. "Come on, gal," he said, still chuckling.

Willie raised his musket and pointed the muzzle at the horseman. "Hold on, there, mister. You ain't taking nobody no place." Willie was trembling noticeably but his voice revealed his determination.

The rider pulled his horse to a halt. He turned in the saddle and glanced toward Bleeker, his eyebrows raised, questioning.

"What are you gonna do, mister?" Bleeker pulled a flintlock pistol from his belt and waved it, suggestively. "There's three of us and only one of you. We got you outgunned. Scoot on over and pick up that gal, cousin."

"There's two of us here, Bleeker." Possum emerged from the trees, holding the Brown Bess musket at the ready.

Bleeker stared down at Possum and chuckled. "Well, looky there. It's my old friend Possum, come to join in the fun. Now, what's your interest here, my friend?"

"These people are my friends. You ain't." Possum kept his expression impassive, his eyes fixed on Bleeker's face.

"Don't matter. We still got you outgunned, three to two. Ain't no need for you to mess with us. Why don't you track on down the road?"

Possum half-cocked the Brown Bess and made a show of checking the prime in the pan. Then he pulled the hammer to a full-cocked position, and thrust the muzzle directly at Bleeker. "When the party starts, I reckon you got the first dance."

Willie took Possum's cue and aimed his flintlock at Bleeker also.

"Hold on, now. No need to get excited." Bleeker shoved his pistol into his belt and gathered his horse's reins together. He laughed aloud, a high-pitched peal of false hilarity. "Boys, I reckon we got us a Mexican standoff here. Let's light out and leave these good folks to their business." He glared down at Possum for a moment. "I'll be looking for you on down the road." The three men turned their mounts westward and galloped away, without another look or word.

Possum released the hammer on his musket. He looked at Willie.

Willie leaned back against the cart, put down his flintlock and used his sleeve to wipe perspiration from his face. "Mine weren't even primed," he muttered. He tucked his trembling hands into his armpits to steady them.

Cassandra strode purposefully around the cart and frowned at Possum. "I want to know," she demanded. "Would you actually have shot him?"

Possum wondered the same thing himself. He looked at his own hands, turning them over slowly, one at a time. They were calm, relaxed. Was he running a bluff on Bleeker? It had worked well enough, but would he have really pulled his trigger?

"I reckon I would have, if the shooting started."

Cassandra nodded. "So would I." She lifted her right hand out of the folds of her dark cotton dress. Possum gawked at the flintlock pistol she held up for his inspection. It must be a larger caliber than his musket.

"Dammit, Sandra, I done told you." Willie reached for her weapon. "Niggers ain't allowed firearms of any kind. You're gonna get us all killed."

Cassandra shoved Willie's hand away. "And I've told you, Mister Kinney, nobody's taking me or my son."

"Where are the boys?" Possum suddenly remembered the children. He looked about, seeking them.

Two heads popped up from the cart, laughing. Small hands pushed aside a blanket. One after the other, they scrambled out and darted to Possum, each winding his arms around one of his legs.

"They was riding in the cart," Bertha explained. "When I heard horses, I flipped that blanket over 'em. Told 'em to hush."

"You done right." Possum suddenly remembered how Davy arranged his expedition to Texas. "We got to get ourselves organized, so we don't get surprised again. We need to have somebody out scouting in front of us. And somebody else keeping watch to the rear." That's the way Davy did it when they were marching through the wilds of Arkansas. A scout and a rear guard. Possum often volunteered to be the front scout. He ventured ahead of Davy's party, reading sign, blazing a tree to mark a safe passage.

"They's only four of us; we can't hardly spare any scouts. And two are women folk." Willie shook his head, downcast.

"I'll scout ahead. You watch the rear. The women can manage the cart." Possum eyed Willie, a questioning look. Was he still frightened after the confrontation with Bleeker?

Bertha interrupted him. "Will, you stay with the cart, keep the mule pulling it. I'll trail just a little ways behind. If I see anyone coming, I'll run and catch up to you." She hiked up her trouser legs and tucked them in her boot tops. "I can run pretty fast, remember?"

Willie smiled at her, relaxing a bit.

"Don't worry. I'll be fine," Bertha continued.

"All right." Possum surveyed the little group for a moment, then started trudging down the muddy road.

"I'll walk with you." Cassandra caught up with him and matched him, stride for stride.

"The mule?" Possum wondered.

"Willie can manage it. He needs a task to settle him down, you know? He did very well, bluffing those renegades like he did, but now he's thinking about what might have happened. Handling the mule will help him settle his mind."

Possum gave her an appraising look, then turned his attention back to the road. Cassandra seemed to be clever enough, but did she plan to talk all the time while he was scouting?

"We better be careful," she said. "Those renegades might try to ambush us. You know, hide in the trees and catch us unawares."

Possum laughed, a whole-hearted guffaw. "Looky at this muddy road. See them horse tracks?" He pointed out a set of hoof prints. "That one with a short stride, that's Bleeker's horse. They've slowed down to a walk now, see? If they turn off the road, or one of them dismounts, we'll know it. I'm a woodsman, I can track real good. This muddy road is like a picture book, if you know how to read it."

They marched in silence, both of them watching the muddy road for the story it told. After a while Possum pointed to the edge of the road and stopped.

"I see it," Cassandra said. The hoof tracks were jumbled, and the clear imprint of a boot heel was obvious. "He dismounted. Is he hiding in the trees?" From her skirts her right hand appeared, her big pistol at the ready.

"Look again," said Possum. "See, all three horses stopped here, but only one man dismounted. And see there? Another boot track, where he remounted."

"But why?"

"I reckon he needed to take a piss. That is—I mean…." Possum fumbled for a polite word.

"I know what you mean."

They resumed walking, Cassandra easily matching Possum's fast stride. The big flintlock pistol vanished again into Cassandra's voluminous skirt. Possum held the Brown Bess musket tucked into his right armpit.

After a half-hour, Possum slowed to a stop and broke his silence. "I need to stop."

"Take a piss?" Cassandra's lip curved into the first hint of a smile, then turned into a frown. "I forgot about your wound. Is it bothering you?"

"I just need to clean mud from these moccasins. Feels like I'm dragging leaden weights. 'Sides, I reckon we're getting too far ahead of the others." Possum leaned the Brown Bess against a pine tree. He removed each moccasin and banged it against the tree, dislodging clods of reddish-yellow clay. Picking up a stick, he scraped at the remaining mud. "Mebbe this evening I'll get a chance to wash these," he mumbled.

Cassandra had found her own stick and was scraping mud from the bottoms of her boots. Possum studied her, taking in the determination that showed in her face and body. She is a fine woman, Possum decided, a wiry strength hidden in a slender body. A good traveling companion.

She felt his gaze on her and stopped her scraping. "What is it?" she asked.

"Nothing." Possum began pulling on his moccasins. "Nothing," he repeated. What made her so touchy, he wondered. A bad experience? He shook his head. He knew so little of women. He'd spoken to girls he met at church on Sundays, but he felt uncomfortable in their presence. All dolled up, curly hair in ribbons, giggling to each other, watching him. When he spoke, they answered meek and polite, tittering. He didn't know what to say, how to talk to those girls.

Cassandra was different. To Possum she seemed forward, not silly and giggly like the Tennessee girls. He thought she was ready to challenge anyone at any time. Cassandra was serious. She made sense when she talked with him.

Possum studied her surreptitiously while they walked the road, side by side. At last, curiosity got the better of him.

"How'd you come to be here? In Texas, I mean."

Cassandra marched along, head aloft, offering no reply. Possum returned his attention to the hoof prints in the muddy road.

"I was hired as a tutor on the Groce Plantation," Cassandra said abruptly. "Mr. Groce wanted his own children and the others on his plantation to be proficient in the three R's. I signed a five-year contract. We arrived on the plantation just in time to flee from the Mexicans."

"What a damned rotten—that is, I mean—what bad luck," said Possum. Listening to Cassandra, he suddenly realized his own deficiencies in proper English. He shook his head, disgusted with himself.

"Bad luck indeed. I thought we would be safe here, since Mexico had outlawed slavery. Now, I find myself in this new Republic, which seems destined to pursue its glory with cotton production made on the backs of slaves."

Possum trudged ahead, thinking. He hadn't considered what the future might hold for any of them. His only aim was to find Davy Crockett. Nothing else mattered to him, but now he wondered about Cassandra's situation.

"Seems to me, you might just want to travel right back to New York." An idea occurred to him. "When I find Davy, we'll go back to Tennessee. Mebbe you could go with us."

Cassandra stopped dead still. "Mister, are you crazy? I wouldn't get twenty miles into Louisiana before I was snatched up and plopped down on a plantation. Or worse."

Possum frowned. "How did you get here?"

"I took a ship, that's how. And that's how I intend to go back, if you Texians would allow me to board one without first grabbing me up for a slave. Didn't you hear what those so-called soldiers were saying?"

"I heard." Possum dared a quick glance at Cassandra. Chin up, she marched quickly to the forefront. Possum watched the swirl of her skirt around her hips and long legs. Suddenly, Davy Crockett and San Antonio seemed far away.

Chapter 9

Cassandra gasped, a prolonged throaty sound, yanking Possum's attention away from his study of the Harrisburg road. She pointed at two men who stood quietly, unmoving, shadowy figures among the pine trees crowding the edge of the road. They were garbed in worn, patched trousers and buckskin pullover shirts. Red turbans wrapped in Cherokee style covered their heads. Possum realized that they were Indians, the first Texas Indians he'd seen since traveling with Davy.

Cassandra slipped around behind Possum, putting him between herself and the Indians. They didn't appear to have any firearms or powder horns. The shorter man sported a silver cavalry sword dangling from a crimson sash wound around his waist. The taller one had his hand on the head of a large hatchet crammed into his trousers. They didn't seem especially threatening to Possum.

A creaking of the cart wheels announced the approach of Willie Kinney, rounding the bend in the road. The Indians stared at the cart. Willie grabbed the reins and halted the mule.

For a moment nobody moved.

Would these Indians understand the Cherokee language? Possum shifted the Brown Bess to his left arm and searched his memory for Cherokee customs governing the greeting of strangers. He straightened his spine and coughed politely to announce his intention to speak. He made a broad sweeping motion with his right arm, palm down, away from his body, a standard Cherokee greeting of peaceful intentions.

Both Indians responded with similar but abbreviated gestures, hurriedly given. They stared at Possum, waiting.

Possum spoke in halting Cherokee, unused since his childhood. The words came slowly. He tapped his chest with his right hand and said, "(This one is called—)." He couldn't recall the Cherokee term for "Possum." He tried again, this time adding his name in English. "(This one is called) 'Possum'."

The taller Indian cleared his own throat. He threw back his head and frowned. Tapping his own chest, he said, loudly, "(This one is called 'Bad-Eye')."

Had Possum understood correctly? Bad-Eye? The man spoke in the Cherokee tongue, but his accent was poor, unfamiliar. At least he responded in the proper, courteous manner.

Possum repeated the name in Cherokee and then in English. "(Bad-Eye.) Bad-Eye."

"Ugh." The Indian tapped his chest again. "(Bad-Eye)," he repeated.

Possum looked closely. Bad-Eye's right eye was clouded, an opaque gray color.

"This one is called Tongue," said the shorter Indian, tapping his own chest and speaking English.

Bad-Eye mumbled an aside to Tongue and pointed toward Cassandra.

Tongue grinned, and jerked his head to attract Possum's attention. "Bad-Eye says he will trade for the Buffalo Woman. He offers all of his horses for her."

Surprised, Possum made a quick hand gesture, palm held outwards, negating any trade. He frowned at Bad-Eye. Pointing at someone was impolite among the Cherokee. Was Bad-Eye deliberately insulting them?

Smiling, Tongue waved his hands in apology. "Bad-Eye has good eye for women," he said, and gave a short barking laugh. "Heh heh heh." He told Bad-Eye something that caused him to shuffle his feet in discomfort. "Bad-Eye would have to raid the Comanche for many horses if he wished to trade for the Buffalo Woman," Tongue said. "Heh heh heh."

Possum joined in the polite laughter. It was a good omen, a gesture of friendship to laugh with a new acquaintance. He nodded at Willie, urging him to join in. Willie finally managed a weak chuckle.

"(Squaw)?" asked Bad-Eye, pointing at Cassandra again.

Possum scowled; Bad-Eye was compounding his rudeness.

Tongue said, "Bad-Eye asks, is Buffalo Woman your squaw?"

"I'm not anyone's squaw." Cassandra drew herself up to her full height, her loud tone a challenge. She glared at the Indians.

Possum made a calming gesture towards Cassandra, fixing her with a stern look of his own. In Cherokee society, when meeting strangers, women were expected to keep silent until they were first addressed. "Not now," he told her in a low tone. "Introductions come first." He beckoned to Willie, motioning for him to bring the cart forward. Bertha had joined Willie and stood beside him, hands on hips, peering at the Indians.

Following Possum's gesture, Willie grasped the mule's harness and urged it forward. Bertha followed, a step behind Willie.

"You fought the Mexicans." Tongue spoke to Possum, indicating the Brown Bess musket with a jab of his chin.

Possum nodded. "Yes."

"You were wounded in battle."

Startled, Possum nodded again. He shifted the musket to his right arm and put his left hand against his wound, an unconscious gesture. How did Tongue know that?

"You take care of your left side." Tongue jerked his head in Willie's direction. "He did not fight the Mexicans."

Possum indicated Willie with a toss of his chin, in the Cherokee manner. He said, "(That one is a brave man.)" His Cherokee tongue was coming back to him. "(That one is called) 'William'."

"You speak Injun?" asked Bertha.

Possum ignored her.

Tongue reached into his shirt and pulled out a cloth bag. He waved it aloft, swinging it back and forth, smiling broadly. "We have coffee," he said. "We drink. We make talk."

The four men sat cross-legged, facing each other around a tiny council fire. Possum had selected a small glen for their parley, a grassy roadside meadow draining toward Buffalo Bayou. He'd arranged the group so that the two Indians sat with their backs toward the cart, where the women were setting up camp for the night. Possum and Willie faced the Indians. Possum didn't want Bad-Eye to sit where he could observe Cassandra. He feared she might react violently to any advance from Bad-Eye, whatever that Indian's intention. He'd left the Brown Bess propped up beside the cart, where Bertha or Cassandra could reach it if the need arose.

Near the cart, Bertha lit a cooking fire lined with flat rocks. She eased the tin coffeepot among the coals. She opened Tongue's bag of coffee grounds and inspected them, feeling the texture, sniffing at a handful. Possum watched her add a generous measure to the pot as it began to boil. He noticed that she tied the bag tightly and poked it down into the cart, out of sight. Did she think Tongue would forget about it? We might have to trade for the coffee, Possum realized.

The four men watched each other, gazes shifting from face to face. No one spoke. Possum sat quietly, but Willie repeatedly shifted his position, obviously uncomfortable. The little fire added to the warmth of a sultry May evening. The Indians reeked of rancid bear grease, a familiar odor to Possum from his Tennessee experience with Cherokees. Perhaps the stench bothered Willie. If Willie farmed in Texas, he must have had contact with Indians before this. Possum reached over and patted Willie's knee, trying to reassure him.

Possum was unsure how to proceed with this parley. Who was the host and who was the guest? If they were actually on Indian land, then the Indians should be the hosts. But Possum had selected the site, invited them to sit, and arranged ground cloths for them, as a host was expected to do. Protocol was important to the Cherokee, and probably to these Indians as well.

Finally, Tongue rearranged himself and coughed, announcing his intention to speak. Good, thought Possum, he's assumed the role of guest. It was polite for a guest to begin the conversation.

"We are Bidai," said Tongue. "Friend to the Caddo. Friend to the Chickasaw. Friend to the Choctaw. Friend to the Cherokee. We come in peace. We greet our white brothers." He untied the saber from his sash and placed it on the ground, between himself and Possum.

"Ugh. Ugh." Bad-Eye pulled his hatchet free and laid it between himself and Willie, with the handle pointed in Willie's direction.

The Indians watched Possum; it was now his obligation to speak.

"We are Texians." Possum was unsure if this was the proper form, but it seemed right. "Friend to the Cherokee." He paused, looking at Willie, considering how to proceed. "Friend to Davy Crockett," he added. "Friend to Sam Houston."

"Huh!" said Tongue.

"Ugh!" said Bad-Eye.

"We, too, come in peace. We greet our Indian brothers." Possum completed the ritual introductions. He pulled the two flintlock pistols from his belt and laid them down, the handles toward Tongue.

Willie took his butcher knife from its sheath and placed it between himself and Bad-Eye. He glanced anxiously at Possum before settling back down.

Tongue leaned forward, addressing Possum. "Bad-Eye knows of your General Sam Houston. So do I. All Indians know of him. Sam Houston is brother to the Cherokee. Chief Duwali adopted him into the Cherokee tribe. Sam Houston's Indian name is '(The Raven)'. 'The Raven,'" he added in English. Noticing Possum's puzzled expression, Tongue said "White people know Duwali as Chief Bowl."

Willie spoke up. "Chief Bowl. Yes, a good Indian." He bobbed his head in emphasis. "Chief Bowl."

Tongue glared at Willie. He'd offered an insult to Tongue with the phrase, "Good Indian." It was an innocent one, given in ignorance, but demeaning to Indians.

Possum coughed to reassert his privilege as host. "Coffee has been prepared. Let us share the gift of my friend Tongue." He beckoned to Bertha.

Bertha gathered up four tin cups and held them out for Cassandra to pour coffee. Cassandra flicked sidewise glances at the Indians. Her face held a lip-bending scowl. She stood ramrod straight; her trembling hand betrayed her nervousness as she poured the coffee.

Cassandra's had a trying day, Possum realized. First the soldier-slavers tried to capture her, and now an Indian wants to trade for her. He gave Cassandra a smile of encouragement. She ignored it. She poured coffee into a glass and took it with her, off behind the cart.

Taking a cue from Possum, Bertha handed a tin cup to Tongue first, then served Bad-Eye, Willie and Possum in that order. The Indians accepted their cups without looking at Bertha. Women could serve at a council but were not acknowledged, according to Indian custom. Possum smiled and nodded to Bertha. She stood stock still, before realizing that she'd been dismissed. She raised an eyebrow and stalked away.

"Ugh!" Tongue tasted the coffee.

"Delightful," said Willie. He took a large sip and rolled the liquid around in his mouth, his eyes closed, savoring the flavor.

Bertha had served them a strong brew. Possum found it bitter, with less of a spicy tang than the cinnamon-rich Mexican coffee in the army camp. He watched the Indians down theirs rapidly, hot as it was. Willie clearly enjoyed his, so much better than the parched corn brew he'd served to Possum that morning.

Both Indians drained their cups and smacked their lips. A polite expression of thanks or a request for more? Possum was relieved when they set their cups down in front of them. Smacking lips was a polite gesture. He followed their example and set down his own cup.

Willie, oblivious, eyes closed, smiling broadly, continued sipping his coffee slowly.

Tongue reached into the folds of his turban and extracted a small clay pipe. He carefully filled the bowl with a generous pinch of tobacco taken from a worn leather pouch. Bad-Eye reached for an ember and passed it to Tongue, who lit the tobacco with it.

Tongue drew a mouthful of smoke and puffed it aloft. He leaned forward, holding the pipe with both hands, and offered it to Possum.

Possum realized this was a ritual but one he wasn't familiar with. He reached out and took the tiny pipe. Following Tongue's example, he blew a single puff of smoke. He started to return the pipe.

Tongue flicked his eyes toward Willie. Possum took the cue and handed the pipe to Willie.

Willie had caught on. He blew upward the ritual wisp of smoke and passed the pipe to Bad-Eye. Possum nodded to Willie; his thoughtless insult had been passed over.

"We will talk." Tongue leaned forward, cross-legged, his forearms resting on his thighs. He stared earnestly at Possum.

"We will talk," Possum agreed. He assumed that all the necessary rituals had been accomplished. Not in Cherokee fashion, perhaps, but Tongue seemed satisfied.

"What will the Texians do now?" asked Tongue.

The question startled Possum. What did Tongue mean? He glanced at Willie.

"We'uns is going back to farm on the Brazos," said Willie. "We're homesteaders."

Tongue picked up a little stick and scratched a circle onto the dirt. "Will you fight the Americanos now?"

"I ain't fighting nobody," said Willie. "Except Injuns."

Possum leaned back, shocked. Was Willie deliberately trying to provoke trouble?

Tongue raised his hands toward Possum, palms out. "He speaks of the Comanche, the Kiowa, the Apache," Tongue said. "William does not mean the Civilized Tribes. If William travels to the west, he must fight the Comanche. We fight them too."

"Comanche. Ugh," said Bad-Eye.

Tongue gestured toward Possum. "You have defeated the Mexicans. Now will you fight the Americanos? For your land?"

Possum struggled to find an answer. He didn't understand the question. Why would he fight the Americans? He was an American. And maybe I'm a Texian, too. Or am I?

"The Bidai were once a strong people," said Tongue. "We numbered many lodges. We traded with the Caddo, with the Apache. We grew maize, we hunted, even the buffalo in years when the buffalo came."

"Buffalo here?" asked Willie.

"Yes. Sometimes a French visited my lodge. Or a Mexican. And then the Americanos came." Tongue squirmed into a more comfortable position. "Americanos traded with us. Guns for pelts. We traded guns to the Apache."

"Apache. Ugh." Bad-eye sat erect, his eyes still shut.

"The Americanos wanted land," said Tongue. "Our land. The land of the Caddo. The land of the Karankawa." He jerked his chin at Willie. "They took our farms. They pushed Indians away."

Possum nodded. "So it was with the Cherokees in Georgia. Their lands were taken."

"Yes, Cherokees," said Tongue. "They came here, wanting our land. Taking from us. Now the Bidai are few. We can no longer trade with the Caddo or the Apache. I wish to know: Will the Texians now fight the Americanos for land? As they did the Mexicans?"

Possum searched for words of explanation, but he didn't know how to answer Tongue's questions. He stared over Tongue's head toward the cart. Bertha was watching him, hands on hips. The little boys stood with her, one on either side. He couldn't see Cassandra anyplace.

He remembered the plug of chewing tobacco Wallace had given him. He pulled it from his pouch and slowly, deliberately cut off a small chunk. He poked the tobacco into his cheek, and offered the plug and knife to Tongue. Possum didn't favor chewing tobacco but it was an acceptable social ritual to share it. He needed the diversion to give him time to think.

When all four men had shared the tobacco, Possum coughed politely. "The Mexicans want more war," he said, spitting loudly into the coals. He recalled the comments he'd heard from the scout Deaf Smith. "The Americanos come and they want war. They wish to fight the Mexicans." He looked at each man in turn and spit into the embers again. "The Comanches will fight the Texians. There will be war."

Tongue leaned toward Bad-Eye and mumbled to him.

Possum waited for Tongue to finish. Had he answered Tongue's questions? He'd avoided the issue of Indian lands; he didn't know how to address it or what the outcome might be. A sense of urgency rose within Possum, a feeling that he needed to find Davy soon, and leave this troubled country behind.

The Indians continued to consult in low tones spoken in a language Possum couldn't follow. Looking over their heads, he saw that Cassandra had reappeared, her hand concealed in her skirt. She's holding that pistol, Possum knew. Beside her, Bertha had a protective hand on each of the boys.

Tongue and Bad-Eye jumped to their feet. Possum rose slowly, watchful. Willie scrambled up and hopped backwards.

Tongue gave Possum a sweeping, palm-down gesture of peace. "We thank our white brother. He has told us much. We go to our village and think on what he has said."

"Ugh!" said Bad-Eye.

"It is good to talk with our Indian brothers," said Possum, trying to forge a courteous response. "We are grateful for the gift of coffee. We offer you our peace."

Tongue and Bad-Eye stooped and retrieved their weapons. They stalked slowly back toward the Harrisburg road, passing beside the cart, ignoring the women.

"Hey!" Willie shouted. "Just a minute. How about the other Indians? The Tonkawas and Comanches? What's they going to do?"

Tongue hesitated, and then turned back. He smiled broadly at Willie. "The Comanches will kill you."

Chapter 10

Possum called a halt when his little group approached the ferry crossing on Buffalo Bayou, opposite the little town of Harrisburg. He walked to the side of the road and peered into the dusk, searching out a campsite for the night.

Willie grabbed his sleeve. "Why don't we'uns just go on across to Harrisburg right now? Sounds like they's a bunch of folks over there. Mebbe some of our neighbors from down on the Brazos River."

Possum shook his hand away. "Best wait until daylight." He could hear shouts, coarse singing, men's voices raised in argument. He didn't want to walk into the middle of a drunken row. If they waited to cross over the bayou next morning, those revelers would likely be sleeping. He gestured towards a grove of live oaks a few hundred yards down the high bank beside the water. "Let's us haul the cart down thataway."

During the day, they'd met more little groups of travelers on the Harrisburg road. Some, like Willie and Bertha, were farmers who'd fled the Mexicans during the Runaway Scrape and were now returning to their farmsteads. Others were townspeople from Gonzales and other communities in a hurry to return, to discover what was left of their homes after the Mexicans passed through. Groups of riders passed them by, making haste. Other families traveled so leisurely that Possum's party overtook them.

Possum had abandoned his plan of scouting ahead and reading signs. The muddy road displayed a jumbled pattern of hoof prints. They stayed close to the cart. He led the mule by its harness. Willie and Bertha walked together beside the cart. The boys rode in the cart, eyes wide, ogling at strangers. Cassandra stayed near Possum and kept a stony silence. Bertha smiled at the other travelers, striking up conversations, asking for news of the Brazos River area.

Possum unhitched the mule and coaxed it into the oak grove. Pushing and pulling, he helped Willie wrangle the cart into position on the bank of the bayou, directly across from Harrisburg. "Stay close!" Bertha admonished the two boys. They squatted down on their heels beside the cart. Cassandra began unloading the cart for the evening's camp. Willie stood beneath a live oak tree, peering across the water at Harrisburg.

Viewed across the bayou in the twilight, Harrisburg looked like a ghost village of twisted timbers. Several bonfires were blazing, likely campsites of travelers who'd crossed earlier. Back at the San Jacinto battlefield, Wallace had told Possum how Santa Anna had ordered his troops to burn Harrisburg to the ground. Wallace had laughed about the story. He said Santa Anna was angry when he didn't catch the Texas government unawares. President David Burnet and his cabinet had skedaddled two days earlier.

Bertha gathered pieces of wood for a campfire. "We gotta see about supplies," she called to Willie. "We's getting low on flour."

"I ain't got no specie left. We gotta make do."

Bertha glanced at Possum. "Maybe we can trade," she said softly.

Possum joined Willie beneath the live oak. He stared into the early evening darkness at the revelry across the bayou. Light from a bonfire revealed a cluster of tents and carts. He was sure he heard Bleeker's whining voice raised in high-pitched laughter, rising above the singing. Possum smiled at the loud voices raised in raucous song. What would Davy Crockett have done? Why, Davy would have jumped right on the ferry and crossed over. He would have yanked out that fiddle and taken charge of whatever celebration he found there. Possum laughed aloud. Davy always told him, over and over, "Be always sure you're right and then go ahead." I ain't Davy, Possum reminded himself. And I ain't sure I'm right.

The wiry little ferryman talked constantly, his hands pulling the boat along, shirttail flapping loose. Possum and Willie helped him pull the ferry boat across Buffalo Bayou. A cable stretched from shore to shore; the ferry boat rode under it, propelled by the efforts of its passengers. Light rain drifted down on them, a westerly morning shower, sprinkling into their faces. Possum had wrapped a piece of canvas around the lock of his Brown Bess. Cassandra carried it for him. Bertha held the children by the hand.

"I usually charge a dollar a trip to folks whose got money," said the boatman, eyeing Cassandra and the Brown Bess. "I can see you're a soldier. San Jacinto, right? Well, I don't charge anything to carry our brave veterans across old Buffler Bayou. Not this spring, anyway. Next year may be different. Depends on how fast we can rebuild Harrisburg. The Mex army done burnt it to the ground. Santa Anna's orders, they said."

"Can we get us some supplies in Harrisburg?" asked Bertha. "We's running short on food." She reached out to the mule's neck, comforting it. The mule stood splay-legged, flinching with each wobble of the boat. Possum had taken the precaution of unhitching the animal from the cart. He'd chocked the cart's wheels with pieces of wood. It was a short ride across the bayou, but losing the cart would be a disaster for them.

"Oh, sure, a store is opened up again," the boatman said to Bertha. "A stable and corral, too." He eyed the mule. "Looks like you'uns could use another mule. Maybe you'd like to trade? A horse might do you better. Might be you'd like to spend a few days here, rest up. We'uns could use some help with carpentry in Harrisburg."

Willie said, "I reckon we need to get back to the farm. We gotta get a crop into the ground soon."

"Where's your farm? On the Brazos? Are you folks headed west? I hear tell the Indians are running wild on the Brazos. You could take the Velasco road south or go on toward Columbia. They say that the capitol of Texas is in Columbia now. Soldiers is getting land grants from the government down in Columbia. You ought to go by Columbia. Here we are. Welcome to Harrisburg. Watch your step, ma'am."

Possum and Willie held the boat steady while Bertha, holding each boy by the hand, stepped up onto the plank landing. Cassandra followed behind, head held high, cradling the Brown Bess in her arms. Possum led the mule off the boat, tied it to a post, and returned to help Willie with the cart.

"Y'all take care," said the boatman.

Evidence of the Mexican army's occupation was everywhere. Possum took note of the remnants of burned buildings, wreckage pulled down, a battered Conestoga wagon with wheels missing. New storefronts, raw planks of lumber hastily assembled, faced the bayou.

Possum hurried his group onto a covered porch, out of the rain. He retrieved the Brown Bess from Cassandra. She knelt and wiped the children's faces dry with her red bandana. Her son was beginning to blubber. "Hush, Marcus," she whispered. "We'll eat breakfast soon."

Bertha searched under the cart's canvas cover and found some corn pone. "This'll have to do. Sonny, Marcus, chew on this pone. Can't get a fire going in this mess."

They huddled together on the porch, chilled and shivering now, peering up and down the street. Harrisburg looked deserted to Possum. Last night's revelers must have taken shelter from the rain, but where?

He spun around when a door creaked open behind him.

"Morning, folks," said a smiling giant of a man, all chest and stomach, his enormous head a bush of hair and whiskers. "Y'all come in the store, out of that rain. I got a fire going in the stove. Coffee be ready soon."

Bertha stalked through the store, looking closely at the sparsely-stocked shelves. The storekeeper had introduced himself—Bear Sullivan, he'd said, proprietor of the best store in Harrisburg. Possum studied him, sipping a cup of freely-offered coffee. Bear's name was appropriate; he was bear-sized and walked with a bear's deliberate pace. Willie warmed himself by the stove. Cassandra took the children aside, into a corner, where they sat on the floor.

"They was a big doing's here last night," said Bear. "Lots of folks traveling through Harrisburg these days, headed west or south. Some old boys had themselves a shindig. Couldn't say much for it." He stroked his bearded chin. "I don't deal in no liquor," he added. "But they's lots of corn squeezins going around here."

Willie spoke up. "I could use a taste."

Possum said, "I thought it best that we wait and cross the bayou early this morning. When the town was quiet."

Bear nodded. "I think you done right. You folks headed out? Going west? Take care, now, Comanches been raiding along the Brazos River bottoms."

"We need supplies." Bertha pointed to a shelf. "You got flour? And coffee?"

Bear hurried over to help her. "Yes, ma'am. We's a little short on coffee. Two Injuns slipped in here and made off with most of it."

"Two Indians?" asked Possum.

"Aye. One of them, a big one-eyed devil, kinda scared me. He acted a bit daft."

"I'm going outside," Willie announced. "Gonna see to the weather."

Possum found a small bag of oats on a shelf. He stepped out onto the porch to feed them to the mule. Standing quietly in the rain, the animal ate the oats out of a bucket, huge mouthfuls. Possum took the bucket away, lest the animal eat too fast. After a moment he led it to a water trough at the edge of the porch.

Waiting for the mule to drink its fill, Possum glanced down the alley between the store and a burned-out building. He saw Willie there, standing on the lee side of the store, out of the rain, head to head with another man. The stranger's back was turned toward Possum. He jumped, startled, when the man laughed, a high-pitched giggle. It was Grady Bleeker, Possum realized.

Cursing himself for his carelessness, he hurried back to Bear Sullivan's store and found the Brown Bess propped against the counter. He yanked the canvas wrap off the lock and checked it quickly. The powder seemed dry enough.

Possum glanced around the store, checking on the rest of the party. Bertha was talking animatedly with Bear Sullivan. Both boys sat on the floor in a corner, their faces screwed up, weeping softly. He didn't see Cassandra anyplace.

He tucked the rifle under his arm and half-walked, half-ran out onto the porch and into the alley. He slowed his pace when he approached the two men. Huddled together out of the rain, they seemed to be sharing a joke. Willie peered across Bleeker's shoulder; his eyes widened when he saw Possum.

Bleeker spun around and faced Possum. "Well, look who's come to meeting," he said. "It's Mr. Possum. Me and your friend here just finished a little bit of business."

Willie stepped aside, out and away from Bleeker, into the rain, greeting Possum with a nervous grin.

"Gonna take that colored gal off your hands, Mr. Possum. I just bought her." Bleeker tried to chuckle; the laugh turned into a high-pitched giggle.

"She ain't for sale." Possum spoke in a low, tight voice, his expression rigid.

"Do tell. Well, I guess she was, wasn't she?" Bleeker looked at Willie, grinning broadly. "I done paid for her."

"She's a free woman. A free Black. You can't buy her." Possum twitched the muzzle of his musket toward Willie. "Best return his money, Willie. Do it now."

"Just a minute," said Willie. "We'uns done struck a deal. We shook hands." He favored Possum with a pleading glance.

Bleeker scowled heavily at Possum, brows lowered, head thrust back. He took a deliberate stance, feet apart, his hand on the pistol crammed into his belt. "You better lay off, my friend. This is the Republic of Texas; it ain't Mexico any more. Ain't no free niggers here. Your friend and I done made a pact. You ain't no part of it. You'll just back away, if you know what's good for you."

Possum thrust the muzzle of the Brown Bess toward Bleeker's stomach, a mere hand's breadth away. "Willie, give him back his money." Possum matched Bleeker's scowl.

Big-eyed, Willie held out a small leather pouch toward Bleeker. "Sorry, Mr. Bleeker," he mumbled. "I guess I done wrong. Here's your money back."

For a moment no one moved. Possum and Bleeker eyed each other; Bleeker with his hand on his flintlock pistol, and Possum clutching the Brown Bess with the muzzle pointing at Bleeker. Willie stood stock still, his arm extended, the little bag of money held out to Bleeker.

"No, goddammit," exclaimed Bleeker. "That gal is mine, and I'm gonna have her. I know all about you, Mister Possum, and your lies about the Alamo fight. You better not push on me. I can bring you down anytime I want."

Possum raised the Brown Bess to his shoulder, pointing the muzzle full at Bleeker's face. He pulled the hammer to a full cocked position; a loud click echoed up and down the alley. A red fury overwhelmed Possum, causing him to tremble. His vision narrowed and his breath came in gasps. The thought occurred to him—one little tug on this trigger, and I've freed myself of this bastard.

Bleeker snatched at the bag of money, ripping it from Willie's outstretched hand. He backpedaled down the alley, fear replacing the fury on his face, his bluster vanishing in the face of Possum's rage. He ducked into the charred timbers of a tumbledown wreck of a building, then poked his head out to yell at Possum.

"One day I'm gonna meet up with you when you ain't got that Mexican popgun. I'm guessing your powder's done got wet, but I ain't taking no chance on it. Not today." Bleeker disappeared into the wreckage.

Possum half-cocked the Brown Bess and stared into the pan. Bleeker was right; the powder looked damp. The musket probably wouldn't fire. He took several deep breaths, trying to calm himself.

Willie stood still, watching Possum. "It ain't like it seems," he mumbled.

"You little sonofabitch. I got a mind to whip you good. I might do it yet." Possum shoved Willie with his left arm, pushing him back against the wall. "Get back to your family. Go on."

Willie squeezed past Possum and hurried down the alley and around the corner, toward the porch.

Possum leaned against the wall, out of the rain. With his thumb, he wiped the wet powder from the musket's pan. He rubbed his finger across the touch hole, trying to keep from trembling. He shook his head; he'd misread William Kinney altogether. Davy's face sprang to his mind. Davy wouldn't have made that mistake, would he? Or would he? Well, Davy would have cut the traces with the Kinney family as soon as that kind of treachery popped up. That's what I'll do, he decided. I'll take off on my own, for San Antonio.

But what about Cassandra? Possum felt his anger rising again. I can't leave her with this bunch. I'll take her with me. If she'll go. Sure she will, when she finds out that Willie tried to sell her. She can bring her son, too, a nice little boy. They'd make good traveling companions.

If this rain would just quit.

Chapter 11

They were waiting for Possum on the store's porch, out of the rain, crowded together under the roof. Bertha Kinney stood in front of Willie with her shoulders thrown back. She clutched her boy Sonny against her with her right arm. Her left hand gripped Marcus's little fist. She faced Possum, daring him to rebuke her as he'd done Willie. Bear Sullivan leaned against the open doorway of his store, a quizzical expression on his face.

Possum propped his musket against the store's wall. He stalked to the cart and flipped back the canvas cover from one side. Tiny streams of rainwater trickled from the brim of his hat and ran into the cart. He reached inside the cart for his haversack and began cramming his belongings into it.

"What are you doing?" demanded Bertha.

"Leaving. I don't want no more to do with you people." He started to untie the mule's reins from the hitching rail.

"Hold on, there, Mister Possum. Don't go just yet. We gotta talk about things. About Cassandra. You don't know what's going on."

"No, ma'am, it ain't up for discussion. Where's Cassandra, anyway?" He glanced at the door. Was she inside? Bear's body blocked the doorway.

"It was her notion. Her idea. Selling her, I mean. She wanted to do it," Willie whined from behind Bertha. She scowled at him over her shoulder.

Possum stopped fussing with the mule and stepped back under the eaves, shaking water from his coat sleeves. He yanked off his hat and beat it against his thigh, spattering rainwater on Bertha. "Her idea?" he said. "You expect me to believe that Cassandra asked you to sell her? To Bleeker? Hell, no. She wouldn't do that. Where is she? What've you done with her?" He looked back and forth between Bertha and Willie.

"She's hiding. You see, she said she needed the money. For ship passage for herself and her boy," said Willie.

"That's right," added Bertha. "She said we'd split it. Said she'd find us when she escaped, and we'd give her half the money. She wanted to take Marcus back to New York on a ship." She tugged the child's hand.

Marcus's face showed the ravages of a long spell of crying. Silent now, he huddled close to Bertha.

Possum looked from Bertha to Willie and back again. "That don't make sense. In fact, it's downright ridiculous. Escape from Bleeker—how did she plan to do that? What kind of stupid lies are you telling me?"

"She said she'd kill him. She'd kill Bleeker and get away," said Willie.

Possum stamped his foot in disgust. "And then what? What did she think would happen? Slave killing her master?" He gestured towards the bank of the bayou. "She'd hang from the nearest tree. Even in Tennessee, they'd hang her. And especially in this wild Texas country. Now, tell me, where is she?"

Bear pulled himself away from the door face, straightened up and interjected himself between Possum an Bertha. "You're right, son, I wouldn't believe it myself unless I'd overheard them planning it. They're telling you straight. I seen your gal scoot off down toward the bayou. I 'spect she's hiding in the brush down there on the bank." He cast a glimpse toward the skies, the downpour still raging. "And she's skin-soaked by now, I'll wager."

Possum followed Bear's gaze across the road toward the trees, his thoughts churning. The idea of taking Cassandra along to San Antonio no longer appealed to him. He wanted to get away from all of these fools. His emotions ran from relief that Cassandra hadn't been taken away by slavers to an increasing anger at her for dreaming up such a bizarre scheme. She'd seemed so—so alive, so—well, attractive. Unlike anyone he'd ever known. Self-reliant and clever. In spite of what they'd told him, he believed that the Kinneys had cooked up the plan, presented it to Cassandra, encouraged her to try it. He shook his head. This had all turned out poorly.

He crammed his hat down on his head and reached for the Brown Bess. Bertha put a hand on his arm. He shook it loose and reached for the mule's lead. Time to set out for San Antonio, alone this time.

"Look, son," said Bear, "You don't want to be starting off down the road in all this foul weather. You'll damn near drown in all that rain, if you don't get lost first. Tell you what—I got a nice little shed in the back that can accommodate your cart and that fine animal. I'll rent it to you for, say, two dollars a night. That's a fair price. There's room for all of you'uns to hunker down for the rest of the day, if you've a mind to. Dry out a bit. Wait for the rain to let up."

Bertha and Willie exchanged glances. Possum studied his soggy moccasins, considering the offer of shelter. He was angry and wanted to leave right away, but what Bear said made sense. Rain continued to beat down on the cart's cover. Water pooled in depressions formed in the canvas. The mule blew a disgusted snort.

"Mister Possum. I was gonna ask for your help with supplies." Bertha spoke softly but urgently. "Me and Willie is out of money. Mister Bear here let me have some things on a promise. If you could find it in your heart, we'd sure be obliged."

Possum stared out into the muddy street. What would Davy do in a spot like this? Or Pap? He thought he knew.

"Mexican silver be okay?" he asked, frowning at Bear.

Bear's shed was only slightly larger than the cart. Possum crowded inside. He insisted on sheltering his mule there with the cart, which left little room for anyone else. Bertha elbowed her way around Possum. She uncovered the cart and sorted through the contents, hanging the wetter garments along the walls of the shed. The boys took shelter under the cart, in the straw. Bertha offered them cold corn pone and water.

Possum pulled off his moccasins and wrung the water from them, as best he could. He kept the Brown Bess close at hand. He'd become distrustful of the Kinneys, uncertain what to expect from them. He rubbed down the mule with handfuls of straw. The mule, fed and watered, tolerated the attention quietly.

Once they'd maneuvered the cart into the shed, Willie disappeared. Possum wondered if he'd gone in search of Grady Bleeker again. The two men seemed to have struck up an unlikely acquaintance. Willie was a puzzle. He would submit to Bertha's scolding on trivial matters, but he acted decisively at other times. He presented himself as a simple farmer from the Brazos River valley. He seemed uncomfortable on the road, nervous in the presence of strangers. And Indians. He'd acted uneasy when they met Tongue and Bad-eye on the road. According to Bigfoot Wallace, the Brazos River valley was infested with Indians. Maybe Willie'd had some bad luck with Indians.

Bear stuck his head into the shed. "Got a fresh pot of coffee boiling, and cornbread and side meat cooked up. Be obliged if you'd join me for a little dinner. Hate to eat alone."

"Be along shortly," said Possum.

Bertha routed the two boys out from under the cart and herded them off toward the store. Possum watched them go, studying Bertha's determined gait. She still wore the same ill-fitting man's clothes she had on when they met. What had got her dander up? Bertha hadn't spoken a word to Possum since the confrontation on the porch earlier. He didn't mind her silence. San Antonio was uppermost on his mind. Best that he get clear of this crazy outfit he'd fallen in with. Except he was worried about Cassandra's absence.

He continued grooming the mule, wiping her cheeks below her ears. "Pap's Sally liked this kind of attention. Guess you do, too, don't you?" Pap might be grooming Sally right now. Funny to think he and Pap might be grooming their mules at the same time, a thousand miles apart. Possum's chest constricted, remembering his home so far away. For a moment, sadness overwhelmed him. Would he ever see Tennessee again?

The mule rubbed her head against his arm, jarring him out of his reverie. "What's your name, darling? What should I call you. Damn, I been so busy, I didn't think to give you a name. Guess I'll call you Sally. Like that other fine specimen of feminine mulehood." He rubbed the mule's nose. "Sally. You like that name? Do you wanna take me to San Antonio, Sally?"

"It is good to talk to mules. And to horses. They understand more than we think."

Startled by the voice, Possum drew back and reached for the pistol tucked into his belt. A shadow in the doorway resolved itself into the figure of a man. Tongue stood still, arms at his sides, silhouetted against the daylight.

How long had the Indian been standing there? Now that he was aware of him, Possum detected the odor of rancid bear grease, the same smell he'd noticed at their previous meeting. Perhaps the stench of wet mule covered it up. Something to consider for a tracker.

He gestured. "Come into the shed."

Tongue took one step forward and stopped. There wasn't room for more. "I bring greetings from Bad-Eye," he said. "Bad-Eye sends you a gift of two horses. He would bargain with you further. For the buffalo woman."

Possum laughed. "She isn't mine to bargain for. I must refuse the horses."

"No, they are a gift. Bad-Eye asks that you think—consider—a trade. Is that the proper word—consider?"

"The word is proper. I can't accept the horses." Possum made a gesture of denial, his palm down, sweeping away to the side.

Tongue moved even closer to Possum, who stepped away, his back now against the shed's wall. His hand found the pistol in his belt. He wondered if it was primed with dry powder. Tongue seemed taller, somehow. In the shed's gloom, Possum couldn't see if Tongue still wore his cavalry saber.

"Take horses from me," said Tongue. "A trade, for a bargain."

Sally the mule gave a little snicker and shuffled her feet, uneasy now that Tongue had moved so close to her. Possum stretched his arm and patted her forehead. "What do you mean? What bargain?"

"I want—I go with you to San Antonio. Take me with you. I be your guide. We ride the horses. I talk with other Indians we meet."

"How did you know I was going to San Antonio?" Possum didn't remember saying anything about it to the Indians at their first meeting. Tongue was full of surprises.

"I hear many things. I watch. I—it would be good to see San Antonio. To watch what happens there."

The idea of proceeding on horseback appealed to Possum, and the idea of an Indian guide made sense, in a way. "You know the road to San Antonio?"

Tongue thrust his chin westward, an Indian gesture.

This offer was a complication Possum hadn't anticipated. He intended to part company with the Kinneys, but not until Cassandra was found. Since her son Marcus remained with the Kinneys, Possum was certain she'd return, sooner or later, if she was free to do so. An anger burned within him; he wanted to confront Cassandra about that silly plan to sell herself. He'd played it over in his mind, how he'd lecture her. Yet he worried that she was lost or worse, taken by Bleeker and his crowd. Perhaps he should go and search for her. Tongue might be able to help with that.

Tongue waited quietly, studying Possum's face, as though he could see the conflict raging in Possum's mind.

"We'uns need the shed. You skedaddle now." Bertha spoke from the doorway, her voice harsh. Possum glimpsed a bedraggled Cassandra huddled behind her.

So she'd come back at last. Possum's shoulders sagged; relief swept over him. He leaned to one side, trying to peer behind Bertha, wondering if Cassandra was hurt.

"Go on, now. Clear out." Bertha gestured toward the store. Her left hand pushed Cassandra further into concealment behind her back.

"Cassandra," said Possum, his voice demanding her attention.

Bertha said, "Not now. We'll talk later." She noticed Tongue and frowned at him. "Why's that Indian in here?"

"We struck a bargain." Possum offered his right hand to Tongue, who grasped it in his and shook it up and down, vigorously, three times. Indeed, Possum realized, a bargain was struck, for better or worse.

"We're going to San Antonio."

Chapter 12

The rain had slacked off to a heavy drizzle, but the skies were still dark. Sitting on the edge of the porch in front of Bear Sullivan's store, Possum watched the herds of purple clouds race across the sky, hurrying along to disappear behind him, over the store.

"Weather coming in from the Gulf of Mexico," said Bear, propping himself up in the doorway, blocking entrance into his store. "Them clouds are blowing away, moving out." He looked pointedly at Tongue, who squatted beside Possum, pipe in his mouth, tiny wisps of smoke carried away by the breeze. "Rain'll be gone by morning. It's gonna clear off."

Possum spit a little wad of tobacco into the street. He used his small knife to scrape damp gunpowder from the pan of one of his pistols. With the knife's point, he cleared the touchhole. The Brown Bess leaned against the store's wall behind him.

"Don't I know you? Wasn't you here last week?" Bear roused himself and took a step in Tongue's general direction.

"He's my guide," said Possum, without looking up. He shook a dab of fresh gunpowder into the pistol's pan and released the hammer. "He's taking me on the trail to San Antonio." He hefted the pistol for a moment and then tucked it into his belt.

"Don't hardly need a guide to find San Antonio," Bear muttered. "Just follow the road west." Possum didn't reply, and Bear returned to guarding the door frame.

Possum rose to his feet and stretched his arms over his head. Bear had given him a plate of food, a stew of beef and potatoes. He'd shared it with Tongue, ignoring Bear's frowns. Possum was certain that Tongue and Bad-Eye had paid a recent visit to the store, helping themselves to supplies, including the coffee they'd shared with Possum and the Kinneys. Bear had mentioned a visit by two Indians, and Possum had recognized Bad-Eye from Bear's description. Possum knew that townspeople often failed to identify Indians as individuals. Woodsmen were more accustomed to dealing with Indians, trading with them and learning bits of language. But Possum himself was too new to Texas to be able to tell the local tribes apart. He hoped that Tongue would teach him to do so.

"Ugh." Tongue gestured with his chin, indicating the bayou. The little ferry boat had brought three riders across, and they were urging their horses up the bank. Possum squinted at them; they looked familiar.

"More soldiers," said Bear. "Business is gonna get lively." He vanished inside.

Possum glanced over his shoulder, checking on his Brown Bess. He sat back down on the edge of the porch, drew his small knife and cut off another chaw of tobacco.

The horsemen reined up in front, studying Possum and Tongue. "I remember you," said one man, the rider in the middle of the group. "You were at San Jacinto. You was wounded, wasn't you?"

"Aye." Possum whittled a chaw from the plug. He thought he recognized the speaker. All three men wore slickers over their clothes and the familiar Texian slouch hats.

The man dismounted. "The army's headed south. We gotta get back to the Colorado River valley, get our crops in the ground. We skedaddled when Ben Rusk tried to sign us up for another round of fighting Mexicans. Is this store open for business?"

"Aye."

The other two men slid from their mounts. "Too much rain," said one, making for the store.

"It's let up a bunch," said Possum.

The other man stopped and studied Tongue. "Lots of Indian trouble up around Nacogdoches, they say. And west around Bastrop. Caddos, Wacos killing settlers and stealing horses." He gestured toward Tongue with a nod of his head. "He savvy English?"

"Some." Possum popped the chaw into his mouth. He tested the knife blade with his thumb.

"I heard tell that companies of rangers is forming up. The government is hiring Indian fighters. I might join up. You interested? They's gonna need guides. I hear they pay pretty good."

"I'm gonna head out to San Antonio."

"Well, you can fight Indians and Mexicans both at San Antone. Say, you might meet up with the Texian army down that way. I think they're supposed to bivouac down near Victoria. Them boys is still itching to fight Mexicans." He offered Possum a salute and followed his companions into the store.

Tongue gained his feet. Possum looked up at him, brows raised. "Indian troubles up north a ways? Nacogdoches?" Possum remembered passing through that strange little town with Davy, on their way to the Alamo.

"Always, the young warriors want to—to prove themselves. Make war. They steal horses, take captives, raid other tribes and pale-eyes. Mostly steal horses."

"Not your tribe, though."

"Yes. Also my people, the Bidai. It is easy for young men to raid the pale-eye farms. They gain much—honor? The old men cannot control the young."

Possum turned a wary eye at the two horses Tongue had offered him. Tied loosely to a rail, they looked innocent enough. Well-conformed, solid, healthy. Were they stolen?

"Not those horses. Heh heh heh. Bad-Eye traded for them." Tongue made a hand-up gesture: all is well.

"Traded with a raider, most likely. No telling where they came from." Possum frowned. He worried that somebody they met down the trail would recognize the horses, or one of them, as missing property.

Willie Kinney hurried down the muddy street and sloshed along right in front of the porch. Head down, he ignored Possum and Tongue and rounded the corner towards Bear's shed in the rear.

"Wonder what's got into him?" said Possum. He gained his feet, peering after Willie.

"Ugh." Tongue knocked the dottle from his pipe, which he replaced in a fold of his turban.

Willie reappeared accompanied by Bertha, the two of them emerging from the shed. They stepped onto the porch and stopped behind Possum.

"We's leaving in the morning," Bertha announced to Possum's back. "Willie found some of our neighbors from the Brazos River settlements. They was camped out the other side of town. We's all gonna travel together, for protection."

"Good idee," said Possum, turning around to face them. "Me, I'm headed for San Antonio. Good luck to you." Where was Cassandra? He peered back the way they'd come, trying to see toward the shed, seeking a glimpse of her. Worry was beginning to creep up on him, replacing his anger at Cassandra. He wanted to know that she was safe, if nothing else.

"The thing is," Bertha continued, "we'uns need to use your mule, Mr. Possum. We can't hardly pull the cart down these muddy roads, just the three of us."

The three of them? That means Cassandra will be with them, helping out, Possum realized. She must be all right, then. Was she hiding?

Willie said, "That mule's been a big help for us. We's grateful for the use of her."

I should have seen this coming, Possum realized. Once the Kinneys got that mule hitched to their cart, they wouldn't want to let it go. Well, since Tongue had brought horses, he didn't need the mule, did he? Thing was, he'd grown fond of her, named her Sally and all. He looked down at his feet, considering what to say.

"Miss, where is farm you go to?" asked Tongue.

Bertha gave him a sharp look and a frown, then turned back to Possum.

"You said your farm is somewhere on the Brazos, ain't that right?" said Possum.

"That's right," Willie chimed in. "Not 'xactly on the river. In the Brazos basin, kinda. About three creeks southwest of the Brazos river, depending on how you go."

"Thing is," said Bertha, "we'uns can pay you for the mule. Buy her from you. Once we get back to the farm. We got some coins hid out there. We tucked it away pretty good when we pulled out ahead of the Mex army. Come with us, and we'll buy the mule from you."

"No, thanks. I'm going to San Antonio."

"It is the right way." All eyes turned to Tongue. "It is west, the way to San Antonio. We go with them?" He waived his arm, waiting for Possum to respond.

"You can come along, too," Bertha said, still frowning at Tongue. "You can talk to them other Indians, can't you?"

Willie hopped from one foot to the other. "Yes, yes. Find out if any Indian raiders are prowling along the Brazos, what they're doing, where they plan to strike. That's wonderful. We can pay you, too."

Possum and Tongue exchanged glances. To Possum, it seemed to be a workable plan. But Cassandra was utmost on his mind. Worry and anger mixed together consumed most of his attention. Where was she? He felt he had to know. He turned his attention back to Bertha. "Where's Cassandra?" he asked.

"She's in the shed, hiding. She's ashamed of what she done. I think she's afeered of you."

Possum pressed between Bertha and Willie to collect his Brown Bess. "I'd best talk with her," he said.

He found Cassandra in the shadows, her arms wrapped around the mule's neck, her face buried in its loose mane. She was dressed in man's clothing, evidently Willie's clothes because they were too small for her. Her black skirt hung from the walls; it was still dripping rainwater. Her son Marcus clung to her, his arms wrapped around her leg. Sonny stood close to them. Big-eyed, he watched Possum.

Possum's heart wrenched at the image. His anger vanished as though it were an unworthy thought. The picture of dejection, she still radiated a nobility even in the cast-off clothes she wore. He felt a swell of kindness, of admiration, overwhelm him. He'd never thought that a woman, any woman, could raise such strange emotions within him. Now, he only wanted to help her, any way that he could.

"Cassandra," he said softly. "Cassandra?"

She released the mule and turned her head in his direction. Her face was swollen from weeping. She blotted her eyes on her sleeve and sniffed loudly. Taking a deep breath, she drew herself erect.

"I am grateful to you, sir, for preventing me from making a grave mistake. For saving me from the terrible situation I was placing myself in. In my desperation, I took the only way I could conceive. It was poorly considered. I must find passage back to the American east coast, to New Jersey, for Marcus if not for myself. I hoped to raise the money by allowing Mr. Kinney to sell me. I thought I could escape and rejoin him and his family and Marcus. You stopped me. You, sir, saved me, and Marcus as well." She reached down to comfort Marcus. A sob escaped her throat; she wiped her nose on her sleeve.

"Cassandra..."

"Willie told me that you were furious with him and threatened him bodily harm. It was not his fault, sir. Do not blame him for my foibles."

Possum wasn't sure what a foible was, but he got the general idea. "Willie seemed right pleased to be doing business with Bleeker. I guess he encouraged you, right enough. And Bertha, too, I'll bet."

Cassandra slumped, eyes downcast, silent for a moment. Then she pulled herself erect and looked Possum in the face, a hint of a smile on her lips. "I fear I have come between Mr. and Mrs. Kinney. He has become quite solicitous of me, even managing to touch me at times. Mrs. Kinney has taken note. It may be—perhaps she would be pleased to rid herself of me."

That idea hadn't occurred to Possum. I haven't been observant enough, he realized. Davy aways had a sense for how people got along. I should have paid more attention. He grinned to himself. I guess Cassandra has addled me a bit.

Cassandra noted Possum's grin. "It is serious; it is not amusing. I am dependent upon the Kinneys. I'm alone in this country of yours, a woman, a black woman, without rights of citizenship. The Kinneys have carried us along with them and have treated us well."

"What will you do now?" Possum hesitated to ask. He was still determined to go on to San Antonio, but didn't like the idea of parting with Cassandra. He searched her face, the flicker of emotions passing across it.

"I don't know." The answer hung there, in the shed's dank air, between the two of them. Possum had a premonition; this was a turning point for him, in his life. Cassandra was waiting for him to speak. He could turn away from her, go to San Antonio, look for Davy Crockett. Her eyes locked with his; his heart rose in his throat.

"Why not—why not come along with me? I am gonna go with the Kinneys to their farm place. Tongue, the Indian, is with me now. He'll act as guide on our journey. You and Marcus—well, you'll be among friends." Possum realized that this didn't solve her problem—how to get ship to the east coast—but it answered her needs of the moment.

"Are you certain?"

What is she asking? I made the offer, didn't I? Possum drew himself up to his full height. "Yes, Cassandra, I'm certain." He smiled at her.

Cassandra smiled in turn. "So am I."

PART TWO

Chapter 13

"Knee high by the Fourth of July."

That's what Pap always said about his corn crop. Possum remembered Pap standing in the cornfield, his lanky frame silhouetted against the Tennessee sky, checking the crop's height against his pants leg.

Well, Willie's corn wasn't quite knee-high, and today was certainly later than July Fourth. Possum sat on the stump of an oak tree, squinting into the sun at the cornfield. He knew it was the month of July. He'd seen Scorpio riding high among the summer stars, and the Teapot rising up behind Scorpio. The actual date was anybody's guess.

I've turned twenty-one, Possum realized. My birthday is July fourteenth but I don't know exactly when that date fell this year. The Kinneys didn't have a calendar. He brushed his hand through his short red beard, thicker now than the scraggly growth of hair on his pate. My knees are higher up than Pap's knees, too, he thought with a smile. I guess I've grown into manhood.

His smile faded as he thought of Pap. Did he get his crop in this year, back in Tennessee? Pap had begun to move slowly. His strides had shortened, and he walked ever more deliberately. Plowing those fields would have been painful for him this springtime. Possum sighed, trying to ease the guilt that settled over him. I should be there, he told himself, but I can't return to

Lawrence County, not just yet. I gotta find Davy first. Davy will know what to do, what to tell people.

He squinted down the rows of corn. Willie's crop looked good and healthy, not quite ready to tassel out. They'd taken turns, Possum and Willie, urging Sally through the acres of the Kinney farm. Pap would be proud of me, Possum realized, working so hard without his oversight.

Possum leaned forward from his seat on the oaken stump and grabbed a handful of dirt. Black and rich, it trickled through his fingers. He glanced toward the cabin where Bertha and Cassandra toiled in the vegetable garden, bent from the waist, pulling weeds in the morning sun. Tongue worked beside them, helping cultivate the vegetables, a little distance removed from the two women.

At first, both women had kept their distance from Tongue, not looking in his direction or addressing him. That began to change with the vegetable garden, when Tongue showed Bertha that he was a proficient gardener. He gathered native plants in the woods and meadows and showed Bertha how the Indians used them. Cassandra asked Tongue about medical uses for his selections. She compared his ideas with her knowledge of the Jamaican flora.

Possum shifted his gaze to the Kinney's cabin. Solid, with logs carefully fitted, seams sealed with river clay, the cabin had doors of pine on leather hinges and small gun ports in each wall. Possum was taken aback when he first saw it. Willie had said they'd been farming here in the Brazos valley for the past two years. The cabin was certainly older than that, and Willie couldn't have built it himself. Not only that two years wasn't enough, which it wasn't. Willie just didn't have the temperament to build a cabin. How had he managed it?

Willie Kinney was still a puzzle to Possum. He fussed all along the last leg of the trip, increasingly anxious to reach his farm. The trek up the Brazos River went smoothly enough, but once they left the river road and struck out cross-country, progress slowed to a crawl. There wasn't much of a trail to follow; they had to backtrack more than once. Maneuvering the cart across three shallow creeks challenged Sally, even with all three men helping her pull the load.

How did the Kinneys manage to get that cart out of the woods during the Runaway Scrape, when all the Brazos settlers were fleeing toward Louisiana ahead of the Mexican army? Possum badgered Willie about it, until Willie confessed that he'd had three horses at the time. He claimed the horses were stolen by Indians up near the Sabine, before the family started the return trip. Possum decided that Willie must be concealing a good bit of his adventures during the Runaway Scrape. Willie just didn't want to talk about it. He didn't answer Possum's questions; he changed the subject.

When they'd crossed the last creek and finally reached the farm, Willie broke and ran past the cabin to the little corral beside it. He wrestled a post out of the ground, reached into the posthole and pulled out a leather bag. Grinning ear to ear, he shook the bag and was rewarded with a clinking of coins. "My gold!" he shouted. "Nobody found it while we were gone."

That wasn't the only surprise, either. A small chicken house beside the corral had a floor made of rough-cut pine slabs which Willie quickly yanked up, exposing a cellar filled with household items he'd cached away. Immediately he pulled out a jug, uncorked it and helped himself to a generous swig. Only then did he offer to help unload the cart.

Possum found a well-made shed beneath a live oak tree, back behind the log cabin. He appropriated it for his own quarters. Tongue shared it with Possum but preferred to sleep outdoors most nights. He seemed immune to the nightly swarms of mosquitoes that rose from the creek. Possum declined Tongue's offer of bear grease for protection, preferring to keep himself covered with clothes and his floppy hat. Occasionally, an evening breeze kept the mosquitoes off of them. Sleep came easily after a hard day's toil in the cornfields.

Possum turned his attention back to the garden, where Bertha was proclaiming an opinion in a loud voice. She looked more formidable now that she'd donned a dress in place of her husband's clothes. Bertha had taken charge of the cabin, cleaning out the debris that had accumulated in their absence, directing Cassandra to help with this and that. Cassandra didn't take well to orders given by Bertha, but she didn't object aloud.

Bertha let it be known that she ruled that roost. She cooked meals with Cassandra's occasional help. Willie's place was at the head of the pine-plank table, with Bertha sitting at the foot. Cassandra and the two boys sat on stools along one side. Possum was welcome to sit at the other side of the table. Tongue was not allowed inside the cabin at all—Bertha's rule that applied to all Indians, she said. Possum carried food outdoors to Tongue, and usually ate outside with him.

Willie had disappeared early on this summer morning. Whatever other faults he might have, Willie was a good father. He was considerate of both boys. He'd assign them little tasks, whenever he could get the boys away from Bertha's supervision. This morning, he'd taken the two boys away toward the creek, down in the woods, to fish for the little perch that hid there in the pool.

Willie was able to catch fish at times, but he never made any attempt to hunt for red meat. That chore he left to Possum and Tongue. Possum and Tongue ranged through the woods in the Brazos valley, exploring, hunting and trapping. They'd found a flock of the Kinney's chickens roosting near the cabin. Bertha corralled the birds, and now they had breakfast eggs on a daily basis. She hadn't permitted Willie to kill even one of her hens. Tongue had pointed out tracks of pigs in the mud beside the creek. Laughing, Possum and Tongue herded a half-dozen pigs back to the farm and into an improvised sty.

They found recent moccasin tracks as well. Tongue identified some of them as Tonkawas or Wacos. He tried to explain to Possum how the moccasins of different tribes left distinct impressions in the mud. Possum couldn't tell them apart. Tongue insisted that none of the tracks were made by Comanches. Tonkawas and Wacos were dangerous, he said, but not in small bands.

Exploring the woods, they found two other homesteads near the Kinneys'. Tongue didn't want to approach them, and Possum didn't either. They crept along beside cornfields, ready to duck into the woods when anyone appeared at the cabins. Possum thought it strange that Willie seemed unaware of his neighbors in the Brazos valley.

Possum found himself watching Cassandra's tall, willowy body as she pulled weeds. She wore a calico-patterned dress, probably a discard of Bertha's. Possum couldn't keep his eyes from straying to Cassandra's well-formed calves, displayed when she bent from the waist. He'd grown fond of Cassandra and believed that she was fond of him, too. He still didn't know what to make of her. He was puzzled by his own emotions. She was a colored woman, after all, a different race of people. Was he falling in love with her? He didn't have any way to judge his feelings; he'd never been attracted to any girl before.

On the trail he'd paid attention to Cassandra, sometimes drawing her into conversations about her life in New Jersey and Jamaica. In turn, she'd asked him about Tennessee and his farm there. Here in the Brazos valley, they often sat together in the evenings, outside the cabin or on the bank of the creek, talking of little things. He thrilled when she touched his hand or leaned on his shoulder. Once he'd put his arm around her while they sat together.

What would Davy think? Or Pap?

Possum had begun to wonder about Pap and the Indian woman, Lena, who'd stayed with them on the farm for a year. She had appeared at their doorway, ill with fever, holding her little boy by the hand. Pap sheltered them in the barn and cared for Lena, getting her through the fever, helping her regain her strength. The boy, Sa-lo-li, became Possum's companion during that year. They'd run the woods together, trapping and fishing the creeks. Possum learned Indian techniques for trapping small game. Of necessity, he picked up Cherokee language phrases. He was sorry when autumn arrived and Lena left for Indian territory in Oklahoma, Sa-lo-li marching beside her.

Thinking back on it, Possum wondered if Pap had taken a liking to Lena. He didn't remember Mother ever helping with Lena during her illness. Pap had always seemed so serious, so stern. Could it be that he'd found favor with Lena, an Indian woman?

Tongue was now standing straight, motionless, staring at the woods behind the cabin. Possum smiled at the sight. What was the Indian up to now? He'd learned so much from Tongue, about the habits of the deer and the bear and the small game.

In turn, Possum had taught Tongue about the use of flintlock firearms. Tongue knew the basic facts about flintlocks but had never fired one. When the powder in the pan was ignited Tongue would turn away. Possum gave Tongue one of his pistols to work with.

Tongue's English improved, and so did Possum's. Cassandra corrected his grammar and enhanced his vocabulary. Tongue listened eagerly to the informal lessons. Cassandra spoke Spanish as well, and Possum was anxious to become proficient in Spanish phrases. When he reached San Antonio, a knowledge of that language might help him to find Davy. Tongue had a working knowledge of Spanish.

Possum rose to his feet, staring at Tongue who remained motionless, eyes fixed the woods. What was going on?

Abruptly, Tongue turned to the two women and grasped each by an elbow. He hurried them around the corner of the cabin towards the door. Possum started loping toward Tongue, who shouted to Possum over his shoulder.

"Comanches!"

Chapter 14

Three Indians approached the cabin, walking their horses through the cornfield, riding abreast, glancing this way and that, advancing cautiously. Possum faced them from the cabin's doorway. He flicked a glimpse toward the woods by the creek and saw Willie crouched there with the two boys. Possum made a downward gesture with his hands, a warning to Willie, who immediately shoved the children into a thicket of undergrowth and followed them, disappearing from sight.

"Get in here!" Bertha yanked Possum by the elbow, pulling him inside the cabin. She closed the door and shoved a wooden latch in place. "There," she said. "It's locked now." Frantically, she searched here and there. "Where's Willie? Are the boys with him?"

Tongue was peering through one of the gun ports. Cassandra handed Possum his Brown Bess and his powder horn; she'd already half-cocked the hammer, ready for priming.

"What do they want?" Possum looked at Tongue. He thought he knew the answer. Most likely, they only wanted a little food or tobacco. He didn't feel threatened by them. Comanches or not, three Indians made for only a small raiding party. They're just exploring, seeing what we have here, Possum decided. Still, he poured a dash of gunpowder into the musket's pan. Best be ready for the unexpected. Like Davy always said.

"Bigger war party, many Indians, other side of creek. Comanches." Tongue's command of English had slipped, Cassandra's lessons forgotten under stress. "Many warriors, Comanche raid," he mumbled. "Horses. Plunder." Tongue fumbled for words. "Three come here. Look at us. Look for plunder. Horses. Maybe firearms."

Bertha tugged at Possum's arm. "Willie? Did you see Willie?"

Possum shrugged her off and peered through a gun port. How could Tongue know about a big war party? Had he seen them? Possum stepped back and finished priming the musket. He noticed Bertha attempting to load Willie's flintlock, fiddling with the ramrod. Cassandra appeared at his elbow; he pulled one of the pistols from his belt and handed it to her. "Just in case," he said.

"One come," said Tongue. He backed away from the gun port.

Cautiously, Possum peered through the port. One of the Comanches dismounted in front of the cabin. He couldn't see where the other two had gone. The lone Comanche marched right up to the door, out of Possum's line of sight through the gun port. The Indian hammered on the door and shouted something Possum couldn't understand.

Tongue responded in shrill shouts, evidently in the same language. The Comanche repeated his demands with more banging on the door, and Tongue answered him ever more loudly, trembling visibly.

Possum thrust the muzzle of the Brown Bess through the gun port. He couldn't quite see the Comanche at the door because of the narrow angle, but he was sure the Indian could see the musket's barrel and would realize that they were armed and ready.

With a shout and a final thump on the door, the Comanche walked back to his horse and mounted it. When he came into view, Possum sighted along the barrel at the Indian, taking aim at his chest. Tongue tapped Possum's shoulder gently, saying "No, no, no."

"I ain't gonna blast him. Not if he don't cause trouble." Possum shrugged Tongue's hand away. He glanced at Bertha, who had poked her flintlock's barrel out of the other gun port. Possum was pretty sure her weapon wasn't loaded.

"What was he saying?"

"Want food. Tobacco. Tell us come out of cabin."

Possum hoped the Indians would just move on. He didn't want a fight, not unless he was forced into it. Tongue's hand kept flicking at Possum's shoulder. Tongue didn't want to get into a shooting match, either. Possum's palms were getting sweaty. His breath came in short gasps. Tongue's tension was contagious. Don't show any fear, Possum told himself. Others here depend upon me.

"Our horses!" cried Bertha. The other two Comanches reappeared in front of the cabin. One led the Kinneys' three horses by ropes looped around their necks. The other Indian tugged at a rope, leading Sally the mule, who kicked and bucked and pulled loose. She galloped away through the vegetable garden, still bucking. The Comanches laughed at the sight. They sat straight upright, unafraid of the weapons pointed at them.

"Shoot 'em!" Bertha yelled at Possum.

"They take. They go. Good." From behind Possum, Tongue offered his assessment. Possum agreed with him. If these three Comanches were part of a larger party of warriors, as Tongue believed, then a few animals was a small price to pay for their lives. Possum withdrew his musket from the gun port.

"Damn!" Bertha pulled her own gun barrel out of the port. She stepped away from it, scowling at Possum. "Damn you," she repeated.

Cassandra pushed Bertha aside to peer through the gun port. "Oh my God! No!" she screamed. Her face pressed to the port, Cassandra could see toward the woods. Possum leaned close to his own gun port and saw that Marcus had burst from his hiding place. The boy ran toward the cabin, head down, his little legs churning.

The Comanches had turned and were riding away through the cornfield, leading the Kinneys' horses. At first, the Indians didn't notice Marcus. Then, one glanced back over his shoulder. He turned his horse around and began to gallop back. Possum poked the Brown Bess through the gun port and cocked it.

The cabin door burst open wide, blocking Possum's field of fire. He pulled the musket away from the gun port and peered out, trying to see what had happened. He spied Cassandra running; she had charged out of the door and was sprinting away, in the opposite direction from Marcus.

Possum quickly scrambled to the open door and stood on the sill, uncertain what he should do. Cassandra was offering herself as bait, attracting the Comanches' attention. The Indian was wavering, too, looking first at Marcus and then at Cassandra. She dashed across the front of the cornfield, skirts held high and dark legs flashing in the sunlight. Abruptly, the Comanche made his decision and urged his horse after Cassandra. Possum raised his musket but hesitated; Tongue was behind him again, muttering, "No, no." The Comanche leaned from his steed, grabbed Cassandra and pulled her across the horse's neck in front of him, face down. He galloped back to his two companions, yelling "Hey, hey, hey, ho, ho."

Little Marcus had stumbled and fallen in the dirt. He scrambled to his feet and, crying and limping, started for the cabin where Possum waited in the doorway.

The remaining Comanche was unencumbered by stolen horses or a captive woman. He urged his horse across the cornfield at full gallop. He twisted down, reaching for Marcus. Possum didn't take time to think. Before Tongue could object again, he aimed the Brown Bess and squeezed the trigger. A puff of smoke from the pan, a crack of an explosion, and the Comanche pitched backward off of his horse. Bertha stretched out her arms and Marcus ran into them.

"Bad," muttered Tongue, shaking his head. "Now other Comanches come."

Possum busied himself reloading the Brown Bess. He cast a quick glance at the two remaining Comanches who sat on their horses on the far side of the cornfield, watching him. After priming the pan, he lifted the musket and thrust it in the general direction of the Comanches. They turned their horses and disappeared into the far woods.

Bertha said "Marcus, your mother done a noble thing." She held the child close. Possum wondered at the triumphant expression on her face.

Willie hurried up to the cabin, hunched over, scooting along with Sonny. The boy broke away from him and sped toward his friend Marcus.

"That was a good shot," Willie said. He reached for his own musket. "Loaded but not primed," Bertha told him. "We lost the horses."

"We'll get other horses, Mother. It's a small loss."

Possum stalked across the yard and knelt down beside the dead Comanche. The musket ball had taken him squarely in the chest, probably piercing his heart. Death must have been instantaneous. The Comanche's face was painted, red and black stripes, a touch of a white stripe across his eyes. His hair was gathered into a topknot. He was naked except for a breechclout and tattered hip-high moccasins.

"Ugly one, ain't he?" Possum looked up to see Willie standing across from him, hands in his pockets. "Ugliest Injun I ever seen."

"Kwaharu tribe, plains Comanche," said Tongue, leaning past Willie. "War paint. Older warrior, not—hasty?"

"Not brash, mebbe? That what you mean?" Possum shoved the Indian's body, rolling it over.

"Hey, bow and arrows. Get that quiver for me," exclaimed Willie.

Possum tugged at the leather strap, freeing the quiver from the Indian's shoulder. He handed it to Willie.

"Comanche want take boy-child back to village. Make into Comanche warrior." Tongue held up a hand for silence. He looked toward the woods, listening.

"You hear anything?" asked Possum.

"Big war party gone now. They move on. Go back up river. Maybe somebody come." Tongue kept his attention fixed on the grove of trees.

"They oughta leave a clear trail," said Possum. "One that'll be easy to follow, if there's that big a bunch of 'em. Come on, Tongue. Let's get started. I'll go look where Cassandra got snatched up. See what the horse's track looks like." Possum started across the yard.

"No follow," said Tongue. "Too many Comanche."

"He's right," offered Willie. "A big war party like that—you'd never stand a chance."

"Mebbe I could sneak up, you know, late at night. If I found Cassandra, I might spirit her away." Possum looked back at the dead Comanche. The Indian's horse had returned to nuzzle its owner's body. "Willie, grab that horse," he said. "I'll take it and start right away."

"Trade," said Tongue.

"Trade the horse?"

"No. Trade for woman. Trade for Cassandra."

"He's right," said Willie. "We could ransom her. Comanches trade captives for guns, liquor, and other things they want. We'll get us a trader, mebbe a hunter who trades with Comanches. We'll get her back."

Possum studied Willie, who stared down at his feet. "Willie, I heard they mistreat women. Torture them. Burn them. I think we need to act fast."

Tongue said, "Buffalo Woman smart. No hurt."

"I ain't taking no chance on it. Willie, hurry up and grab that horse like I told you, before it runs off. I'll get my outfit together. You coming or not?" Possum asked Tongue.

"White man come." Tongue gestured with his chin at a rider who emerged from the woods in the direction of the creek. He approached slowly and stopped his horse beside them.

"You folks all right?"

"Lost our horses," said Willie. "And a woman."

"Goddammit, Kinney, you always had your priorities backwards."

"Didn't mean nothing by it." Willie's head drooped down.

"Who're you?" asked the horseman, peering at Possum. "Ain't seen you around."

"George Hanks, called Possum. This is my guide, Tongue. We's bound for San Antonio. Lending the Kinneys a hand with the corn crop."

"Cyrus Godfrey," said the rider, eyeing Tongue carefully.

"He's Bidai. Step down." Possum made the offer; he didn't think Willie was going to invite the man to dismount.

Godfrey threw a leg over the saddle and slid to the ground. "We're neighbors. The other side of the creek and down a ways." He looked Possum up and down. "Guess I seen your tracks near our place, a few days ago."

"We been out hunting game. The Comanches hit you too?"

"About a dozen came at us sudden-like. We fought them off pretty good. We were six muskets, took turns shooting. They tried to burn us out, but we doused the fire."

"Heard guns. Smelled smoke." Tongue nodded.

Possum stared at him. He hadn't heard any gunshots. Tongue must have acute hearing. Either that, or he was a liar.

"Anybody hurt?" asked Willie.

"My boy taken an arrow in his shoulder, that's all. Did the Comanches take Bertha?"

"No, just a negro woman working for us."

Possum glared hard at Willie. Is that the way he thought of Cassandra? A servant? Just a servant? His temper rose; he clenched his fists. I might give you that beating yet, he said to himself. I owe you one.

Godfrey glanced down at the dead Indian. "I see you got one of the bastards. We wounded one at our place. The others drug him off."

"Mr. Godfrey, are your folks all right? Did the Comanches attack you, too?" Bertha came up behind Willie, bringing each boy by the hand.

"We'll make out all right, Mrs. Kinney. By the way, I seen your brother down in Columbia a while back. He said he'd be wanting his farm back." A slight smile played across Godfrey's lips.

"Oh, did they come back to Texas?" asked Willie. "I thought they was bound for New Orleans."

"He's back, all right. Wondered if you'd made it through the Runaway Scrape. Said something about you taking his horses." Godfrey stepped closer to Willie and, smiling, poked him on the shoulder.

Willie backed away. "Don't know about no horses."

"Well, I'm sure he'll be coming back this way soon. With his family. As soon as he finishes his business in Columbia."

Understanding dawned on Possum. This farm must belong to Willie's brother-in-law. That would explain the neatly-built cabin and the cleared fields, jobs Willie just didn't seem capable of. What would happen when the rightful owner returned? Well, he thought, that's not my problem.

He offered his hand to Godfrey. "Pleased to meet you, sir. I'm taking off after the Comanches. I'm gonna rescue Cassandra before they get too far away."

"Don't be a damned fool," said Godfrey. "They's too many of them. A troop of Rangers will be coming up from Columbia before long, on the trail of those redskins. You might join up with the Rangers. But alone—you wouldn't stand a snowball's chance."

"Ugh," said Tongue, nodding.

"You ever been up in the hill country?" asked Godfrey.

"No." Possum shrugged his shoulders. He looked at the sky. Mid-afternoon, he judged, plenty of daylight left. "I need to get started." He turned to Tongue. "You coming or not?"

"Need more men." Tongue's chin jutted out, his shoulders thrown back.

Possum pulled his fingers through his beard, considering his options. Without Tongue's help he couldn't accomplish much; he didn't know enough about the habits of the Comanches.

"You certain them Rangers will take up the trail?" he asked, looking at Godfrey.

"A Comanche raid this size? Hell, yes, they'll be all over it. Why don't you ride on down to Columbia and go with them when they set out?"

Possum's shoulders slumped. It hurt to delay, but Godfrey's suggestion made sense.

"Down river, yes. I go too." Tongue brightened up.

Chapter 15

The Columbia ferry across the Brazos River was put away for the night. Possum could make it out in the evening dusk, tied up at a pier on the far riverbank. It looked deserted. Possum tried a few halloos, but couldn't raise any response. He and Tongue settled down to sleep under a big pecan tree. He'd hoped to spend this night across the river in Columbia. He itched to get riding, to rescue Cassandra.

Possum and Tongue had trailed their way down the north bank of the river until they reached the Harrisburg road and found the Columbia crossing. Possum rode Sally the mule. Tongue followed reluctantly, astride the Comanche Indian's horse.

Bertha had raised loud objections when Possum saddled Sally. Their horses were stolen, and they needed the mule to work the farm. She poked Willie into adding his whining plea. Possum ignored them. Willie reached for the rawhide halter on the Comanche horse, but Tongue vaulted onto it and followed Possum.

The Comanche raid had thrown Tongue into a panic. Nervous, he stayed close to Possum, especially when they passed near a farm or homestead. Some cabins they saw had been burned out. Most farms showed signs of the Indian attack. Possum had half expected Tongue to disappear, perhaps to make his way back to his tribal area near the Trinity River. Thus far, Tongue stayed with him, ever watchful, saying little. Neither of them mentioned going to San Antonio.

They weren't alone while waiting for the ferry. A party of Indians was camped near the riverbank. Tongue said they were Tonkawas. At Possum's urging, he crossed the road and talked with them. They knew about the big raid, of course, but they hadn't seen any Comanches nearby. Tongue said the Tonkawas hoped to sign on as scouts for the Ranger company recruiting in Columbia. The Indians started a small campfire to wait out the night. Possum wondered if he and Tongue would be invited to join the Tonkawas. Tongue said no, they weren't invited, and settled beneath a blanket at the base of the tree. He tied his horse to the tree right beside him and kept the Tonkawas in view. Possum followed Tongue's example, staking Sally where he could watch her.

Possum tried to sleep, but the image of Cassandra running across the cornfield kept coming back to him. He dreamed of her each night. His sense of helplessness, his inability to pursue her captors, pestered him like a sore blister. Tongue kept assuring him that the Comanches would find her too valuable to hurt, and that she was smart and would protect herself in captivity. She could be bought by a trader, or bartered to another tribe of Indians. Eventually she would be freed. Reluctantly, Possum agreed to bide his time, but he intended to go after her with a Ranger company whenever one was organized.

Even with his feeling of urgency, Possum had delayed leaving the Kinney farm. He felt obligated to bury the Comanche warrior he'd shot. Tongue objected, claiming that it was bad medicine to touch a Comanche, even a dead one. Godfrey the neighbor said it was a foolish gesture. Throw the Indian in the creek, he'd said. Possum ignored them and proceeded to dig a grave.

Possum had never killed a man before. The Comanche was his first, and it preyed on his conscience. At the Alamo, he'd fired into a group of bodies, never knowing if he'd actually hit one of the Mexican soldiers, much less killed one. It's just an Indian, said Willie Kinney, but to Possum it was more. It was a man whose life he'd taken. Not without cause, but a death nevertheless. Possum felt that, in a way, it marked his twenty-first birthday. It proclaimed his accession into manhood. What would Pap think, Pap who'd never harmed anyone?

Tongue had watched while Possum dug the narrow grave, rolled the warrior's body in a blanket and buried him. Possum didn't offer any prayer, just stood silently for a moment with Tongue shivering at his elbow. "Comanche near creek," Tongue told him. Possum doubted it. He saw no one there. He thought Tongue was reacting to the odor of the dead Comanche.

It was Tongue's sharp sense of smell that allowed him to detect the Comanche raiders. He told Possum that each tribe had a distinct odor, and he could smell and identify Indians before catching a glimpse of them. Tongue said that Possum had a distinctive smell, also, but not as strong as the odor of an Indian. Tongue chuckled when Possum sniffed at his own armpits.

He awakened on the riverbank with a start, confused for a moment. He threw off his blanket and propped himself up on his elbows. The river seemed calm in the early morning light, wisps of fog trailing across it. He saw a figure standing on the dock across the river. The boatman? The Tonkawas were ambling down the riverbank; they'd seen the man, too. Possum poked Tongue with his foot. Time to get up.

Columbia, the provisional capitol of the Republic of Texas, was a sea of mud. Possum sat on a roughhewn bench outside a blacksmith shop and watched the constant parade of Texians slosh up and down the streets, squishing through the red mud. The official business of the Republic of Texas competed with an array of trappers, hunters, farmers, Indians, soldiers and others, no two dressed alike. He wondered if one of these might be an Indian trader, a man he might send to look for Cassandra. The Tonkawas from last night sat huddled together on the other side of the street. Tongue gave his horse's reins to Possum and sloshed across the street to talk with them.

The blacksmith suggested that Possum wait until later in the morning before seeking out a Ranger company. Three-legged Horace Peavey, who was in charge of recruiting, had caroused late into the evening and wouldn't be rising this early. Plenty of time, said the blacksmith, and plenty of room in the Rangers, from what he'd seen of them. He pointed out a short, fat man with a bandaged left leg, who hobbled carefully through the mire with the aid of an improvised crutch. The blacksmith said the Comanches had attacked his upper Brazos farm. He'd taken an arrow. Now, the man was anxious to get into a Ranger company. He couldn't join until his wound healed. Possum rubbed his own wound, covered by an ugly scar. It was stiff but no longer sore.

A tall officer marched past, his boots slinging mud, his elbows poked out, arms swinging in a military stride. Three men hurried to keep up with him, surly-looking rascals following in a row. Possum squinted at the officer; something about him was familiar. The man's name came to him suddenly. He gained his feet and yelled, "Colonel Wharton! Colonel Wharton."

The officer stopped, looking this way and that. "Yes?" he called. "Who asks for me?" His eyes locked with Possum's. "Oh, I remember you, son. From the San Jacinto battle. Wounded, weren't you? Well, come on, soldier, we're going to the Land Office. You've earned your acres, a gift from a grateful Republic. Fall in, there." And Wharton marched down the street, oblivious of the muck, tall hat askew and frock coat bobbing behind him, twin pistols hanging at his sides. Head down, Possum fell in at the end of the line, stepping carefully to avoid the deeper puddles.

His attention focused on his moccasins, he bumped into the man in front of him when the little troop came to a halt. A gray-bearded scarecrow turned around to spit a brown stream of tobacco. He scowled at Possum.

Colonel Wharton marched up the steps to the porch of a wooden building and pushed open a door. "Here's some more San Jacinto veterans, soldiers all. Ready to claim their land. March in, boys." Wharton stood aside and beckoned them inside.

Possum halted on the steps and began scraping the mud from his moccasins. He felt a hand on his shoulder and Wharton said, "Your turn, soldier. Don't fret about that mud. Jerome don't give a damn about dirt on his floor."

A dour-faced man sitting behind a pine-plank table beckoned to Possum. "Come on, come on," he said. "I ain't got all morning." He grabbed for a sheet of paper and dipped a pen into an inkwell. "Name?"

"George Hanks." Possum frowned and looked aside. The name sounded strange to his ears; he'd used it so little. Had he said it right?

"What company was you in?" The pen poised over the paper.

Possum chewed on his lower lip. He didn't know if he was ever really in a company of the Texian army.

"Well?"

"Goddammit, Jerome!" exclaimed Wharton. "He was in my company. Give him his goddamn land."

"All right. Sign your name." Jerome pushed the paper across toward Possum and handed him the pen. "Right there at the bottom."

Possum labored to write his name, slow but sure, concentrating on each letter. He hadn't written anything since—well, since he had come to Texas. The skill returned, bit by bit. He handed the paper back.

Jerome took the pen and scratched something on an official-looking piece of paper. "Here's your deed. File it at the courthouse down the street, or in Houston, or anyplace. You are the proud owner of 640 prime acres in the Texas hills. Hope you can speak Comanch'." He passed the deed to Possum while looking at Wharton. "Any more rag-tag veterans of San Jacinto outside, waiting for their riches?"

Wharton took Possum by the elbow. "Pay him no mind," he said. "I'm ready for a hooker of the real stuff. How about you? Fancy a whiskey? I'll take you to my favorite tavern."

Long pine planks stretched across two barrels served as the bar in Wharton's favorite saloon. The clientele hailed him when he entered, cheering and raising their jars of clear whiskey. Wharton shoved Possum toward a place at the bar, elbowing his way ahead. Possum found himself standing next to a buckskin-clad giant who was waving the biggest Bowie knife he'd ever seen.

"God dammit, Charlie, put down that Arkansas toothpick." Wharton slammed his fist down on the bar. "Whiskey for this soldier, Buck. And me, too." He slapped Possum on the back. "A veteran of San Jacinto, wounded in the fight, suffered side-by-side with General Sam. Give him your best."

The bartender placed two glass jars in front of them and poured from an earthen jug.

"This here's Buck Wilson. Makes the best corn likker in east Texas." Wharton grabbed his jar and took a taste. "Damn, that's good."

Buck nodded to Possum, who nodded back. He sipped cautiously from his jar.

"Ain't that smooth?" Wharton popped Possum on the back.

Possum nodded, but he thought it was the worst corn liquor he'd ever tasted. If that's what passes for good whiskey in Texas, he'd do well to set up a still. In Tennessee, they'd run this guy Buck out of town on a rail.

"One more," hollered Wharton. Possum took his jar and carefully eased his way back from the crude bar. The man Wharton called Charlie had pulled out the Bowie knife again and was cutting slices out of the air. Other customers were giving him as much space as they could.

Possum pushed his way through the throng and made for the door. He looked for a place to set down his jar. There didn't seem to be any tables or chairs, or even many places to stand.

He found his progress blocked by a short man smiling up at him. Possum took in the man's tailored suit. Wide dark lapels on an open coat exposed a brocade vest.

"Pardon," said Possum. He tried to slip past but the little man blocked his way. He grinned ear to ear and gestured toward the bar.

"Buy you another?"

Possum shook his head, no. His stomach was rebelling at the sharp liquor. Again, he tried to push his way past, but the man side-stepped so as to stop him.

"I heard you were a veteran of San Jacinto and wounded in the fight to boot. I'd like to show my appreciation."

"Thankee, but no."

"Name's Frank Lively. Is that your land allotment you got there?" Gently, he reached across and pulled the paper from Possum's belt. "Yes, you got the full allotment, I see. But it's way off there in Indian country, isn't it? I think Texas should treat its soldiers better than that, don't you? This land of yours is far to the west, a hundred miles from here. Texas owes you brave men a mighty debt but pays you with Comanche land." He removed his cap and wiped his brow. "Wish you'd let me buy you a whiskey to show my personal appreciation for your bravery. And maybe we can do a little business." He grabbed Possum's arm and turned him around toward the bar.

Frank Lively was surprisingly strong. His fingers dug into Possum's biceps and shoved him back to the bar, crowding him in next to Charlie again. Lively slipped between Possum and Charlie. With his elbow, he shoved Charlie aside, ducking to avoid a swoop of the Bowie knife. "Set up the bar, Buck," he called. He was answered by whoops of joy and jars banging down on the planks.

"Let's talk a little business." Lively spoke softly, his lips near Possum's ear. "I'd like to talk with you about your land allotment. It won't be much use to you way off in Indian country. I'm an agent for a German company of settlers, a land company. I speculate in Texas properties. I might consider making you an offer for yours." Lively smiled up at Possum, eyes all a-twinkle.

Another jar of the vile whiskey was slammed down in front of Possum. He studied the little trader. What would Pap think, or Davy? He took a cautious sip of the corn whiskey, considering what to do. He hadn't expected the land allotment. If he sold it to Lively, perhaps he could use the money to ransom Cassandra.

An image of Pap came to him: Pap in Lawrenceburg selling his tobacco crop. Bargaining with the Nashville buyer, chewing on a grass stalk, driving a bargain. That memory brought a quick smile to Possum's face, a smile he quickly erased.

"Mebbe I could sell it. I ain't decided."

"I'll make you a prime offer, soldier. If you're interested." Lively smiled, his fingers tapping a tattoo on the plank bar. His other hand clenched Possum's deed.

Possum didn't have a grass stem to chew on, as Pap had done. He found a small piece of jerky in his pouch and tasted it. He waited and chewed.

"Tell you what. I'll give you two hundred for it. If you're interested. It's way off in Indian territory, probably worthless for farming. What do you say?"

Buck the bartender had stopped in front of them. Possum locked eyes with him. Buck frowned.

"Guess I oughta take a look at it. That land might be well-watered, suitable for grazing or farming." Possum kept watching Buck's face.

"Now, you don't want to charge out there into Indian country, not right now." Lively took Possum's arm again, squeezing it gently. "Sell it to me right now, today, I'll go to—say—four hundred. That's more than fair."

"Well now, I don't know." Possum shook his elbow loose. He reached over and poked at Lively's brocade vest. "Looks like you already got a passel of land deeds tucked in there. I can see them sticking out."

"I told you, I'm a land speculator. I'll go to five hundred dollars. Think about it. A good horse, a good rifle." He looked Possum up and down. "You could use some clothes."

"A thousand dollars." Possum kept his gaze on Buck's face. Buck stared back, wide-eyed. "Yes, a thousand," Possum repeated.

"Why soldier, I could buy prime land right here in Columbia for a thousand dollars. But I like you. I'll go to seven-fifty. That's the top I can offer."

"All right. Seven hundred fifty dollars. In gold."

"Gold! No, I can't do that. In Republic of Texas script. No, not gold."

Buck turned aside, hiding a smile. I'm on the right track, Possum realized. He sipped his whiskey and waited.

Lively shuffled his feet. "You don't know what you're asking. Texas script is good, good as gold."

Possum chewed slowly on his bit of jerky. Be still, wait, as Pap would do. Lively fussed with his vest, twisting a button. He sighed deeply.

"Gold. Well, I guess I could go two hundred in gold. That's more than it's worth."

"Seven hundred."

"Dammit. Two hundred fifty."

Possum shook his head no. He snatched his deed out of Lively's hand, shoved the whiskey jar away and turned as if to go.

Lively caught his sleeve. "All right," he said loudly. "Here's my final offer. Four hundred dollars in gold. That's it."

Stillness descended on the barroom. Only Charlie with the Bowie knife muttered drunken curses. The other patrons watched Possum and Lively, waiting for the outcome.

Possum looked at the floor, then at the ceiling, and finally toward Lively. "Five hundred gold. No less."

"That's way too much." Lively shook his head. "But I like you. I'll go four-fifty in gold for your deed. You're breaking my heart, but I'll do it."

The barroom broke out with cheers. Possum accepted several slaps on his back. Buck, laughing, reached across the bar to shake his hand.

"Come along, soldier. Let's go find us a banker." Frowning, Lively steered Possum toward the street.

Chapter 16

The horsemen materialized abruptly, looming out of the darkness and plodding down Columbia's muddy street, riding slowly through splashes of light spilling from the storefront windows. Silent, dark apparitions, big men astride horses whose necks drooped in fatigue. Alarmed, Possum stepped back into the shadows of the livery stable and stared at the strangers.

The leader tugged his horse to a stop. He raised an arm, flinging back the Mexican *serape* from his shoulders. Behind him, his men reined in their mounts.

"Step down," called the leader.

They dismounted and stretched, arms raised above their heads, twisting their torsos. Some removed their big floppy-brimmed sombreros and wiped dirt-streaked faces on their sleeves.

"Stable boy! Come here." The leader's voice had the ring of command in it.

Possum looked over his shoulder and caught a glimpse of the Mexican stable boy high-tailing it out the back and into the night.

"He ain't here right now." Possum stepped cautiously out of the shadows. "The owner's gone down to the boarding house. For supper."

The leader peered at Possum. He kneaded the horse's head behind its ears.

Possum felt drawn to the man. His demeanor spoke of strength, of competence. He reached out and took hold of the horse's reins. "I'll stable him for you, mister."

"Thankee." The big man gestured to his followers, a wave of his arm. "Rangers, clean 'em and feed 'em."

The troop dismounted and led their steeds into the gloomy stables. They moved stiffly, silently, tending to their horses.

"You work here, son?" asked the big man.

"No, sir. I'm just waiting. For a friend. Are you the Texas Rangers everybody's been waiting for?"

"Waiting? Well, mebbe so."

The captain's horse pulled back when Possum tried to steer it into a stall. It nipped at him viciously.

"I'll do it." The Ranger grasped the bridle and stroked the horse's flanks. "He's a one-man *caballo*. He's used to me. Nobody else rides him." He eased the horse into position and slipped a feed bag over its muzzle.

The Rangers gathered around their leader. "Micah, where we gonna bed down?" The speaker wiped his sleeve across his mouth, which was almost hidden by a full black beard.

"Down by the river. Caleb, you check and see how the supplies are holding up. Somebody track down the goddamn owner of this corral. See that saloon right down there? That's where we'll meet up presently. You men get supper at that boarding house. I gotta find Judge Peavey." The leader swung his saddlebags over his shoulder.

Possum stepped forward. "Would that be the man they call Three-legged Horace? I think you'll find him down there in the saloon."

"Damn if that don't make sense."

"Sir, I'd like to join the Rangers." Possum spoke without thinking. Joining a Ranger troop to pursue the Comanche raiders was his goal in coming to Columbia, but so far he hadn't found anyone to help him. He'd been advised to seek out Three-legged Horace. Possum found Horace too drunk to sustain a conversation. This Ranger captain, well, that was another matter.

The Ranger captain looked Possum up and down, taking in Possum's new clothes and pistols.

"You're a mite young for Ranger duty."

"I'm twenty-one." Possum took a deep breath. "Name's George Hanks. Possum will do."

"Micah Pace." The Ranger didn't offer his hand to Possum. He gazed down the street toward the saloon. "Peavey does the recruiting here. Talk with him if you wanna join the Rangers. You think that's where he is right now? In that saloon?"

"Yes, sir."

Pace strode off down the middle of the street.

After a moment's hesitation, Possum followed. He wanted to talk more with this man. Joining the Rangers ought to be easy. Surely they needed men. The rumors he'd heard in Columbia told him that a company of Rangers would soon be formed, and they were looking for volunteers. He'd been told, as Micah Pace confirmed, that Judge Peavey—Three-legged Horace—would be in charge of recruiting. But was Peavey ever sober?

Other rumors had been circulating about a company of Rangers who would appear in Columbia, experienced Indian fighters who would lead the expedition against the Comanche raiders. Was this what Micah Pace's troop was supposed to do? There weren't many of them. Possum had counted seven. They looked tough enough for Rangers, all right, but they were so few. Wouldn't they want recruits, able young men like Possum? Big

Foot Wallace had termed him a soldier. So had Deaf Smith. Sam Houston himself had called Possum "soldier."

Possum felt anger rising in his bosom. He quickened his gait to catch up with the Ranger. Micah Pace had simply brushed him aside. Well, he'd confront Pace again and ask him to reconsider.

He was on Pace's heels when the big man pushed his way into the crowded saloon. Pace halted just inside the doorway, his head swiveling from side to side as he surveyed the hubbub. The crowd's babble diminished; eyes turned toward the big man. After a moment's hesitation, Pace elbowed his way though the saloon toward the plank bar. He cleared himself a space there and turned around to address the assembly.

"Men," his voice boomed, "I'm Captain Micah Pace of the Rangers. I'm looking for Three-legged Horace Peavey."

The throng slowly parted to clear a passageway to the far wall, where two men shared a table. Possum recognized Colonel Wharton, who held a jar halfway to his lips, his gaze fixed on Pace. The other man had been pointed out to Possum several times in Columbia. He was Three-legged Horace, the man Possum needed to convince if he wanted to join the new troop of Rangers.

Pace heaved himself away from the bar and stalked toward the two men. His heavy strides rang on the wooden floor. "Judge Peavey," he announced loudly, "we've arrived from San Antone. You asked for a troop of Texas Rangers. Indian fighters. You got 'em. We're here."

The barroom fell silent, as though holding a collective breath. The sound of a man's laugher drifted in from the street. Men holding jars of whiskey crowded closer, intent on the scene playing itself out before them.

Three-legged Horace crouched on the edge of his chair, his deformed right leg bent at the knee and projecting straight out behind him. A small wooden artificial leg was attached to the knee and reached to the floor. He did indeed appear to have three legs. Horace fixed Pace with a bleary eye. His jaw drooped down, his mouth open.

Wharton sprang to his feet. "Micah Pace! Wonderful to see you. Join us! Have a jar of this marvelous whiskey."

"Colonel Wharton." Pace nodded and addressed Peavey. "Judge Peavey. Horace. What are your plans?"

"You caught Horace at a bad moment," said Wharton with a chuckle. "I don't think he plans to do anything besides drink more whiskey. If that."

Indeed, Horace's head was beginning to slump toward the table.

"Goddammit," said Pace, "I'm supposed to coordinate my activities with this skunk. He wanted us to train a bunch of you wanna-be Indian fighters. Well, I never did trust a judge much, anyway." He poked Horace on the shoulder, and watched him slump down even further.

"Don't know what's got into him," said Wharton. "He's been drinking for two-three days." He looked up at the horde of men crowding up to the table, trying to catch every word. "Captain Pace, let's step outside and palaver. We're putting on a show in this here saloon."

With a final long look at Peavey, Pace turned around and led Wharton through the mob and toward the doorway. Conversations resumed; voices reached a crescendo. Possum tried to follow Pace and Wharton. He pushed his way through and peered over heads in front of him. He felt a hand against his chest, holding him back. A sneering Grady Bleeker confronted him.

"Well, looky here, if it ain't our old friend Possum. Acting grown-up. Look at that beard he's sporting. Ain't that a bobcat's howl? You gonna have a drink with me and the boys? Think yer ready for a real man's drink? What about it, boys?" Grady Bleeker laughed loudly and kept pushing against Possum's chest, holding him back while the crowd drifted toward the plank bar.

Possum recognized Bleeker's two companions from the San Jacinto road hovering behind him. Their fixed stares belied Bleeker's cheery humor.

As he pushed, Bleeker said, "Got himself some new duds, too, I'll wager. And a big Bowie and one of them new pistols."

Possum's clothes were clean and new. So were the Bowie knife and the pistol. The pistol was a new, long-barreled percussion-cap gun, a model that didn't have to be primed. He wondered how rapidly he could yank it from his belt with Bleeker standing so close to him.

Bleeker kept pushing at him, shoving him backwards, until Possum's back hit the saloon wall. Bleeker's hand found Possum's chest again and lingered there. "Old Possum and me share a secret, don't we, Possum? We..."

Possum grabbed Bleeker's little finger and twisted it back, hard.

Bleeker winced and stepped away. His hand pulled a vicious-looking knife from someplace in his shirt.

His hand on his own Bowie knife, Possum stared at Bleeker, flint-eyed. His other hand found the handle of the big pistol. Now there was room to draw it. He flicked a glance at Bleeker's two friends.

Bleeker chuckled, breaking the spell. His knife disappeared back into his shirt. Rubbing his painful finger, he grinned at Possum. "Well, well, our boy's got his strength back. Say, I meant it about that drink. How about it?"

"No thanks."

"Lookee here. No hard feelings. You and me, veterans of San Jacinto, we oughta be friends, like. You got some height and meat on your bones since the battlefield, don't you?"

"Got my strength back. Like you said."

"Yessiree, you have!" Bleeker waved his hand again. "Got yourself a better outfit, too." Bleeker's worn shirt and tattered pants contrasted with Possum's new clothes.

"You still got that colored gal? Hey, no hard feelings," he said, when Possum scowled and yanked his knife half out of its scabbard. "Just asking. We ain't trading niggers no more, are we, boys? Niggers is too much trouble. We got something better." His gaze fixed on Possum's knife, Bleeker eased nearer. "Mustangs" he said softly. "Down south, beyond the Nueces River, there's lots of wild horses to be rounded up. They's a few Mexicans we'll trade with."

One of Bleeker's friends chuckled at that. Possum eyed him. Bleeker made a shushing motion.

"We's gonna do a little trading, this side of the border, know what I mean? Those Mexicans don't know they ain't in Mexico no more."

Possum put his left hand on Bleeker's shoulder and eased him to one side. He eyed Bleeker's friends and shoved between them, slowly, his right hand on the Bowie knife.

"Think about it," Bleeker called after him. "We'll be in town a few more days."

Possum quickened his step, glad to get away with no further trouble. Maybe Bleeker will really go south and rob Mexican traders, he thought. I hope he goes soon.

Possum had debated with himself over the best use of his newfound wealth from the sale of his western land allotment. Should he prepare himself for a wilderness expedition with the Rangers to try to rescue Cassandra? Or use the money in an attempt to ransom her?

The ransom idea seemed less likely now, the more he learned about its prospects. He had talked with two Indian traders, one a Tonkawa and another who looked to be half Mexican. They both counseled patience. Comanches often swapped off their captives to other tribes, they said. Wait; in time, some trader will find her, and she'll be freed. But they didn't meet his eyes when they spoke; they looked down toward the ground.

He soon realized that his inquiries about Cassandra were met with long deliberate stares, once he mentioned that she was a black woman. Negroes were property in Texas. White men did not develop romantic attractions to negroes, use them as they might. Was he stepping across a boundary by insisting on rescuing her?

In the end, Possum chose to use his funds to equip himself for the trail. A wiry little merchant sold him sturdy pants and shirt, boots, and a wide-brimmed hat. He dickered with the gunsmith for a pair of large saddle guns, percussion cap pistols, and a long rifle. The same smith converted his two Mexican pistols and the Brown Bess musket from flintlocks to percussion fires. He felt ready and anxious to join a Ranger troop and pursue those Comanches. Was Micah Pace an alternative to dealing with Three-legged Horace Peavey?

Possum found Ranger Pace eating a late supper at the boarding house. He was sharing a table with Colonel Wharton. The two had their heads together over plates of stew. Possum stood in the doorway, wondering if he should try to join them. He'd like their advice: How to proceed with Judge Peavey?

The landlady emerged from the kitchen, wiping her hands on a soiled white apron. She frowned at Possum. Was it too late for supper? Pace and Wharton were the only other customers. Possum kept an eye on the landlady and eased his way to a table near the door, seating himself. She gave an exaggerated sigh and brought him a plate and cup.

The coffee was hot and the stew tasty, but Possum had little appetite. He fidgeted in his chair. At last he laid down his spoon and rested his elbows on the table, cupping his forehead in his hands. Was he doing the right thing by abandoning any effort to ransom Cassandra, choosing instead to join with the Rangers? What would Davy do? He brought up the image of Davy Crockett, the assured Davy, smiling and clapping him on the back, encouraging him. Go ahead, Davy would say. But ahead where? And how? For once, Davy seemed to be deserting him. I really am on my own, he realized. I must make my own way.

Was Davy in San Antonio, wounded, maybe? Or a prisoner down in Mexico? Everyone said he was dead. All the Alamo defenders were slaughtered; that's what they all believed here in Columbia.

Well, it wasn't quite true, was it? I'm alive, he reminded himself. Deep down inside, Possum felt that Davy was still alive, too. "I will come for you, Davy," he mumbled to himself. "I swear. When I can."

He looked up suddenly, aware that a heavy silence had fallen in the dining room. He glanced toward Pace and Wharton. The men had stopped talking and were staring at Possum. Was I talking aloud, he wondered.

A hand grasped his shoulder. He looked up to see a man standing beside him, frowning down. He placed the face; it was Jerome, the clerk from the land office.

"Is this the man?" asked Jerome.

"That's him." The voice came from Possum's back.

Possum looked over his shoulder. "What?" He craned his neck to peer behind Jerome, and recognized Cyrus Godfrey, the neighbor from the Kinney's farm. The man who'd appeared after the Comanche attacks. What was going on?

"You are the one they call Possum." It was a statement, not a question. Jerome kept his hand on Possum's shoulder.

Possum nodded, frowning. His hand crept to the handle of his Bowie knife. Confused, he couldn't seem to think.

"I'll take that." Jerome brushed Possum's fingers aside and grabbed the knife. With his other hand he yanked the pistol from Possum's belt.

"Stand up. Mister Possum—whoever you are—you are under arrest."

Chapter 17

"Jerome, what the hell do you think you're playing at?" Colonel Wharton burst to his feet and charged across the dining room, shoving chairs out of his way.

"Making an arrest." Jerome pulled himself up to his full height. "I got a sworn warrant for this man."

"Sworn for what?"

"Thievery."

"Goddammit, this man's a San Jacinto veteran. He's no thief."

"You back off, Wharton." Jerome pointed a grimy finger at him. "You ain't the law here. Judge Peavey is. I'm acting for him."

Wharton brushed Jerome's hand aside and shoved his chin at him. "Did he tell you to arrest this man?"

"I'm gonna hold him until the judge can see him."

"Three-Legged Horace Peavey couldn't see a three-masted schooner right now. You know that, Jerome."

Micah Pace eased himself up beside Wharton. "Mister, I'm Captain Micah Pace of the Texas Rangers. Exactly what is this young man accused of stealing?"

"A horse."

"No, I..." Possum started to object but a memory suddenly erupted. The image of himself, taking his neighbor's horse for the trip from Tennessee to Texas. Old Man Abernathy would have been spitting mad. It was only a sway-backed, spavined old nag. Taking it would be a good prank on Abernathy. Boys were always playing tricks on him. Could he have traced me all the way out here to Texas? Possum shuddered. He looked from face to face. All four men were staring at him.

"This man is *not* a horse thief." Wharton turned his attention back to Jerome. "I'll vouch for him. A San Jacinto veteran don't steal horses."

Pace laid his hand on Wharton's arm, urging him to one side. "Horse stealing is a serious crime in Texas. A hanging crime on the frontier." Pace spoke softly, deliberately. "Who is this man's accuser?"

"Willie Kinney." Jerome waived a hand toward Cyrus Godfrey standing behind him. "His neighbor, Cyrus here, done brought me a signed paper." Jerome shifted his grip to Possum's upper arm and tried to turn him toward the door.

"Wait!" Possum broke his silence. This was a different matter entirely. It had nothing to do with Old Man Abernathy or his broken-down nag. "I never stole nothing from Willie Kinney. It's a mistake. He's lying." He tried to pull away from Jerome.

"He says," Jerome interjected, waving the piece of paper. "He says you also stole some of his gold."

"He paid me! For helping him with his farm. And for hauling him and Bertha back to work it." Possum's glance passed from face to face. "I let him use my mule to pull his damn cart all the way from San Jacinto." His gaze settled on Jerome, a plea for understanding. The dining room had grown cold. Possum tried to shake free, but Jerome's grip only tightened.

The landlady joined the group, shoving her way forward, her hand held out, demanding payment for Possum's supper.

Jerome grinned at her. "You'll get your chance, Martha." Again, he tugged Possum's arm, directing him toward the door.

"Come along now, mister. Don't make me no trouble. Soon as I can find him, I'll hand you over to Judge Peavey. I just gotta lock you up until then."

Possum hunkered against a wall of the little one-room jailhouse, hugging himself, his thoughts racing in all directions. What the hell is that goddamn Willie Kinney up to? Me, steal a horse? The Comanches took his horses, not me. What game is he playing at? After me helping him, and all I did for them. Why would he do this? Jerome had cleaned everything out of his pockets except for his plug of tobacco. Possum clutched it tightly. It was something to hold onto, the only thing he had left.

Sweat beaded on his forehead; it was sweltering in the tiny room, but Possum felt chilled. Little thrills of fear ran up and down his spine, competing with anger. He'd heard rumors of rough frontier justice. How could he defend himself against this pack of lies?

Glimmers of light filtered through the only window and splashed against the opposite wall. Possum made out the image of a big man sprawled on the floor in the corner of the room. He was propped up against the wall, his hat pulled down over his face. Possum wasn't certain, but he believed the man was the one they called Charlie, the knife-waver from the saloon. Was he asleep or was he unconscious? He was breathing softly, a light snore. At least he was alive.

Possum hauled himself erect and grabbed the bars covering the window. He tested them, shaking and pulling hard. He couldn't move them. He pressed his face to the bars and peered out. He could see down Columbia's main street, where a few lights still shone. He took a deep breath. The dank evening air smelled of mud, but it was far better than the stench in the jailhouse. Charlie hadn't been able to hold his liquor.

He pulled away from the window when something blocked his view. It took a moment for him to realize that a head was pressed against the window, trying to peer in from the outside. He sensed a familiar odor, grease mixed with something else, perhaps sweat.

"Tongue?" he whispered. It had to be Tongue.

"Bad. Very bad. Very bad talk. You must leave here." The voice came softly, urgently.

Possum slumped down for a moment, the tension draining from him, relieved by the presence of a friend. "I ain't exactly able to go no place right now. Mebbe they'll let me out come morning. I don't know."

"They say 'hang.' Drink much whiskey. Talk loud."

"Hang me? I didn't do nothing. Why hang me?"

Tongue shook the bars. "Door locked. I try. No open."

"These bars ain't gonna give neither. Tongue? Tongue?"

Possum could see down the street again. The Indian's head had vanished. Possum shook the bars again.

"Tongue?"

"Ugh."

Tongue clinked something between the bars, something metal. Possum grasped it and probed it with his fingers. It was a horse pistol. "Is this one of my new pistols?" he whispered. He stuck it down into his trousers. "Tongue," he called again but this time there was no answer. He held his cheek against the bars and searched through the darkness. A shadow slipped away across the street, fading into the trees. The Indian had taken a dangerous chance, slipping that pistol to him. Tongue is a true friend, he thought. I have no other, not right now.

Possum settled down to wait for the morning. He explored the pistol with his fingers. Yes, there was a cap in place, on the nubbin. No doubt Tongue had passed him a loaded weapon. The feel of the butt in his fingers was reassuring, even though he could hardly shoot his way out of the jailhouse. He played over schemes in his mind, scenarios in which he might escape from Columbia. He visualized flashing the pistol and holding Jerome hostage while he escaped, or taking Judge Peavey himself captive and fleeing on horseback. Dreaming up plans, even improbable ones, helped raise Possum's spirits. Davy always had a plan, and maybe one or two plans in reserve. What would Davy do here? Possum grinned. Davy would talk Jerome into trading places.

A series of loud bangs woke him. Disoriented, he stared at Charlie, who was assaulting the door, banging on it with all his strength. Sunlight streamed through the window, casting a shadow of bars on the wall.

"Jerome? Goddammit Jerome, let me outa here!" Charlie was yelling as loud as he could.

Possum struggled to his feet, just as the door flung open and Charlie lurched through it, bursting outside. Immediately he staggered back in, propelled by Jerome who shoved him back against the far wall.

"Just settle yourself, Charlie. You ain't going no place but to see that three-legged judge. I brung you coffee and beans. You all right?" The question was aimed at Possum.

Possum nodded his head, eyeing the coffee pot.

"I need a whiskey," Charlie muttered.

Jerome placed two pots on the floor and produced utensils from his pocket. "Eat it up. I'm gonna take you to wash your faces. Then we'll look for the judge."

"I ain't done nothing wrong," said Charlie.

"Me neither," Possum added. He watched Jerome's back disappear through the doorway and heard the bolt slam into place. Possum ignored the food and Charlie. He held tightly to the window bars, looking across the street for any sign of Tongue.

"This coffee ain't bad." Charlie was slurping it down as fast as he could.

Possum reached down and grabbed a tin cup from the floor.

Judge Three-Legged Horace Peavey huddled on a wooden bench outside the land office, which appeared to be the seat of all government in Columbia. "Once more," said the judge. He leaned forward, to allow a lanky Texian to pour a bucket of water over his shaggy head. He shook his mane and ran his fingers through it. Red-rimmed eyes peeked from a rugged face. He ran his hand across his face and stared about the courtyard.

A crowd began to assemble, men drifting in from the street, some pushing forward, others hanging back, all eyeing Peavey. The judge fixed his gaze on them when a few laughs attracted his attention. He felt about himself and located a scarred gavel. Scowling, he pounded on the bench beside himself.

"All right. Let's get it done. This court's in session. Jerome, where are you, you rascal?"

"Here, your honor." Jerome elbowed a path through the pack of spectators, hauling Charlie and Possum along with him, each grasped by the upper arm. He yanked them to a halt in front of Peavey. "Got two cases this morning, Judge."

The judge closed his eyes and surrendered himself to a fit of shuddering. "Again," he commanded.

Another bucket of water splashed over Peavey's head. Jerome backpedaled, snatching his prisoners away from the cascade.

Possum staggered and grasped his stomach with both hands. The pistol Tongue had slipped to him was jammed down into the front of his trousers. His shirt hung free, outside of his pants, covering the weapon. He pressed his hand on the butt of the pistol, keeping it from slipping.

He glanced at Charlie. Do I look that bad, clothes rumpled, all awry? I suppose I do. He poked at his hair with his left hand; the right covered the hidden weapon.

Peavey wiped a sleeve across his eyes and squinted at the prisoners. "Charlie?" he croaked. "What the hell?"

Charlie tried to step forward but Jerome held him back.

"I ain't done nothing, Horace. I mean Judge."

"Drunk and disorderly, creating a disturbance." Jerome pronounced the charges firmly, and a titter from the crowd followed.

"Shit, Judge, you was there! You seen me. I didn't do nothing. Remember?"

This comment brought fourth a loud roar of laughter.

Peavey banged his gavel again, scowling at the little crowd, quieting it down. "Jerome, mebbe you oughta clear the yard here?"

Jerome looked around him. The crowd quieted down, waiting. He shook his prisoners' arms; he couldn't release his hold on them. He had no one to help him.

Charlie was weaving slightly, held in place by Jerome. Peavey frowned at Charlie, squinting his eyes. He ran his tongue over his lips. "Sentence..." he began.

"I need a drink," muttered Charlie, his voice faint. That comment sparked another bout of laughter from those close enough to overhear it.

"Aw right." The gavel banged officiously. "Drunk and disorderly. Fine is fifty dollars."

A grown erupted from the mob. Fifty dollars was a heavy fine.

"I ain't got no fifty dollars!" The complaint faded into a wail.

"Jerome, what did he got on him?"

"About thirty-five dollars, Your Honor."

"Fine is remitted to thirty dollars." The gavel banged again. "Who's this other scoundrel?"

"George Hanks. Goes by the name of Possum. Charged with horse stealing." Jerome shoved Possum forward and turned to grab at Charlie, who was pulling away from him. Claps on the back followed Charlie. Jerome himself was beginning to laugh. Possum kept watching Judge Peavey. Was this what passed for a courtroom? A trial?

"Order." The gavel banged again. Peavey fixed Possum with a severe frown. "Young man, horse stealing is a serious crime in Texas. Where you from?"

"Tennessee." Possum blurted out. "And I…"

"Is horse stealing allowed in Tennessee?"

"No, Your Honor, but…"

"Just answer the questions. Whose horse did you steal?"

"I never stole no horse! It's a lie!"

The gavel banged. "How 'bout it, boys? You think he's telling it straight?" Peavey addressed the crowd, speaking over Possum's head.

"No! Lies! Hang him!" The mob whooped, offering advice, laughing. A bearded giant waved a noose in the air. "Let me have him. I'll teach him how we handle horse thieves in Texas."

Bang! Bang! Bang! Went the gavel. "Now boys, let's make a fair trial out of it. You can all act as a jury. Jerome? Who brings the charge against this—who did you say he is?"

"Possum, Your Honor. I have a sworn statement by Willie Kinney."

That name brought a round of groans from the crowd. Possum jerked around to look. They must know Willie.

"Old Willie Kinney, huh? Let me see your paper." The judge made a show of examining Willie's statement, looking it up and down, holding it sideways so the morning sun would strike it. "Looks all right," he said, handing it back.

"A moment, Your Honor. A man should have the right to question his accuser." With a wave of a cigarillo and doff of his hat, a tall stranger pushed his way forward and stopped beside Possum.

"Do you wish to teach me the law?" thundered Peavey.

"Somebody needs to." The shout came from the crowd of spectators. It led to another round of laughter.

The judge looked the stranger over, taking in his tan visage, his finely-cut suit of clothes, neatly trimmed black hair and moustache and ingratiating smile. Possum's eyes widened when he recognized Captain Torreón, the wounded Mexican officer from the San Jacinto battlefield.

Peavey banged for silence. "Who might you be?" He frowned at Torreón.

"I am Juan Torres, a citizen of San Antonio. I am curious about the law code in this new Republic of Texas." He made a small bow, again waving his hat and his cigarillo.

Possum caught his breath. He was certain the man was Torreón from the San Jacinto battlefield. Now, he is Torres, is he? Had he become a Texian?

"Will this new Republic follow the code of its mother country, Mexico?" Torres continued. "Or will it adopt the code of the Americans? Or a combination of the two?"

The gavel banged for silence amid the sound of grumbling. Torres took no notice; he raised his eyebrows and motioned with his cigarillo for the judge to respond.

Peavey straightened up from his crouch on the bench. His eyes came alive, sparkling with sudden interest at this challenge. "I ain't well versed in the laws of Mexico. But I take your point." He studied Torres carefully. A smile crept across his lips. "Jerome, where is this man's accuser?"

"He ain't here, Your Honor. He been wounded."

Peavey looked intently at Jerome, eyebrows raised, waiting.

Jerome shuffled his feet. "Well, he taken a Comanche arrow. In the arse."

Hilarity erupted. Peavey joined in the laughter, rocking back and forth on the bench, picturing Willie Kinney butt-shot. Possum stared at Jerome, open-mouthed. Willie Kinney wasn't wounded during the Comanche raid.

The gavel rang again. "Tell us more, Jerome. How did that take place?"

Jerome shrugged. He looked around and spotted Cyrus Godfrey. Pointing at him, Jerome said, "He's the one told me about it."

"I'm Cyrus Godfrey, neighbor to the Kinneys. Bertha herself told me the story," Godfrey stated with a thrust of his chin. When Peavey gestured for him to elaborate, he continued. "She said two Comanche bucks surprised Willie down by the creek.

Shot an arrow in him, in the butt. They didn't bother the cabin. They stole a little nigger boy."

"Wonder what Kinney was doing at the time?" Peavey joined in the howl of laughter that followed.

Possum didn't laugh. He looked down to conceal his elation. He rubbed his hand across his face, hiding a broad grin that had emerged. Old Tongue had gotten it right. Cassandra was not in danger. She had taken her situation in hand. She must have managed to insinuate herself into the Comanche band. And then dispatched a party of Indians to capture her son and return him to her. Possum choked back a giggle.

After a moment he raised his head and joined in the general hilarity, although his laugh was one of relief.

Chapter 18

The thought of Willie Kinney with an arrow shot into his butt was enough to lighten the mood of the onlookers. No more scowls, no more waving of a noose in Possum's direction. Raucous laughter filled the courtyard.

Willie's predicament wasn't what brought a smile to Possum's face. His thoughts were of Cassandra. How had she managed it? He tried to picture the woman dressed in Indian clothes. Maybe adorned as a native priestess. She'd told him about the Jamaican black magic; "Obeah," she'd called it. Sitting with Cassandra on the bank of Willie's creek, Possum had listened to her speak softly of her island's strange beliefs. The melodious tone of her voice intrigued him more than her stories of witchcraft. Maybe she'd used a chant, a ceremony or ritual to impress her Comanche captors. He looked over his shoulder, searching in the mob for a glimpse of Tongue. Had he been listening to Godfrey's story?

Thump! Thump! Thump! The banging of Judge Peavey's gavel on his little bench brought Possum out of his daydream. The volume of laughter subsided. The crowd moved closer, ready for the next event in their morning's entertainment. The bearded giant produced his noose again but changed his mind and poked it back into his shirt.

Possum studied Torres out of the corner of his eye. A light smile played across Torres's face. His stance, his garb, the cheroot waving in the air, all radiated confidence. Is he truly a lawyer, or is he playacting? When did I become his client? Possum bit his lip. What was Torres up to? He knows my secret, that I survived the Alamo massacre. Maybe he is more of a danger to me than this silly trial.

Torres raised his voice. "Your Honor. Your Honor. Judge."

The judge extended his gavel toward Torres. "Speak," he commanded.

"Where is this steed my client supposedly took without permission?"

"Where's the goddamn horse, Jerome?" The judge belched and wiped his mouth with his sleeve.

Jerome shrugged his shoulders. "Don't rightly know." Frowning, he searched left and right as though the horse might appear. This was an unexpected development.

Exclamations of disgust from the audience rose to create a hubbub. The judge stared at Jerome, who stared back. Possum straightened up. This was going to be a stalemate. He sighed with relief, but tensed again when he saw Micah Pace stroll up and put his hand on the judge's shoulder. He spoke in a low voice. People nearby surged forward, trying to listen. Possum couldn't make out Pace's words. Pace turned and gestured to the street, where one of his Rangers was leading Possum's Comanche horse forward. The crowd stirred, making a pathway. The noise settled down to a low murmur. What now?

"I believe this is the animal in question, Your Honor," announced Pace.

"Jerome, is this the stolen horse?"

"Is it?" Jerome turned the question to Godfrey.

"I don't know, Your Honor." Godfrey shook his head.

The judge pointed the gavel at Possum. "Is this your horse, son?"

"It is," Possum nodded. "Your Honor," he added belatedly.

"Where'd you get it?"

Torres was tugging at Possum's sleeve, but he spoke up anyway. "I took it from a dead Comanche. A Comanche I killed myself."

That statement brought a rumble of approval from the crowd. Possum threw back his shoulders and stared defiantly at the judge.

"Caleb?" called Pace.

"It's an Indian pony all right, Captain," said Ranger Caleb. "No doubt about it. This horse's mouth never felt a bit. It's hooves are unshod. And it's skittish from the left side. Comanches mount from the right." He reached up and patted the horse's right shoulder; it jerked its head, tugging the reins.

Jerome and Peavey exchanged glances. He raised his gavel and held it hovering over the bench, considering what to do. The watchers fell silent.

"Horace," said Jerome. "Maybe I got it wrong, kinda. Look at that paper again. What does it say about a horse?"

The judge put down the gavel and held the warrant close to his face, holding the paper high so sunlight would strike it. His right hand slipped a pair of gold-rimmed glasses from his shirt pocket. He hooked a loop over each ear.

In the silence, someone coughed. Possum started; he was sure the cough was Tongue's. A signal, or merely to announce his presence? He glanced quickly over his shoulder but couldn't see the Indian anyplace.

The judge burst to his feet and stumbled away from the bench. He shoved away the attendant Texian who reached to steady him. "Jerome, goddammit," he thundered, "It don't say 'horse.' It says 'mount!'" He grabbed the gavel and shook it in Jerome's direction. "Is there another horse?"

"You got another horse?" asked Jerome.

"No. No sir, I don't."

"Judge. Your Honor." Cyrus Godfrey waved his arms. "I remember now. I seen him ride away from Willie Kinney's farm on a mule." He pointed at Possum. "Willie told him not to take it. Said he needed it to farm his crops." Godfrey sneered at Possum.

"It's my mule. That's how come I rode it here." Possum stood straight, arms folded, chin thrust forward.

Judge Peavey sat back down and gaveled for quiet. "All right. Let's see if we can't bring this to an end. Is the mule in question here?"

"My mule is at the stable," Possum offered.

With a nod to Jerome, Peavey banged on the bench. "We're in recess for a minute. Jerome, go fetch the goddamn mule." Peavey laid down the gavel and rubbed his wrist. He motioned away the lanky Texian who approached with another bucket of water.

Torres took Possum by the arm and moved him to one side. He crowded close to Possum, chest to chest, staring him in the eye.

"What?" Possum asked.

Torres took the cheroot from his lips. "If you are smart," he whispered, "you will pass that pistol from your trousers to mine." The corners of his lips curled upwards. He returned the small cigar to his mouth.

Possum stood still, staring into Torres's dark brown eyes. Perhaps it was for the best. Leaning close, he slipped the pistol out of his pants and shoved it behind Torres's wide leather belt. Torres nodded his head and took a step backwards. "That is good," he whispered. "You shouldn't be armed at your own trial. Not even in Texas."

"Why are you here, Torreón? Or Torres, if you'd rather," asked Possum.

Torres slipped a cheroot from his jacket pocket and proffered it to Possum who shook his head no.

"Please, I am Torres now, a native of San Antonio. And a Texian. A Tejano. You would do well to remember that."

Possum nodded slowly, his eyes fixed on Torres's. He recognized the implied threat. "Are you a lawyer now?"

"Yes. I have decided to study the law. A suitable occupation for a gentleman, don't you think?" He gestured toward the street with his cheroot. "Is that the animal?"

Sally the mule plodded onto the courthouse lawn, sleep-eyed, ears drooping, escorted by Jerome on one side and Caleb on the other. Possum laughed aloud. For once, the mule was co-operating. He took a step toward Sally but Torres stopped him. "Leave it," he said softly.

Judge Peavey hammered away on the bench. "All right. We are back in session. Is that your mule?" he asked Possum.

"Yes, Your Honor. Sally."

"Where'd you get it?"

"Judge. Judge. Your Honor." Grady Bleeker pushed his way out of the crowd of onlookers and insinuated himself in front of Peavey. "I know that mule, Your Honor."

"Go ahead. What's your testimony."

Bleeker rubbed his chin, half concealing a sly grin. "First time I seen it, it was hitched to a cart. A poor family of Texians was making their way back to the Brazos." He flung a gesture at Possum. "This young feller wasn't anyplace to be seen." His grin widening, Bleeker eyed Possum.

A wave of anger rushed over Possum. The frustrations of the night in confinement, the stupidity of this ridiculous farce of a trial, all became focused on Bleeker's unwanted intrusion.

"Go ahead, Bleeker, you sonofabitch," he yelled. "Tell the judge the whole goddamn story. I loaned 'em the mule. You know that. Tell him!" Possum lunged in Bleeker's direction. Jerome grabbed him by both arms, holding him back.

Bleeker backed away, hands raised as if to protect himself, a mock grimace of fear moving across his face. "Keep him off me, Judge," he said. His grimace shifted to a sneer.

"Your Honor," Torres interrupted, "I believe this matter can be easily resolved." He stepped between Possum and the grinning Bleaker. "If you will look on the lower part of the animal's left ear—there, where it is attached to the head—you will observe a small V-shaped earmark."

Ranger Caleb searched the mule's ear as instructed, and nodded toward Judge Peavey, pointing at the earmark.

"That," said Torres, "is a Mexican Army mule from the supply train of Santa Anna's army. My client captured that animal on the field of honor. On the battlefield of San Jacinto, where he received a wound, fighting for Texas." He stepped away from Possum and puffed vigorously on his cigarillo.

Judge Peavey gaveled for silence and motioned Possum forward. "Son," he announced, "I'm dismissing these charges. I find that the mule is truly yours, spoils of war. Now hold it, hold it," he continued when cheers erupted. "Your character seems of a better nature than Willie Kinney's. Many of us know Willie." He gaveled for quiet once more. "I ain't saying nothing about the charge of stealing gold. That stands unproven. If Willie wants to appear and swear out another warrant for that, I expect you to appear and defend yourself. We stand adjourned."

Thump.

The crowd dispersed in several directions. The noose-waving giant hurried over to Possum and pounded him on the back. Captain Pace and his Texas Rangers cornered Judge Peavey before he could escape. Jerome divided his attention between Possum and Charley, who were pulling in opposite directions. He held each man by an arm. Charley tugged away toward the saloon, ignoring Jerome's demand that he pay his thirty-dollar fine. Possum, still furious, tried to pull away in Bleeker's direction. Jerome kept a firm grip on Possum's upper arm.

"Let go of me," Possum demanded. "You heard the judge. I'm a free man."

"I did. The charge of thievery still hangs over your head. Dammit, Charley, quit it!" Jerome tightened his grip on Charley.

"I'm gonna give you your goddamn money. Let me be." Charley jerked his arm free.

Possum pried Jerome's fingers off of his own arm. "The judge didn't say for you to hold me."

"All right." Jerome held his finger under Possum's nose. "But you stay here in Columbia until this all gets sorted out."

Possum searched through the diminishing throng, looking for Bleeker. He spotted the man, scurrying away with his two companions. Possum started in pursuit.

"Hold up," said Jerome. "Let's go and get your damn belongings. Come on, Charley, you too."

At the jailhouse, Possum checked his bag of possibles and threw the strap across his shoulder. Still scowling at Jerome, he made a show of examining his Bowie knife and saddle pistol.

"It's all there. I ain't no thief," muttered Jerome.

"It'd better be." Possum stalked back to the courthouse lawn. Bleeker had vanished. He searched through the remnants of the crowd. Where was Torres? He had Possum's other saddle pistol, and he had questions to answer.

Judge Peavey, still straddling the wooden bench, beckoned to Possum. After a moment's hesitation, Possum eased up to the judge, who was still talking with Captain Pace.

"Son, I believe your story," said Peavey. "I don't doubt that your mule is your own property. Or that you got that Indian pony off a dead Comanche. But tell me—what did you plan to do with that pistol hidden down there in your pants?"

Possum started in alarm, wide-eyed, his anger at Bleeker suddenly dissolving. He realized that Peavey was grinning at him. Peavey must have taken notice of the concealed saddle gun, but he hadn't mentioned it during the trial. Pace was smiling at him, too.

"I'm glad your lawyer took it away from you. Although it might've made the morning a bit more interesting."

Possum shuffled his feet. "I…I…"

"Anybody dumb enough to get tangled up with Willie Kinney…How come Jerome didn't take that firearm away from you when he locked you up?"

Possum hung his head, unable to explain this without putting Tongue in jeopardy.

Peavey waived a hand, dismissing any answer. "But that ain't the only thing I'm wondering about," he continued. "How did you find that Mex lawyer?"

"He kinda found me," Possum mumbled.

"But you knew him. Didn't you?"

Possum nodded. How was he going to explain Torres?

"Was he on the Kinney farm? With you?"

"No." Possum shook his head. Best get it out in the open. "I met him at San Jacinto."

Peavey and Pace exchanged glances. "Likely one of Seguin's company of Tejanos," said Pace.

"Probably from down around San Antonio. One of the old Mexican families there," added Peavey.

Pace frowned. "Don't know about that. I don't recall seeing him there."

"He seems to have skedaddled, anyway. Where are you from, son? From your speech, I'd guess Tennessee."

"Yes, sir."

Peavey waited for a moment, watching Possum. He chewed on his lip, wondering what to say. He didn't want to try to explain why he was in Texas. He couldn't very well mention Davy Crockett, or the Alamo.

"Well, it ain't any of my business. Just forget about that gold-stealing charge. Keep your hair combed and stay outa trouble." Peavey waived a dismissal.

"Just a minute. Tell me, son, what do you plan to do next?" Pace asked, before Possum could make his getaway. The Ranger fixed him with an intense gaze, his dark eyes held steady and brooding.

"I'm gonna go to San Antonio." Possum blurted it out. That's what he'd concluded last night at supper, before Jerome found him. Go to San Antonio and look for Davy. Even before he heard that Cassandra had sent the Comanches to get Marcus, before he'd concluded that she was safe, he'd decided on that plan.

"Thought you might have an idea about seeking out this man Willie Kinney," said Pace. "Settling a score."

"No, sir." The idea hadn't occurred to Possum. He'd pushed Willie out of his mind altogether. Grady Bleeker, now, that was another story, one he wasn't finished with. He shook his head. "My business with Willie is finished."

"Good." Pace nodded. "Best to move on." He tugged at his beard. "You'd said something about wanting to join the Rangers."

"I might. I mean, I still would like to." In fact, now that he felt reassured about Cassandra's safety, he didn't think it was such a good idea.

"Well, you might wanna look me up in the morning. I'm bound for San Antonio myself."

Possum hurried back to the street, eager to get away from probes into his past. Peavey's questions weren't unreasonable, but they weren't easily answered. I gotta make up a good story, he decided, a tale that would explain why I'm here in Texas. That Ranger captain ain't gonna give up until he gets some answers. I don't want to be caught in that situation again. He was uncomfortable with the idea of making up a downright lie. Pap always said, tell the truth, it's easier that way. But this truth was one he couldn't tell to anyone. The Alamo battle had become a legend. He mustn't dispute it.

Possum felt Tongue's presence even before the Indian spoke.

"We go now? Stay here very bad."

"Didn't you hear the judge? It all worked out all right. I'm free. But you're right, we go now. I'd like to locate that lawyer Torres. He has my saddle gun, the one you slipped to me last night."

"Mexican gone, too."

"Is he? Where?"

"Ride out." Tongue gestured. "Setting sun."

"West? Maybe we'll find him in San Antonio."

"We go San Antonio?"

"Yes, my friend, we go San Antonio."

PART THREE

Chapter 19

Texas Ranger Caleb Dewitt's voice was a gushing cascade of words, tumbling over themselves, reminding Possum of the bubbling fountain in the square at Lawrenceburg. Caleb's stories flowed in spurts of yarns and tales, bits of lore in a never-ending stream, churned out to the accompaniment of creaking saddle leather. Possum rode beside Caleb at the tail end of the troop, well behind the main party. Caleb called it "riding drag."

Captain Micah Pace was Caleb's opposite, thoughtful and reserved, a deliberate speaker. He arranged his convoy of travelers as Davy Crockett had done, with scouts in front and behind. The party was made up of horsemen with assorted pack animals. Mexican riders segregated themselves from the others; their delegation included several women wrapped in concealing *serapes.* Pace himself took the lead position, breaking trail down the La Bahía road. Possum wondered if Caleb's constant chatter was what got him assigned to rear guard.

"Now this here's the best part of south Texas." Caleb's arm swept an arc across the landscape. "Red, lookit that good grass out there, hip-high. Herds of wild cattle and bang-tail mustangs call it home. 'Course all kinds of game and varmints, any kind you'd like to see, they all tromp through it, too. Well watered, good forage. When you get further south, the grass gets sparse, and pretty soon you get to a desert. Wild Horse Desert, they call it. Nobody out there but outlaws and Mexicans, though. Down on the other side of the Nueces River there ain't nothing but bandits, all the way to the Rio Grande. We ain't going that far, though. Just as far as Victoria."

"Uh-huh." Possum half-listened to Caleb. He stood in his stirrups, looking for Tongue. He spotted the Indian riding beside Pace at the head of the column.

Pace had singled out Tongue and offered to make him a scout for the Rangers. To Possum's astonishment the Indian accepted. Tongue had appeared frightened of the Comanches during the raid on Willie's farm. Why, now, would Tongue want to scout his way into their lands? Possum could see that the two men were in heavy conversation. Or Tongue was, at least. The Indian gestured here and there, his arms flailing. Pace sat erect in the saddle, elbows drawn to his sides, facing straight ahead.

Tongue agreed enthusiastically with Possum's conclusion that Cassandra had arranged for a Comanche party to visit the Kinney farm and capture her son Marcus. Whatever her situation with the Comanches, Cassandra must have reached a compromise that allowed her some control. Tongue was confident that Cassandra would make herself a valuable member of the tribe, perhaps through her exotic appearance and behavior. Possum wasn't convinced she was safe, but he no longer felt the urgency to rescue her. Tongue believed that Cassandra would find a way to communicate. As a Ranger scout, Tongue would be in a position to locate her. Is that what motivated him to accept Pace's offer?

The caravan's destination was the south Texas village of Victoria. Micah Pace agreed to provide escort and protection for a mixed group of travelers. The frown on his face revealed his concerns about the venture. The night before they'd left Columbia, Pace had gathered the Rangers around a campfire, where he introduced Tongue, a scout. Possum he referred to as "Red," a new Ranger. Pace explained that the troop would take an indirect route back to San Antonio. The old timers groaned at this idea, but Pace explained that some of the travelers had offered payment for an escort, and no other was available at the time. This information was met with nods of understanding. Funds were short for the Ranger troop. Supplies ran low.

Furthermore, Pace explained, he needed to evaluate the potentially violent conditions in Victoria. Rumors of clashes between Anglos and Tejanos had reached his ears. Victoria was an important stop on the La Bahía road. The town gave access to the important port at Linnville. Bandit activity had increased there, due to renegades of both nationalities.

"So, we will commence to Victoria," Pace explained, "and then ascend the north bank of the Guadalupe River to Gonzales, and thence to San Antonio. We will gather information along the route. We will stay alert for the presence of Mexican troops, or Indian raiders, or scoundrels of any stripe preying on citizens."

"Ain't the Texian army mustering at Goliad?" interrupted Caleb. "Might be we should investigate that, too."

"Them's the worst of the lot. Real scum, some of 'em," offered another of the Rangers.

Pace shook his head no. "Leave the army be," he said. "Colonel Wharton told me there's a General Barrett there, trying to work up an invasion of Mexico. Old Sam wants him to drop the idea. We're best out of it."

Possum had been delighted when Pace offered him a provisional assignment as a Texas Ranger. Accompany us to San Antonio, Pace had said, temporary duty, see if you are suited for the Ranger life. Possum wasn't fooled by the offer. It was a conciliatory gesture for stealing Tongue away from him. Nevertheless, he accepted immediately. Even a temporary assignment to that elite group was a thrill for a young man. The Texians in their party treated him with the same deference given to the other Rangers. Possum enjoyed that respect, although he was well aware that it wasn't earned.

Squatting on his heels beside the fire the night before the caravan departed, Possum had felt at ease in the company of the Rangers. What would Davy do? Would he join the Rangers, if invited? Why, Davy would most likely look for that army forming up in Goliad. Invading Mexico—why, that would be a fine adventure for Davy Crockett. Maybe, just maybe, Micah Pace has a better grip on life than Davy does.

When Possum elected to ride beside Caleb, Pace nodded his approval. Alone with Caleb, Possum wanted to ask questions about the Rangers, how they operated, what were their responsibilities, who decided on their orders. As it turned out, questioning Caleb was unnecessary. While listening to him, Possum kept his eyes open for telltale signs along the road. The riders in front of him churned up the mud but not so much that Possum couldn't detect a broken horseshoe here, a splayfooted gait there.

The other Rangers rode on both sides of the travelers, keeping the party moving forward, encouraging stragglers to keep moving. A small group of well-dressed Mexicans rode shoulder to shoulder, immediately behind Pace. After them came a handful of men who claimed to be traders, headed for the ports along the Gulf of Mexico's waters. Finally, a dozen desperate-looking riders said they would join the upstart Texas army which was mustering at Goliad.

Bleeker and his two companions rode among the would-be soldiers. Possum tried to keep them in view. He'd had an evening to cool his temper, and he'd decided that there was nothing to be gained by challenging Bleeker, at least not now. Maybe

Bleeker really didn't know that Sally the mule belonged to him, and was giving honest testimony at the trial. Possum doubted it. The man clearly enjoyed himself with his lying comments to the judge. Let it go, he counseled himself, at least for the present. But he felt wary of the man and wanted to keep an eye on him. Grady Bleeker was like a thorn in his foot, a nagging presence that would have to be dealt with. Maybe he'd join the new Texian army and try to invade Mexico. Possum snorted. The skunk would find some way to profit from that military venture if he could. Likely he'd avoid any actual fighting.

"What're you thinking, Red?" Caleb studied Possum in sideways glances. "Something stuck in your craw?"

"Wondering about those soldiers. The ones who want to invade Mexico."

Caleb turned away to spit. "Micah said they want to sack Matamoros for whatever gold they can find. He thinks they'll split up over any plunder. Likely wind up prisoners of the Mexicans."

"Humph." Possum concentrated his attention on the tracks in the mud, trying to pick out Bleeker's mount. It wasn't likely, with all the jumble of hoof prints.

"Micah said them Mexican travelers plan on leaving us when we get to Victoria." Caleb gestured at the Tejanos with his chin.

"Are they going all the way to Mexico?"

"Uh-uh. See the tall old man? There, with all the other Mexicans huddled to him. He's Señor Benavides, an *alcalde* in Victoria. Got a big house there." Caleb spit again. "He might not have it for long. They's making it uncomfortable for Mexicans."

Possum shifted in his saddle for a better view. The old man rode ramrod stiff, shoulders back. Silver glinted from his narrow-brimmed hat. A youngster paced along on either side of him. A few others followed in their wake.

"Too bad, all that trouble I heard about," said Caleb, shaking his head. "Poor Victoria. Fortunes of war, I guess. That village was home to Mexicans and Anglos alike, and they got along, ran their affairs together. They helped supply General Fannin's troops when he passed through on the way to Goliad. You know, women knitted scarves and such things. Well, General Urrea upset all of that."

"How?"

"After he massacred the Texian soldiers at Goliad, he marched his army into Victoria. All the Anglos fled, upcountry to join Houston's army, or over to the bay. Urrea's soldiers ransacked the Anglos' homes."

"Didn't Urrea have to pull out? When Santa Anna surrendered?"

"Sure. I hear tell Urrea's down in Matamoros now, with what's left of his army. He's the one those soldier boys is gonna meet up with if they go charging down there. Thing is, Red, when the Anglos came back to town they were mighty aggravated about their houses being wrecked. They blamed their Mexican friends. Thought they should have stopped Urrea."

Caleb fell silent, frowning, lost in thought.

"What about Señor Ben-something? The old man up there." Possum stood in his stirrups for a better glimpse of the tall Mexican.

"Benavides. Don't know, Red. I reckon he's a tough old rooster."

The caravan approached a grove of live oak trees. Micah Pace raised his arm, signaling a halt. Caleb galloped ahead. Possum urged his horse forward but stopped well short of the rest of the group, where he dismounted. He wanted to keep plenty of space between himself and Bleeker. He looked behind himself, back down the road and off to the sides. The open country made him feel exposed now that he found himself at ground level.

Caleb led his horse back to the rear. He was chewing jerky. He offered some to Possum. "I got to ask you," he said, "how come they call you 'Possum'? Don't seem to suit you."

"Oh, a friend gimmie that name. 'Cause I grinned so much. He thought I looked like a possum."

"Ain't seen you grinning very much lately. Possum's more of a kid's name. Micah started us calling you 'Red.' With your beard, it suits you. Hair's a bit thin, I guess, but you got plenty of red beard. You oughta trim it down some. When we get to San Antonio, I can find you a good barber."

Possum grinned at Caleb.

"'Red'," Caleb laughed. "That's a good name for a Texas Ranger. 'Red'. 'Course you could use your real name. What is it, anyway?"

"George Hanks." Possum flinched; he hadn't meant to blurt it out.

"That name's all right, too, I guess, but I like 'Red' better. Mount up, Red, Micah's signaling for us to get moving again."

Maybe he's right, thought Possum. I wasn't much more than a boy when I struck out for Texas with Davy. I'm a grown man now. Named 'Red'. He straightened his shoulders.

"Tell me more about the Mexicans," he said. "The ones traveling with us." Caleb had fallen silent, slumped down, dozing in his saddle. The afternoon sun beat down out of a cloudless, hazy sky. Possum was perspiring under his floppy sombrero. He'd removed his serape. His shirt was plastered to his back. Caleb seemed unperturbed by the heat. Possum frowned at him; he wasn't checking his back trail like he was supposed to. Get him talking again; that'll keep him awake. He repeated his question. "What about the Mexicans?"

"What about them?" answered Caleb.

Possum shifted in his saddle. What was it that piqued his curiosity about the Mexican family? He frowned; he couldn't put his finger on it, but he was attracted to them somehow. "Are they farmers?" he asked.

"Ranchers more likely. They's two boys and a girl—a young lady—riding with Señor Benavides. Along with some servants; they're the ones that ain't dressed so fine. The youngsters must be offspring of old Benavides."

"If they live in Victoria, I guess they must be Texians. Not Mexicans."

"Who knows?" said Caleb. "Lots of them just call themselves Tejanos. I'm not sure what that means anymore. They used that name when they was citizens of Mexico."

"And now they're what? Texians?"

"After the revolution? It's a disputed territory down here, Red. Claimed by Texas and Mexico both."

"Below the Nueces River, like you said?"

"Micah says anyplace south of San Antonio is disputed by the Mexican government. Such as it is; there's lots of fussing in Mexico right now. Sooner or later, they're gonna straighten themselves out and bring an army back here. We'll have to fight them all over again."

"Were you in the Texian army?" Possum thought it was a reasonable question, but it drew a dark scowl from Caleb. He kicked his horse into a gallop and rode up beside the caravan. He advanced until he'd reached Pace at the front of the column.

Guess I'm riding drag now, Possum sighed.

Something big crashed its way through the tall grass, leaving a trail of broken stems behind it. Possum pulled to a halt, puzzled.

"Bear," a Ranger yelled. "Look at him go. A young boy, this year's cub grown up. Mama ran him off."

The bear broke into the clear and halted, mouth agape, drooling, startled by the travelers. Possum heard the zing, zing of lariats. Nooses settled over the animal's head. Shouts of joy, "*Ay Ay Ay*," rang out among peals of laughter from the Rangers. Two young Mexican lads, Tejanos, had roped the bear. A flip of their lariats and the bear was freed. Snarling, it turned tail and crashed back into the safety of the grass.

The two Tejano lads raced their horses back and forth alongside the party, flicking the horses' rumps and weaving among the slower Rangers.

Caleb appeared at Possum's elbow. "Best horsemen you'll ever see," he said. "Look how they sit them horses. Natural as everything. Born to it."

Possum nodded. "They're slick, all right."

"Only Comanches ride better, and I ain't too sure about that. Look at them saddles, Red. High cantle in back, big pommel with a huge saddle horn. Stirrups slung low on leathers. And them pointy-toed boots. Better than your moccasins for this country."

Their unusual clothing intrigued Possum. Narrow-legged trousers ornamented with silver conchos down the sides. Short, fitted jackets worn under their *serapes*. Black, flat-topped hats with stiff brims. Possum glanced at Caleb, taking in his broad-brimmed floppy sombrero and his shapeless serape with a tattered fringe. Tejanos dressed better than Rangers.

They rode better, too, although Caleb seemed able to sit the saddle for hours at a time, rocking gently, at ease. Possum wondered how Caleb would fare at a full-out gallop. Could he ride like the Tejanos? Embarrassed, Possum rearranged his *serape* across his shoulders and tugged his hat tighter. The appearance of those two youngsters put the Rangers to shame. He watched, envious, as the two Tejanos reined in beside their father.

Chapter 20

Late in the afternoon, fluffy clouds scooted across the sky, riding a coastal breeze. The wind picked up, carrying a hint of salt air. The caravan approached a row of trees, a landmark rising above the sea of grass, their canopies marking the bank of one of Texas's slow-flowing creeks. Where the road crossed the creek, Micah Pace raised his arm, calling a halt. "We'll camp here for the night."

"Still plenty of daylight, Captain," called one of the volunteer soldiers.

Pace ignored him. He led his horse to the creek bank and allowed it to drink. "Caleb, scout the area."

Caleb tugged his steed aside and galloped out into the grassland, past the pecan grove, looking this way and that.

Possum dismounted and examined the ground for tracks and other signs.

"We'uns need to get down to Goliad. We don't wanna miss the campaign against Mexico." The soldier stayed in his saddle, flicking his reins in an impatient gesture.

"You are free to proceed on your own," Pace called over his shoulder.

"We done paid you. Escort us to Goliad, like you agreed."

Pace disregarded him, still tending to his horse.

"Dammit, Ranger! Do your duty or give us our money back!"

One of the Rangers who'd dismounted took hold of the soldier's bridle. "I don't think you ought to tell the captain his duty," he said calmly.

"Let go of my horse, you sonofabitch!"

The Ranger released his grip on the reins. He reached up and grabbed the man's belt. "Lemme help you down," he said, yanking him out of the saddle and dropping him on the ground. The Ranger stood over him. "We'll camp here tonight. Like the captain said."

Bleeker's high-pitched laughter filled the sudden silence. "There's gonna be enough fighting for every man's son, once we get closer to Mexico. I'm a bit saddle-weary myself." He extended a hand to the surprised lad. "Grady Bleeker. San Jacinto veteran. Looking to fight some more Mexicans."

"Ross Farrier." The man struggled to a sitting position and extended his hand.

Bleeker took it and hauled him to his feet. "Not worth a fracas," he said. "Come and have a hooker with me and my cousins."

Possum walked his horse down to the creek to water him, stopping beside Pace. "Captain, you'd best keep an eye on that man Bleeker. He likes to stir things up. He's been a trouble-maker."

"I know. Just stay clear of him. We'll reach Victoria tomorrow about noontime. Those varmints can go their own way."

"Red! Red!" Caleb galloped up and skidded to a stop. "Come take a look at the campsite I found over there."

The signs weren't hard to interpret. A small party of Indians had camped there recently. The remains of a fire, the moccasin tracks, the debris said it all clearly.

"Fish heads. Looks like bass," Possum nodded. "One of them coastal tribes, you think? Or mebbe Apaches?"

"Karankawas, most likely. Kronks." Caleb pointed to the moccasin prints in the dust. He grabbed a stick and stirred the remains of the cooking fire. "Last night's fire, or maybe this morning. They probably caught fish right out of the creek here. Kronks are mostly harmless now. They used to be trouble. People thought they were cannibals, one time. They're tall for Indians but not much on fighting, not anymore. Not a lot of them left, either."

Possum stared up and down the stream bank. "Ain't they some Apaches in these parts?"

"These local tribes—the few of them left—don't amount to much. A few leagues to the west, you might run into Apache or Comanche raiding parties. And they's trouble enough. That's been our job as Rangers—punishing Indian raiders. They range west and south of San Antonio. Captain Jack Hays chases Comanches to the north, and Micah leads us south against the Apaches. Comanches and Apaches don't get along. The Apaches are getting pushed out by the Comanches. They're mean sonofabitches. 'Course, a few renegade Indians show up here and there, ever now and then."

The verbal stream rolled on and on. Caleb had stories of Indian battles he'd fought, campaigns he'd witnessed. Possum nodded occasionally. He kept his eye on Bleeker, who was playing up to Farrier and the other soldiers. He'd produced a jug of whiskey. Possum watched it pass from hand to hand. Was Bleeker trying to stir up trouble? Those men were angry, and liquor wouldn't help. But then, it rarely did.

Captain Pace insisted that supper come first, before setting up camp for the night. Each party of the caravan made its own eating arrangements. Pace's strategy worked; tempers cooled after a meal. Pace separated the travelers. He moved the Tejanos far off to the right, a spot on the creek bank. The soldiers, including Bleeker and his friends, he sent down the left bank to an opening in the trees. The rest of the company stayed with the Rangers, camped beside the trail, between the Tejanos and the soldiers.

Guard duty seemingly divided itself among the Rangers without Pace issuing any orders. Caleb volunteered for second shift. Possum opted for third.

Pace's decision to stop early meant that all chores were completed before dark. The camp, with its three sections, had quieted down by the time dusk settled on the plains. Possum sat cross-legged, propped against his saddle, listening to the tree frogs voicing their evening chorus. A wisp of evening breeze rippled the tall grasses beside the trail. The Rangers spoke among themselves, a soft muttering, as they settled into blankets for the night. A guitar played a soft melody in the Tejano camp. The soldier camp was quiet.

A surge of happiness washed over Possum. He felt a kinship with the Rangers, a feeling he'd missed since his days trekking through Arkansas with Davy. He stretched his arms over his head, yawning, relaxing at last. His saddle-weary body ached, but he found it a comfortable feeling. He grabbed a blanket and rolled up in it, rested his head on his saddle, and drifted into a peaceful slumber.

Someone shaking his shoulder jarred him wide awake from a dreamless sleep. The feeble glow from a dying fire revealed Tongue's dark image. He held his face close to Possum's, his dark eyes catching the firelight. "Come," he whispered and slipped away into the darkness.

Possum followed in Tongue's creeping footsteps toward the Tejano campsite, where a campfire cast long shadows. He hesitated when he saw Bleeker and his two cousins standing face to face with the old Tejano, Señor Benavides. The two Tejano youths flanked their father, one to each side. Behind Bleeker, his two friends stood with rifles held close to their chests, barrels pointed upward. Possum noted that their fingers rested on their triggers. Each of the Tejano youngsters held a pistol, pointed downward.

"Now it's just a logical question, ain't it?" Bleeker was speaking softly. His voice held its customary sneer. "We're headed down to fight Mexicans. You people are Mexicans. Likely you know what they're planning for us, down in Matamoros. We'd like to know too, that's all. We ain't gonna cause you no trouble."

Señor Benavides frowned at Bleeker. Both Tejano boys shook their heads. "We are ranchers," exclaimed one. "We don't know about armies, Mexican or Texian." He tried to peer around Bleeker, to where the Rangers were camped.

"Not so loud, seen-yore. No need to wake them Rangers. We don't want no trouble, like I said. These here men will just look through your gear here and see if there's any contraband, which I'm sure there ain't. No, no," he added, when the Tejano youth started to protest. "You don't want to make any difficulty. Not with that pretty little miss I see back there. Just step aside."

"Hold on there, Bleeker." Possum stepped into the little circle of firelight. "You boys get back to your own side of the camp and let these folks alone." He looked past Bleeker toward the two riflemen. "Run along, boys," he said, grasping the handle of the saddle gun he'd crammed into his belt.

This wasn't the first time he'd stared down Bleeker. Possum felt confident that the man would back down, once he'd made some spiteful face-saving remarks.

Bleeker leaned close to Possum, sneering. Possum caught a whiff of whiskey on his breath. He realized that this confrontation might prove dangerous.

"Mister Possum. Always sticking your nose in where it ain't wanted. I done figgered you out. You're yellow, ain't you? A runaway. You ain't gonna do nothing." He turned away from Possum. "Let's search them Mexicans, boys."

Possum had his pistol half drawn when the roar of a gunshot split the darkness. He jerked in alarm, his head turned this way and that. Bleeker stumbled backwards and bumped into one of his companions. The other waved his rifle about, seeking the source of the gunshot.

Captain Pace stood just outside the firelight, with Tongue at his side. The Indian had roused the captain just in time.

"You men. Return to your own camp." Pace spoke deliberately, in measured tones. "Now."

Bleeker squinted into the shadows. Is he going to challenge Micah Pace? Possum wondered. Bleeker must be drunker than I thought.

While Bleeker stared at Pace, undecided, other Rangers drifted out of the shadows, weapons at the ready. No one spoke. The captain had given an order. It would be obeyed. It needed no explanation.

"All right." Bleeker coughed and wiped his mouth with his shirtsleeve. "But you oughta know, Captain, at least one of your Rangers is yellow-livered. I mean this one." He gestured at Possum. "This one right here. He ran away from the Alamo fight. Just skedaddled. He's a goddamn coward."

"That's a damned lie." Possum yanked his pistol and pointed it at Bleeker's head.

"Oh, you're brave enough with all them Rangers with you, ain't you? But not enough guts to fight me man-to-man. You're just plain yellow."

A wave of rage overwhelmed Possum, making him stagger for a moment. He threw his pistol to the ground. Glowering at Bleeker, Possum yanked his Bowie knife from his belt. "Let's settle it," he mumbled, as much to himself as to Bleeker.

"Come in to me. I been waiting." Bleeker took a wide stance, swaying slightly from side to side. A vicious-looking knife appeared in his hand, as if from nowhere, catching the firelight. He laughed, a high maniacal burst, and waved the blade in Possum's face.

Possum retreated a step, his rage ebbing, replaced by a cooler sense of calculation. He'd mimicked fights with his Cherokee friend, Sa-lo-li, each grasping the other's knife hand, wrestling back and forth. He made a tentative pass toward Bleeker's hand, reaching for it, but Bleeker easily evaded him.

Bleeker tossed his blade from hand to hand, left to right and back again, swiftly, weaving a confusing pattern. He made a sudden feint and Possum stepped backwards, cautious. "Ha ha," Bleeker laughed. "I'll take it slow, don't worry. You're gonna get to know my frog-sticker real well." He belched and stopped his prancing to wipe his mouth with his sleeve. "Ain't she purty?" He held the knife aloft, the point upwards, showing it to Possum.

Possum could hear Bleeker's friends behind him, laughing with their leader. A twinge of fear ran down Possum's spine. This was nothing like the mock fighting he'd done with the Cherokee boy back on Pap's farm. Bleeker's knife looked deadly in the glimmering firelight. A cut-down butcher knife, honed to a point. Possum stepped further back, away from Bleeker, and lowered his Bowie.

"You're a spineless coward." Bleeker staggered. Drool crept down his chin.

"Take him, Grady. Slice him up," said one of his companions.

Cool-headed now, Possum squinted at Bleeker. Was he really stumbling drunk, or was it an act, a come-on.

Micah Pace stepped between them, a palm held out toward each man, stop signals. "There'll be no fighting here tonight." Pace reached out and grabbed Possum's hand. He slipped the Bowie knife away from Possum and tucked it into his own belt. He reached for Bleeker's knife. Bleeker lurched away. The knife disappeared into his shirt.

"You're drunk," Pace announced to Bleeker. "You three, you and your friends, back to your campsite. Mebbe you'd better move another half-mile down the creek bank. It will be light in a few hours. We'll settle this in the morning."

One of Bleeker's friends took him by the arm and dragged him stumbling away, still complaining. The other followed.

Pace made a little bow in the direction of the Tejanos. "Señor Benavides, my apologies that your slumbers were interrupted. I am glad that this Ranger was on hand to take control of the situation." He indicated Possum.

Possum stood up straight. He hadn't thought of himself as acting in the capacity of a Ranger. He'd merely reacted to his anger at Bleeker.

One Tejano lad whispered urgently into Benavides's ear. The old gentleman bowed to Pace and to Possum. "I...thank," he said. *"Gracias a los dos."* The lad took him by the elbow and turned him away.

Waiting at the edge of the firelight, wrapped in a white gown held close, was Benavides's daughter. Tall and slim, almost as tall as Possum, shoulders thrown back and chin held high, she stared at him. Her dark eyes locked with his. Possum caught his breath, transfixed by her image.

Pace grabbed hold of Possum's belt. "Red. Come with me. Now. Come on, Red."

The spell was broken. Possum glanced toward Pace. When he looked back for the girl, she had disappeared into the darkness.

Pace squatted on his heels beside the embers of the Ranger campfire. He motioned for Possum to join him.

"Now listen, Red. Red, that's what they're calling you, ain't it? You and I need to have words. First thing—don't ever let yourself get pulled into a knife fight with a skunk like that drunkard from Louisiana. He'd slit your gizzard before you could make a pass at him. Jim Bowie was a Louisiana man and a knife fighter, and he scared me shitless. You're a Ranger, temporarily, and a Ranger don't ever drop his gun like you did. Shoot first. If your gun ain't loaded—club somebody with it."

"Yessir."

"Now, the other thing. What did that polecat mean? Did you run away from the Alamo fight? Like he said?"

"No, sir. I never ran away from the Alamo. Nossir."

"Hold out your hands, Red. Lemme see them."

Pace took Possum's hands in his. He turned them over and over, examining them in the firelight.

"Thought so," he said. "You're a working man. Done your share of labor. Calluses and thick wrists. That man Bleeker's hands—tiny and smooth as a Mexican whore's. Did you notice them, when he was tossing that knife?"

"Nossir."

"Your hands give me confidence in you, but I need to know more. Tell me right now. Did you run away from the Alamo battle?"

"No, Captain Pace, I've never run away from any fight. I never fled from the Alamo." It was a fine point, true, but Possum certainly didn't leave the Alamo of his own accord, under his own power. He was taken away while unconscious. He hadn't run away.

Pace stared into Possum's face for a long moment. At last he picked up a stick and stirred the fire. A fresh leap of flames illuminated his face. Possum tried to read his expression, but it was stony.

At last Pace threw down the stick and rose to his feet. "I believe you're telling me the truth," he said. "But at the same time, you're holding something back. Something you're concealing. Aren't you?"

With a sigh, Possum looked away. Perhaps he should confide in Captain Pace, but he'd held the secret so long, he just couldn't let it go. No, he could not tell Pace that he'd been at the Alamo. And was taken away, unconscious, not his fault, not his choice. He couldn't reveal his compulsion to find Davy Crockett. Maybe someday he could tell someone. But not now.

"Well then. Every man makes enemies. Bleeker is surely one of yours, and you will have to deal with him in your own good time. But hear this. I think you would make a good Texas Ranger. But I cannot accept you until I know the nature of your secret. Whatever it is, it holds you in thrall. Dispose of it. If you can."

Chapter 21

Heat from the mid-morning sun pushed down on Possum's shoulders, almost like something shoving at him, a pair of hands pressing on his back. Gotta be late August, he thought, maybe September. Last night he'd seen the archer chasing the scorpion across the southern sky. Are we still in Dog Days? He dabbed at his forehead with a bandana, breathing shallowly, trying not to think about the Texas heat. Caleb rode beside him, stirrup to stirrup, silent for once, twisting often to check his back trail.

The caravan had closed ranks, riding close to one another, stirrup to stirrup, heads down, moving slowly along the La Bahía road. No stragglers this morning; the travelers followed directly on Micah Pace's heels. Rangers patrolled the margins, looking this way and that. Only the young Tejanos ventured away from the column, brief excursions into the grasslands, eyes searching ahead and behind. When Possum stood up in his stirrups, he could see Tongue taking the lead, ahead of Pace by a few yards.

Grady Bleeker and his two companions were no longer part of the caravan. They'd left before dawn, Caleb told him. Three of the would-be soldiers left with Bleeker, too. Possum looked for Bleeker's hoof prints but couldn't recognize any in the dusty road. Possum felt a sense of relief that he wouldn't have to confront Bleeker, but at the same time, he regretted that he'd lost the opportunity to settle with the man once and for all. He tightened his grip on the reins; the memory of last night's embarrassment was a bitter one.

Caleb muttered something under his breath and shifted around in his saddle, scouring the grasslands with a slow intense study. Possum squinted into the haze, searching for any movement at all. No breeze disturbed the scene. The flat grasslands seemed to disappear in waves of heat rising on the horizon, little mirages here and there. He looked down and away, squinting, his eyes burning.

Caleb reined in and halted. Hand on his hip, next to his pistol, he scrutinized the trail behind.

"You worried about Indians?" Possum asked.

"Outlaws. Raiders, Mexican or American or both." Caleb ejected a stream of spittle. "We're getting farther south. Ain't much law in this part of Texas, not anymore. 'Course there never was a lot, except when the Mexican army put in an appearance."

"Not so, señor. We have laws and we enforce them. *Buenos días*, Señor Colorado. Señor Caleb."

Possum recognized the young Tejano from last night's misadventure. He was one of the pair who'd raced back and forth yesterday alongside the caravan. The lad reined in at Caleb's elbow.

"I am called Eduardo. Eduardo Benavides. *Mi hermano*—my brother—*es* Emiliano Benavides." The youngster's smile displayed a set of strong white teeth.

Caleb grunted, his gaze sweeping the rear. "You boys twins?"

"*Sí, si! Somos gemelos*. Twins, as you say."

Eduardo's brother Emiliano, grinning broadly, appeared at Possum's side. "*Buenos días, Señores*."

Caleb turned his mount and urged it forward to catch up the caravan. Possum and the Tejanos spurred their mounts after him.

"Seen-yore," Caleb called over his shoulder. "What are you telling me about laws here in the wilderness? What kinda laws do you boys enforce hereabouts?"

"We have the *volantes.* Like you Texas Rangers, the *volantes* ride to protect us from Indians and *bandidos.* As did the *companía volante* in San Antonio, in years past."

"*Volantes?* Flyers?" asked Possum.

"*Sí.* You could call it a flying squadron."

"They was broken up in the last Mexican revolution," said Caleb. He slowed his pace and shifted to check the back trail again. "Like you said, they come before the Texas Rangers. Covered the territory from Laredo to San Antone along the old *camino real.* I heard tell—they give the Alamo its name, they did. It used to be called Mission Valero. This *volante* troop moved in there and named it after their home town, someplace down in Coahuila. The Alamo. C'mon, let's keep up."

"You are right, Señor Caleb. My father, *Don* Benavides, he tell me—told me—of the brave *companía volante de San Antonio,* how they rode to fight the Apache Indians." Emiliano laughed and rattled his spurs. "Still the *volantes* ride. They are summon when there is trouble, and the *caballeros* and *vaqueros* from the *ranchos* ride against it. Soon, I make *diecisiete.* I will ride with the *volantes en próximo.* When I am—seventeen?"

"You look old enough right now," muttered Caleb.

"Yes, this autumn, we are seventeen *años. Venga!*" Eduardo shook his horse's reins and galloped off, racing along beside the caravan. Emiliano scampered after him.

"Lookit them boys ride." Caleb turned his head and squirted a brown stream of tobacco juice. "Not a care in the damn world. How you think they're gonna like being Texians instead of Mexicans? This ain't Mexico anymore."

Micah Pace raised his arm, fist clenched, and called a halt when one of the wannabe-soldiers hopped down from his horse and stumbled into a patch of tall grass beside the trail. His loud retching was followed by laughter from some of the Rangers.

"Guess he had too much of your friend's whiskey jug," said Caleb, chuckling.

"He ain't my friend!"

Caleb eased himself down out of his saddle and stood straddle-legged, massaging his kidneys with both fists. "C'mon, Red, let's stretch our legs while we can. I wanna talk with you."

They walked a few paces back down the Bahía road. Caleb plucked a grass stem and chewed on it for a moment. "Red," he said softly, "you gotta do something about that little shit Bleeker."

Dammit, thought Possum. Micah last night, and now Caleb, wanting to tell me what to do. He scowled, glancing at Caleb sideways.

"He named you a coward. No self-respecting Ranger would put up with that. Now, the boys is wondering, maybe you ain't got the spit to be a Ranger. You gotta find him and whip his ass. Where everybody can see it. Make him take water."

"He's a goddamn liar." Possum's voice rose. "I woulda killed him last night. Micah stopped me."

Caleb sighed and made a shushing gesture, his hand waving. "No, Red, he woulda killed *you.* Even drunk, he's a knife fighter. You ain't."

"What makes you think I ain't a knife fighter?" Possum's hand fell on the handle of his Bowie knife.

"I seen the way you held that Bowie. Bleeker would have cut you to carrion. Micah Pace saved your hide, all right."

"You goddamn Rangers think you know it all." Rage filled Possum's head. The memory of last night's debacle surfaced once again. He felt the humiliation overwhelming him. Trembling, he shook his fist under Caleb's nose. "I'm a Tennessee man. I take care of my business and do it in my own way. We Lawrence county men don't put up with—why, Davy would…" Possum stopped abruptly, chewing at the words. Breathing hard, he stared intently at Caleb. He hadn't meant to say Davy's name.

"Calm down now." Caleb took another suck on the grass stem. "I don't think you're coward. I think Bleeker is. Otherwise, he wouldn't sneak away like the did this morning."

"I mean to kill him. I will. When I catch him." There, I've said it. Possum nodded his head, reinforcing the idea to himself more than to Caleb.

"It won't be a fair fight. He's got those two galoots behind him. You don't wanna back-shoot him either, now that he's branded you. Mebbe one a these gangs of bandits will take care of him for you. Where do you think he's off to?"

"How the hell would I know?" Possum kicked at a clod of dirt in the road.

"Look." Caleb pointed up the road. "Micah's got them mounted and ready to move. Let's go." He grasped Possum's sleeve. "I like you, Red. I just wanna help you be a good Ranger."

Possum jerked free. His ire was still aroused. "Let's get going."

In early afternoon, the party picked up speed, moving into a slow trot. "There's Victoria up ahead." Caleb raised up in his saddle. He shaded his eyes with his hand, squinting into the dust. "Thank the Lord. I'm ready for a glass and a hot meal." He flicked the end of his reins against his horse's rump. "Come on, *caballo*, your day's about done."

Possum slowed his pace, walking his horse. He'd had enough of Caleb DeWitt, at least for now. He searched about himself, making note of his surroundings. That's what Davy always did. Checking the scene, he called it. By now, it was second nature to Possum.

He stopped beside a corral made of twisted logs. Horses, several dozen, stood motionless except for blinking at the hordes of flies around them.

A lanky cow caught his attention. Lean and rangy, she stared at him from beneath horns that reached several feet to each side. Possum laughed at the sight. She must be one of the longhorns he'd been told of, one of the herds of wild cattle ranging through south Texas. The beast snorted in his direction and pawed at the ground. She tilted her head from side to side, displaying the points at the end of her horns. Her eyes blazed a warning, a message of pure hate. Possum's horse shied away from the corral.

He reined it in, chuckling. "Well, old girl, I'd hate to be the man whose job it was to chase you into this corral." Sniffing the air, he added, "If my senses ain't failing me, that's a rendering operation in the building next to you. You're gonna be hide, hair and tallow before long."

The caravan moved into the little village, walking their horses, following Pace's lead. He halted them at a large square in the town's center, a grassy park in which several horses grazed. Possum caught up with the Rangers as they dismounted. He joined them, leading his horse into the tall grass and looping the reins around a low-growing mesquite tree. The grass was dry, seared by the heat, but the horse began to graze eagerly. Good enough, thought Possum. Let's see what this town has to offer.

There didn't seem to be much to Victoria. Just a squalid little village, that's all Possum could see. He watched the Mexicans, the Tejanos, take their leave of the caravan with handshakes all around. Señor Benavides offered several nods of his head to Pace but stayed in his saddle. With a broad wave of his arm, Benavides directed his party away into a side street.

Their horses tended, staked out in the town square, the Rangers hurried across the dirt street to a barroom.

"C'mon, Red," yelled Caleb.

Grinning, Possum waved back no. He drifted across to a hotel with a wooden sign that advertised baths. A cool tub of water was more appealing than a glass of whiskey. He knew that the Rangers would probably splash in the river once they'd drowned their thirst with whatever liquor the barroom sold. Possum looked forward to a scrub in a real bathtub and maybe a clean hotel room for the night.

Hands on hips, Possum surveyed the square and the buildings surrounding it. No sign of Bleeker or his friends, or the other soldier recruits. He noticed Micah Pace striding purposefully across the square to a low-slung wooden house surrounded by a white fence. The door swung open and a tall, thin gentleman emerged to grasp Pace's hand with both of his. They disappeared indoors. Curious, Possum watched for a moment, but Pace didn't reappear.

At the point of entering the hotel, Possum changed his mind. He'd noticed a mercantile store with a flat-topped, Tejano-style hat displayed by the door. He removed his floppy-brimmed sombrero and wiped his forehead on his sleeve. The Mexican hat looked inviting.

"Bienvenidos, Señor. Como puedo ayudarle?" The shopkeeper spoke from the shadows at the rear of the store, where he struggled to his feet. "Ah," he continued as he hurried up to Possum, "I see you are an *Americano.* Welcome to my *tienda.* My very fine store. Forgive me, I was about to enjoy my *siesta.* May I be of assistance to Your Honor?"

"What do you call this style of hat?"

"Ah, the Spanish hat. Some call it a *gaucho.* The gentleman has a sharp eye. That is a very fine hat, made from the finest wool. Try it on, Señor. Oh, a bit small? I have larger ones. Follow me, please."

"Wait a moment," said Possum. "That little house across the square. With the white fence. Who lives there?"

"Ah, that is the home of Juan Linn. John Linn, you would say. Mayor of the City of Victoria. He was an *alcalde* before the war; now he is our mayor. Do you know him?"

"No. I just wondered whose house it was."

"Juan Linn has the respect of Mexicans and Americans alike. You should know, Señor, Victoria is only the third city to be chartered by the new government of the Republic of Texas. We are very proud of our city and of our mayor. We are growing and prospering, thanks to Juan Linn."

Possum pushed further into the shop, his eyes adjusting themselves to the darkness inside. He noted shelves well stocked with various kinds of dry goods. The little rotund shopkeeper followed, gesturing here and there where articles of clothing were displayed.

"You are wondering, why is Victoria so successful?"

Successful? From what he'd seen of it, Possum thought Victoria to be a hot, smelly, poor little village without much to recommend it. He selected a dark-colored cotton shirt and held it up to the light. It looked to be his size.

"I will tell you. We have become successful because we are a major center for commerce. We trade with the *Estados Unidos*, with Mexico, with European countries." He broke off his speech with a wave of both arms, his head down, shaking no. "I should not have said Mexico. But you should see, señor, the warehouses to the east of town, why, they have many kinds of goods." The shopkeeper rubbed his hands together. "Many kinds."

Possum stared at the man. "Who buys them? Here in this village?"

"Ah, those goods are for transport to San Antonio. You must know, we are but twenty miles from Linnville on the coast and Juan Linn's shipping piers." The little man gestured toward the east. "I will tell you, many things pass through Victoria. And the boats, they our carry hides and tallow away to be sold in New Orleans. All must go through Galveston, of course, and be taxed. Our waters are too shallow for large ships. Our flat-bottomed boats cross the sand bars easily."

"Interesting." Possum fingered a pair of trousers. Narrow-cut legs with silver conchos, secured with buttons down the sides, like the ones the Tejano youths wore. He held them against his waist.

"And the people! I tell you, Señor, many *inmigrantes* pass through *Ciudad* Victoria. Many Germans. *Alemánes*. They go first to Galveston. Then, on the shallow boats, they come to Linnville or Indianola over on the Gulf Coast. They all pass through Victoria. *Ricos*, fine gentlemen. They travel to San Antonio and beyond, to new towns in the hills. They do not fear the Apaches or the Comanches." The shopkeeper shook his head. "They are—you would say—determined."

"Do you fear Indian raids here? In Victoria?"

"We are too many, Señor. Juan Linn, he keeps us prepared. But on the trail to San Antonio, that is where Apaches may strike. Of course, they are mostly after horses, but one never knows what an Indian will do. They raid at night. Apaches are devils, but it is the Comanches above San Antonio that are most fearsome. Sometimes they come down from the hills."

"I am bound for San Antonio myself." Possum drifted deeper into the store and stopped at a rack of leather belts.

"Ah, Señor, then you must wait for a big caravan for such a trip. *Como se dice*, 'in numbers there is strength.' *Verdad?*"

Chapter 22

Victoria town looked more pleasant in the evening dusk, when shadows softened its harsh image. Cool breezes carrying an earthy aroma wafted across the town square. Fireflies danced above the tall grass. From the distance came the deep, lowing call of a milk cow. Across the square's pathways, shafts of light streamed from lanterns hung in the windows of the low-slung houses along the town's streets.

Possum strolled beside the square, relaxing and enjoying the ambiance, puffing on a cigarillo and nodding to other gentlemen taking the evening air. Freshly bathed, groomed, his hair and beard neatly trimmed, he sported the newly-purchased attire of a Tejano, from Spanish hat to *vaquero* boots. The boots were uncomfortable. He'd tried on several, and finally settled on a soft leather pair. The shopkeeper insisted that he would soon get used to them and would find them more serviceable than his well-worn moccasins.

"Colorado! *Espérase!* Colorado."

The call came from behind him. It took Possum a moment to recall that "Colorado" was the name given him by the Tejano boys. He turned to see Emiliano approaching on horseback.

"Good evening. *Buenas tardes,* Emiliano." Some of Cassandra's Spanish lessons were surfacing in his mind. He smiled up at the lad reining to a halt beside him.

"Colorado. I am sent—I am to bring you to the *casa* of Don Octavio. For a *baile.* A dance. Please."

"Don Octavio?"

"*Sí.* Don Octavio. Señor Benavides. Señor Octavio Benavides. Don Octavio. My father. Please accompany me."

"A party at the house of Señor Benavides? I gladly accept your invitation." Possum tossed away his cigarillo.

Emiliano hastily dismounted. "You must take my horse, Señor. I will walk beside you."

"Nonsense. I will walk. At your stirrup."

They compromised. Both men walked, with Emiliano leading his horse. With sideways glances, Possum studied Emiliano's clothing. Yes, they were dressed in similar fashion, but the Tejano's suit was decorated more elaborately. It seemed molded to his body. Still, Possum decided that he was appropriately dressed. I'm learning from these Tejanos, Possum thought. Perhaps I will learn to dance.

The approach to *Casa Benavides* led through a path illuminated by flickering torches. A fiddle tune met them on the broad veranda. Possum's breath quickened; he thought of Davy Crockett. Could it be? But, of course, it was not. Emiliano urged him through a hallway and into a large, well-lit patio filled with gentlemen and their ladies. He spied two musicians on an improvised stage, sawing away on their fiddles and accompanied by an oversized guitar. Heads turned in his direction; conversations diminished. Emiliano grasped his elbow and encouraged him through the assembly, where Don Benavides held out a welcoming arm to him.

Stern-faced, Benavides gave a brief nod before waving to the musicians. The fiddles broke into a rousing version of "Yankee Doodle." This prompted a round of laughter from the gathering, followed by sporadic applause. Chuckling, Possum joined in the applause, unsure if it was a salute in his honor or a joke at his expense. Either way, he'd been introduced to Tejano society in Victoria.

Don Benavides presented Possum to his wife, Doña Graciela, a stocky woman whose Indian heritage showed in her high cheekbones and dark coloring. She was dressed in a black gown, with a lace mantilla atop an ivory comb. Doña Graciela and her husband wore somber expressions, ignoring the gaiety surrounding them at their party. Possum found them an impressive pair, dignified, impeccably dressed. When Emiliano took his elbow once again, Possum bowed deeply to Don Octavio and then to Doña Graciela. Each, in turn, nodded to him.

"Now, let us—strengthen ourselves?"

"Fortify ourselves," mumbled Possum. He followed in Emiliano's wake, moving to a claw-footed table at the far wall.

"Yes. Fortify. This punch is made with the finest *tequila*, aged at our *Rancho*."

Possum sipped from a cup Emiliano urged on him. A cool citrus drink, laced with a pungent, unfamiliar whiskey. He sipped again, a bigger drink this time.

"What do you think? Did you ever taste better *tequila*?"

"Never." Actually, Possum hadn't tasted *tequila* before. Strong but pleasant, it was much better than the whiskey he'd drunk back in Columbia.

"Now, we dance. The fandango." Emiliano dashed away.

The taste of the whiskey punch still in his mouth, Possum kept his gaze fixed on Emiliano's back and followed as best he could. Couples were gathering in the middle of the patio. The musicians had exchanged their fiddles for guitars. A few tentative chords echoed across the courtyard. Emiliano slowed his rush and nodded, one by one, to a trio of young ladies sitting in chairs lined up against the wall. Possum caught a glimpse of red and yellow flared skirts and white blouses. The girls giggled at Emiliano and then smiled up at Possum.

The Tejano came to a full stop and Possum crashed into his back. Emiliano grasped Possum by the arm. "May I present my sister, Señorita María *de* Benavides *y* Castillón?"

Possum stared open-mouthed. Was this the same girl he'd glimpsed the night of his confrontation with Bleeker? Seen in the torchlight of her father's patio, seated with her hands folded primly in her lap, her beauty overwhelmed him. Her dark eyes, widely set in her smooth tan face, sparkled up at him. Long coal-black hair, loosely knotted, cascaded onto the shoulder of her white, embroidered blouse. She rose in a graceful swirl of dark red skirts overlaid with black lace. Her lips, full and red as her skirts, parted with the beginnings of a smile.

"Sister, *mi hermana*, I have the honor to introduce the *famoso* Texas Ranger, Don Colorado."

María extended her hand, palm down. An enormous emerald ring caught the light and Possum's eye. "*Encantada*," she murmured. She was nearly as tall as he. Her eyes crinkled, and her mouth curved into a smile.

Possum took her hand and raised her fingers to his lips. He searched frantically for something to say, something that wouldn't reveal him to be the fool he felt he was. He simply held her fingers, perhaps a bit too long for she gently disengaged them. She stepped to his side and placed a hand on his sleeve.

Guitars began a slow melody, a sad-sounding tune strummed in a minor key. "Lead María to the dance," exclaimed Emiliano. "I seek a partner half so *hermosa*." And he hustled away.

Her hand on his arm, María directed Possum into the center of the patio and turned to face him. She produced a pair of castanets and clapped them in his face. Stepping slowly, she emphasized the rhythm of the music with taps of her feet and the castanets. Her heels rang against the stones of the patio and alternated with quick taps of her toes. Swaying gracefully, she raised one arm and then the other, offering sinuous, come-hither movements.

Possum tried to mimic the movements of the other men on the floor, taking back and forth steps, his hands clasped behind his back, certain that he appeared ridiculous. María was an enchantress. She kept her eyes fixed on Possum's.

The tempo of the music increased, and the dancers followed it, moving ever more quickly. María's castanets whirred in time with the guitars; her feet tapped a rhythm on the stones of the patio. Possum abandoned his attempts to mimic the other men. He stood in place, clapped time with his hands, and admired María.

The music came to a thunderous crescendo. Breathless dancers shouted their praise. The hubbub of conversation resumed as people dispersed to the punch bowl or to the garden behind the patio. The musicians laid down their guitars and disappeared.

María slipped her arm into the crook of Possum's. Smiling radiantly, she steered him toward her chair. Suddenly, Don Octavio loomed in front of them. He removed María's arm from Possum's and placed it on his own. With a curt nod, he turned María away. As her father led her off, María smiled back over her shoulder at Possum. Don Octavio gently shook her arm, a caution, and she turned away. Possum stared after her, his pulse racing.

Several taps on Possum's arm turned his attention away. "Emiliano?" he asked.

"No, it is I, Eduardo. I believe my sister favors you. Come, let us have a cigar." He led the way out onto the veranda, away from the glimmer of the patio's torches, into the darkness.

"Your sister María. She is so—so beautiful.

"Many *caballeros* here would agree with you."

"Is she spoken for? Engaged to be married?"

"No, *después de todos*, she is her father's only daughter. Don Octavio guards her well. And Doña Graciela! *Ay, Dios!*"

Possum produced two cigarillos and offered one to Eduardo. So, he thought, there is a chance. He stomped his foot in disgust. What am I thinking? I can't even speak her language. I'll be leaving. Most likely, I'll never see her again. Eduardo held a match to Possum's cigarillo, and he puffed it to life. No, Possum decided, I'm being a fool. A fool desperately in love with a beautiful girl.

Eduardo's brother, Emiliano, loomed out of the darkness, his arm around the waist of a slender girl. Eduardo broke away and began a heated conversation with the pair. Some good-natured poking of shoulders and laughter soon followed. Rivalry between brothers, Possum realized. And yes, the girl is a pretty one. And yes, she appears to be playing one brother against another. He smiled. This competition may not be as playful as it appears on the surface.

A flaring match at the far end of the veranda caught Possum's eye. The flame illuminated the rugged face of Micah Pace. Curious, Possum stalked toward his silhouette. Pace looked around at the sound of Possum's footsteps. "Who's there?"

"Me. Possum. Red."

"Oh, Red. All right."

Possum caught sight of a second figure in the gloom, standing behind Pace. "Sorry, Captain. I thought you were by yourself."

"It's all right. John, this man is a Ranger recruit, called Red. Red, meet John Linn."

"How do," said Possum. "Heard of you."

"I guess we're finished," Linn said to Pace, with a brief nod to Possum. "I'm grateful for your help, you and the Rangers. We will hang on here as best we can."

"Seems like you folks are doing very well."

Possum looked from man to man, waiting. Linn stayed back in the shadows. Pace puffed on his cigar, its tip a reddish dot.

"I'll be leaving now." Linn stepped away, vanishing from sight. Possum stared after him.

"I shouldn't have come here," Pace said. He pitched his cigar away. "We shoulda gone right back to San Antone. I was curious about this coastal country." He took a deep breath, which then emerged as a soft sigh.

Possum started to ask a question but checked himself. This was probably a bad time to pry into Pace's motives.

"You would think," said Pace, "that they'd be satisfied with what they have here in Victoria." He pounded his fist on the railing. "The rest of Texas is struggling with debt. Dammit, these people are living in a pipeline of money. German immigrants pouring into the country, well supplied, on their way to hill country settlements. There's all those mercantile goods passing through Victoria, headed for markets up country. Mexican ranchers are giving way to American commerce. The coastal Indians are tamed, thanks to the old mission padres. Shit, they are even trading with Mexicans, I guess through that trading post on Corpus Christi Bay, although it's against the law.

"What do they want, Cap?"

"A company of Rangers to guard them, that's what they want! They're worried about bandits. And Apaches. There haven't been any raids on Victoria since the Mexican army left." Pace barked a laugh. "Maybe those would-be soldiers whooping it up in Goliad will attack Victoria instead of Mexico."

Possum didn't laugh. The image of Grady Bleeker, sneering, came back to his mind. He could imagine Bleeker organizing a raid on Victoria, stealing whatever he could. He shook his head, clearing the thought away.

"This *baile* that Don Benavides pitched tonight? It's his last one." Pace coughed to clear his throat. "His last in Victoria. He's giving up his house here. He'll take his family and live on his *rancho* on the Nueces River. Or maybe in Mexico, across the Rio Grande. Before the war, old Benavides was an *alcalde* here in Victoria. Most of the old-time Mexican families are moving out. They no longer feel welcome in a town they established."

"Leaving? They are all leaving Victoria?" A chill of alarm ran down Possum's spine. María leaving? And going where?

"That's right, Red. Doesn't seem right to me. They are Texians now." Pace stretched his arms above his head. "We better head back to camp. I want to get a real early start in the morning."

"I must say farewell to Don Octavio and his family," said Possum, wondering if he could catch a quick glimpse of María.

"Don't be too long. See, Red, I promised John Linn I would ride the San Antonio river instead of the Guadalupe on the way back."

"Will that take us longer?"

"Not much. It'll take us right by Goliad where those soldier conscripts are raising Cain. John thinks the sight of Texas Rangers might pacify them. He's worried, too, about bandits and Apaches between the Nueces and San Antonio rivers. I promised Linn we'd scout for him on the way back to San Antonio."

"Don't he worry about Comanches? Ain't they worse?"

"I think the Comanches are pushing Apaches over this way." Pace sighed. "I tell you, Red, I got a bad feeling about that promise I made to John Linn. A real bad feeling."

Chapter 23

Captain Pace herded his Rangers onto the trail by first light, out of Victoria town and across the Guadalupe River. Their route would take them first to the *Presidio* of Goliad and then along the San Antonio River to the city it drained.

The Rangers rode new horses, acquired with the help of Mayor John Linn. Pace explained that he intended to move as rapidly as possible, and fresh mounts would be needed. Possum thought Pace had traded well. His own steed was well-muscled and bright-eyed, a bit frisky but responsive to his reins.

Four potential soldiers rode with them, men who intended to enlist in the Texian army mustering at Goliad. Young Eduardo Benavides and a servant completed the party.

The Tejanos twins had ridden into the Ranger camp just before daybreak. Eduardo asked permission for himself and a servant to accompany the Rangers to San Antonio. Some Legal affairs to settle, he said with a vague wave of his hand. Pace frowned but said he would allow it. Possum stared back toward the town, hoping that María would follow her younger brothers, but the path was empty.

Leaving Sally the mule behind was a problem for Possum. Pace had told him, "Forget the mule; we need to travel fast and light." Possum and Sally had shared many adventures, escaping from San Jacinto, crossing the Brazos to the Kinney farm, then down to Columbia, and finally now to Victoria. On a whim, he suggested that Emiliano take her as a parting gift from him to

María. Instantly he regretted the impulse; Sally was hardly a show animal. But the Tejanos heartily endorsed the idea. Emiliano said he'd have Sally groomed and bedecked with ribbons. They assured Possum that María would be delighted with Sally.

Eduardo took to the trail with enthusiasm, grinning widely, sitting erect on horseback in his stylish Tejano garb. His jacket was heavily embroidered and embossed with silver. New trousers of buckskin were buttoned along the sides from the waist down. A pigtail peeped from a red bandana beneath his flat-brimmed Tejano hat.

His servant was a short, stocky *hombre* Eduardo introduced as Cruz. The man seemed to be a combination of servant, caretaker and bodyguard. A dark-skinned, muscular man, Cruz spoke not at all. His short Tejano jacket, worn and stained, barely covered his frayed cotton shirt. His dirty pantaloons were unbuttoned to the waist, revealing leggings worn from knee to ankle. A wicked-looking bone-handled knife protruded from the leggings on his right side. The red sash around his waist carried a large pistol.

Possum couldn't decide whether Cruz was angry or frightened. He wore a perpetual scowl. His dark eyes darted this way and that. He sat hunched forward in his battered saddle, one hand on his horse's reins and the other held against his stomach, ready for action. He rode close to Eduardo, never pacing him, always slightly to the rear.

The Rangers rode at a near gallop, toward the west, dawn to their backs, along a well-worn trail. They'd arranged themselves in pairs. Each rider kept his eyes fixed on his side of the trail. Possum and Caleb rode side by side. Eduardo brought up the rear, with the silent Cruz close behind them.

After an hour's ride, Pace slowed the patrol to a walk, resting the horses. Possum shifted in his saddle, seeking a more comfortable position. His fresh mount demanded his attention, and his thighs were aching from the effort.

"We will reach Goliad before long," said Eduardo. "Well before *mediodía*. The Captain Pace is—urgent?"

"Seems to be in a hurry, don't he?" Possum looked over his shoulder. The four soldiers had fallen behind and hurried to catch up.

"I have a cousin in Goliad. Perhaps I will see her."

"Captain Pace didn't seem happy about riding to Goliad. I guess we won't visit there for long." Possum cut himself a chew and poked it into his jaw. "Eduardo, how come your horse don't seem to be tired?"

"Oh, this is a well-blooded animal. Is that the right word? He carries some Arabian blood. I am not heavy. There is no problem."

"What about Cruz there?" Possum indicated the servant with a wave of his knife. "His horse don't look like no champion."

"Ha-ha, my friend. No, his horse is a *vaquero's* ride. If it tires, Cruz will run along beside it. He is part *Indio*, you see."

If Cruz heard that remark, or if he understood it, he gave no sign. His eyes continued searching. He closed the distance between himself and Possum. His horse's head eased between Possum and Eduardo. His gaze shifted to Possum's face for a long moment.

Possum felt a little thrill of alarm. Did Cruz think him a threat to Eduardo? Possum turned his steed to the right, leaving more space between himself and the young Tejano.

Possum said, "What kinda name is 'Goliad'? Is it Spanish? Or Indian?"

"It is a—a—a play on the words." Eduardo struggled, frowning, searching his command of English. "The letters would say the name of Father Hidalgo."

"Ah." Possum searched his memory. English class, the school at Lawrenceburg. "It's—an anagram." Is that what it was? The term didn't sound right. "Whatever it means, Goliad is on Pace's shit list."

With a wave of his arm and a shout, Captain Pace urged the Ranger Troop onward. "Gallop!" He led the dash through the scattering of huts that surrounded the *Presidio.*

Possum struggled to keep his horse in stride with the others. He caught only a sidewise glimpse of the squalid little hovels, goats tethered to mesquite trees, chickens frantically escaping his path. What was the damn hurry anyway? Unprepared for Pace's sudden stop signaled with a raised fist, Possum crashed his horse into Caleb's.

"What is this place?" Possum asked.

"*Presidio la Bahía.*" Caleb yanked off his sombrero and wiped his forehead on his sleeve. "You know. It's where the damn Mexican army slaughtered Fannin's men after he done surrendered to 'em. Captain just don't like being here, I guess. He seems all het up."

"No, Señor. The killing took place on *La Ciruelo.* Plum Creek, I think." Eduardo reined in beside them.

"I know that, Eduardo. We just happen to call it the Goliad massacre."

"Remember Goliad!" Possum shouted, laughing. That's what they'd yelled at San Jacinto. Several Rangers turned in their saddles to stare at him.

Pace had called a halt beside the *Presidio's* main gate. Standing in his stirrups, Possum could see over the fort's high stone wall. Several substantial buildings made of limestone blocks sat at the far end of a large parade ground. A few men gathered in front of the buildings.

"Now what's this?" An officious bantam of a man pushed open the gate and strutted through it. "Who are you men?" Hands on hips, he squinted up at Pace.

"Texas Rangers. Brought you some volunteers. Where's your officer?" Pace stayed in his saddle, his hands folded over his reins.

The volunteer soldiers walked their mounts to the front of the column, slipping past Pace. "We's come to join the army," one of them offered.

"I'm Sergeant Lynus. First Sergeant Lynus. Come inside the fort. Who the hell are the rest of you men? Rangers?"

"Call your Officer of the Day." Pace shifted uneasily in his saddle. "I'll talk with him." He stared off into the distance, ignoring the officious little sergeant.

"I'll answer any questions you got, mister."

"Captain."

"All right, Captain then. What do you want?"

Pace didn't answer. He'd asked for the Officer of the Day, and he saw no need to repeat his request. He waited. When a tall, thin officer strode through the gate, Pace swiveled in his saddle to stare at the man. Gold bars decorated the man's army jacket. Trousers with a gold stripe disappeared into knee-high riding boots. A saber dangled from his belt.

"Captain Micah Pace, Texas Rangers. And you are?"

"Lieutenant Murdock." He favored Pace with a careless salute. "What's your mission, Captain?"

"Any Indians or Mexican army activity in this vicinity? What do your scouts report? Bandit raids hereabouts?"

Murdock shuffled his feet. "We ain't—I mean, we have no scouts out at present."

Pace snorted his disgust. "What information do you have, Lieutenant? Anything at all?"

Murdock gestured behind him, through the gate. "We are still getting our company organized. The General will send scouts when he deems it necessary. Perhaps you should talk with him." He scowled a challenge at Pace.

"Rangers forward." Pace raised his arm and trotted down the trace; his troop followed obediently.

The Lieutenant stared after them, hand on his saber.

"Hey, Caleb!" The little sergeant shouted after the Rangers. "Caleb DeWitt. Ain't that you? Howdy, Caleb."

Caleb turned his mount to the far side of the column.

"Come on, Caleb. Join up with our army. This time you can fight the Mexicans."

Once across the San Antonio river, Pace set an easy gait, following a trace that led northwest between the sun-baked prairie and the trees scattered along the riverbank. Possum stayed to the rear of the column with Caleb beside him. Eduardo, with the faithful Cruz, ranged alongside the column.

Caleb rode on Possum's right side, the river side of the trail. "Now them's some fine pecan trees there. Bet there's gonna be plenty of nuts this fall. Indians used to harvest them, you know, different tribes meeting here. Send their women to do the work. The men'd get into fights. Women could work together. Dammit," he said, "Micah's picked up to a gallop again. What the hell is his hurry?"

Possum kept his attention fixed on the vast prairie to his left. The scrawny mesquite trees had given way to a field of leafy cactus, interspersed with vicious looking thorny shrubs. In the hazy distance, a flock of buzzards circled over a find of carrion. The column of Rangers flushed a covey of quail, which whirred suddenly into flight. Pace's horse shied, a sideways stumble, and the captain warned, "Rattler!"

When Pace finally reined into a grove of pecan trees and called a halt, Possum slipped from his saddle and staggered momentarily. "We gonna spend the night here?" he asked Caleb.

"They's a good two hours of sunlight left. I'm guessing Micah is gonna push on."

A thin creek trickled through the pecans. Possum followed the Rangers to its banks and watered his horse.

"Hey," somebody yelled. "They's a dead man here!"

Pace turned the body over. "It's that man Farrier," he announced, "that rode with us from Victoria. Knife cut in the gut. Dead almost a day, I'd guess." Pace stared at Possum for a moment, then turned his attention back to the body.

His meaning was clear. It looked like Bleeker's knife work. Could have been me, Possum realized.

"Anything in his pockets?" somebody asked.

"They're turned inside out," Caleb observed.

Pace straightened up. "We oughta bury him."

Caleb said, "Cap, we ain't got no shovels." He looked around at the ground. "No rocks here—can't make a cairn, neither."

"Toss him in the river?" a Ranger suggested.

"No, no, not since we know who it is. That wouldn't seem right." Pace scratched his chin. "Tell you what. Let's pile brush over him. We need to keep moving. We'll leave a note. When one of those caravans of German immigrants comes by here, they'll have shovels. They can do the burying."

The Rangers scurried about, dragging fallen branches and piling them atop the corpse. Pace supervised. When the heap was finished to his standards, he affixed a note penciled on torn paper to a branch—"R. Farier. We dint kill him. We got no shovils to burry him."

When Pace called a final halt, the sun was low on the horizon but the heat lingered. Possum's shirt was sticking to his back. Exhausted, the Rangers slipped from their mounts and watered them in the river. Pace had selected an open spot near the San Antonio river for their night's camp. The stands of pecan trees had thinned out as the Rangers moved upstream. Isolated clumps of only two or three trees dotted the riverbank. Away from the river, cactus and thorny shrubs had given way to tall grasses, burned brown with the summer heat.

Captain Pace searched up and down the riverbank before selecting a spot for the night. "Open ground might be best tonight," he said. "Stake the horses in plain sight. Double guards tonight. Tomorrow, we'll reach a *ranchito* owned by one of the San Antonio Missions. We'll get fresh horses there."

The river looked cool and fresh where it ran across a limestone outcropping. Possum shed his clothes and joined the other Rangers in the water. He sat on the outcrop, letting the water run over his legs. Eduardo soon appeared there beside him, bare, his brown skin a sharp contrast to Possum's. Cruz took a position on the riverbank where he could watch Eduardo. Eyes darting here and there, always returning to Eduardo, Cruz showed no signs of heat or fatigue. When Possum stared at Cruz, curious about him, the man's eyes suddenly locked with his. Cruz's gaze was intense; to Possum he seemed to lean forward, projecting a forceful warning. Possum broke the contact. He left Eduardo and climbed out of the river.

The second watch belonged to Caleb and Possum. Possum sat with his back against a pecan tree and watched the horses graze in the tall grass. By the light of the quarter moon, he could see Caleb about twenty feet away, crouched on his heels beside another tree. A nighthawk swooped near and another called in the distance. Then another.

Possum glanced in Caleb's direction. The Ranger had risen to his feet. Possum rose also and scanned the group of horses. He saw nothing strange. What was Caleb watching so intently?

Then he saw it. The grass stems were moving, ever so slightly. Was it a predator? A bear, maybe, like they'd seen two days ago? He yanked the pistol from his belt and squinted into the moonlight.

"Indians!" Caleb yelled. "After the horses!" He leveled his pistol and fired as a shadowy form sprang onto the back of a nearby steed.

An Indian rose from the grass immediately in front of Possum. Leveling his pistol, Possum pulled the trigger. The flash of gunpowder temporarily blinded him. He bent over and felt for his shotgun which he'd propped against the tree. An arrow thunked into the tree trunk directly above him.

Another gunshot echoed through the night air. "Did I get him?" yelled a Ranger who'd appeared beside Possum, waving a second pistol.

"My horse is gone!" cried Eduardo, from someplace nearby.

Another gunshot split the night. "Hold yer fire," Caleb called. "We done spooked them." Cautiously, he approached the horse herd, gathering reins as he went. Possum went to help him, keeping his shotgun at the ready.

"Two horses gone," announced Caleb, "And one dead Indian." He handed the reins over to Possum. "Take 'em back to the river," Caleb ordered. "Tie 'em up good. We shoulda brought hobbles with us. Hold on there, youngster," he called as Eduardo rushed out into the grassland looking for his horse. "Them Indians ain't got very far."

"Caleb, you better come here." The call came from their little campsite.

Possum followed on Caleb's heels. A Ranger had kicked the fire into life. By its feeble light Possum made out Micah Pace lying flat on his back. An arrow shaft protruded from his left shoulder. Pace brushed at it feebly with his right hand. Blood soaked his shirt.

"Aw, goddammit," said Caleb.

Chapter 24

"Build up that fire. You and you—take guard duty; watch out for more redskin attacks." Caleb DeWitt took charge of the troop with the same forceful voice that Micah Pace used.

Possum hastened to throw pieces of wood onto the fire. He marveled at the way the Rangers accepted Caleb as their new leader. But then, perhaps each was glad the task hadn't fallen to him.

The Rangers laid Pace on his back close the fire. "It's Apache, all right. Look at that shaft," muttered one.

"Bled a lot. Still bleeding." Caleb took hold of the arrow shaft and moved it ever so slightly. Pace flinched and moaned when he did so. "Cap, it's gotta come out. You know that."

Pace nodded his head. "Pull it out," he whispered.

Grasping the shaft and bracing himself, Caleb tugged on the arrow shaft, hard and then harder. Blood flowed freely around the shaft. Paced hissed through clenched teeth.

"Musta hit a blood vessel," said Possum. "He's gonna bleed to death if we don't stop it."

"It won't come out, Cap. It must be lodged in a bone." Caleb wiped his hands on his trousers. He looked up at the Rangers standing around him and Pace. "I don't know," he mumbled.

"Asalto!" cried Eduardo. *"Gracias a Dios!"*

"What the hell?" yelled Caleb.

"My horse. My fine horse, Asalto. Cruz has recovered him."

Cruz emerged out of the darkness leading Eduardo's steed by a rope around its neck. He held his wicked-looking knife at his side. Blood covered the knife blade and Cruz's hand as well. He passed the makeshift bridle to Eduardo.

"One less Indian," muttered a Ranger.

Pace stirred. "Push it through. Push the arrow through."

"Can't do it, Cap. It's caught on a bone in there." He looked around at the other Rangers for support. Some looked down; others stared away from the fire. Captain Pace was dying right before their eyes, and they could do nothing.

Cruz spoke to Eduardo in a low, raspy whisper. He gestured towards the grassland, an emphatic wave of his arm.

"Cruz says there is a *ranchito* he knows, only a league away on the prairie. They have a doctor, a *famoso* healer."

"Mebbe we could send for him," said a Ranger.

Cruz shook his head and mumbled something to Eduardo.

"Cruz says we must take the captain to the doctor, not the doctor to the captain."

Pace tried to sit up. "Leave me be," he said. "Caleb, get them ready to move out." He slumped back, groaning. "Go on to San Antonio. I'm done for."

"I will carry the captain," said Eduardo. "Cruz and I, we can do it. Cruz knows the way."

"I'll go too." Possum spoke up on an impulse, feeling the need to do something, anything, that might help.

"Guess it's his only chance," said Caleb. He looked around at the other Rangers. "We all oughta go."

"No! Take the patrol to San Antonio, Caleb." Pace was emphatic. Coughing, he waved an arm at Caleb. "I'll meet up with you there. Carry on your duties. Do it!"

"Meet us in San Antonio or in Hades," mumbled a Ranger.

Possum swung into his saddle and reached down for Pace. Two of the Rangers hefted their captain and tried, unsuccessfully, to place him behind Possum. Suddenly Cruz intervened, taking Pace away from the Rangers and swinging him up in front of Possum, who wrapped his arms around him. Cruz trotted off onto the prairie, away from the river, into the darkness.

"Come on," said Eduardo, urging his steed after Cruz. "Asalto! *Vamos.*"

Possum held Pace tightly and spurred his mount into a trot. He couldn't see ahead; he trusted his horse to follow Eduardo's. Pace roused for a moment, kicking his legs and squirming.

"Easy, Captain. Take it easy." Possum tightened his grip.

"Is that you, Red? Are we back on the trail? God, this shoulder hurts."

"It's all right." But was it? Were those Apaches still out there in the grass someplace? He had to put his trust in Cruz's knowledge of the prairies and follow blindly along.

He overtook Eduardo at the top of a small hillock. Cruz had stopped there. In the morning's soft light, Possum made out a cluster of huts about a hundred yards in front of them. A larger dwelling gleamed white in the sun's early rays.

Cruz cupped his fingers in front of his mouth and gave a spine-chilling cry, somewhat like that of a screech owl but deeper and more prolonged. He held up his hand to Eduardo, signaling wait, wait. His call was soon answered with a similar cry. "*Vamos,*" whispered Cruz.

A spindly boy grasped the reins of Possum's horse and led it toward a nondescript, whitewashed shack made of rude pilings.

Possum slipped the unconscious Pace down to a waiting Cruz. Weary from the effort of holding Pace, Possum stumbled when he dismounted.

A tall Mexican steadied him. "You are Señor Colorado?"

"*Sí.*" Possum eyed the Mexican. How has my reputation reached this place? How would they know me?

"Come," said the man. "*Sígame.*" Possum followed him into the shack, where lamplight revealed Micah Pace stretched out on a low cot. A figure crouched over Pace, hunched down, muttering something incomprehensible. Possum searched around the little hut. Where was the doctor?

"*Colorado, aquí es* Don Pedro de Olmos. *Un famoso curandero.*"

The figure straightened up and nodded to Possum. Don Pedro de Olmos was entirely bald. A gray beard reached halfway down his rough blue shirt. His dark eyes glittered from a wrinkled brown face. He lifted Pace's head and held a clay bowl to his lips. "*Beba,*" he whispered. "Drink of it."

"This man is a—a witch doctor? What have we done?" Possum grasped Eduardo's arm. "Why didn't you tell me? Tell us?"

Eduardo shook loose, frowning. "Don Pedro is a powerful healer," he stated firmly. "Do not doubt him."

"Dammit," growled Possum. But what other choice did they have? Pace would had died in any case. But a faith healer? Possum shook his head in disgust.

Don Pedro crossed the room to a tiny altar, where he lit two candles. Religious symbols were pinned to a crooked *serape* dangling from the wall. Possum recognized the Virgin but couldn't identify other symbols. When Don Pedro turned to face them, he held a piece of flint in a shaky left hand.

"It come out." He looked Possum in the eye and waved the makeshift scalpel. "Come out," he repeated, and knelt at Pace's bedside.

Possum gestured after him, to no effect. Did he understand English? Questions flooded Possum's mind, but he didn't know how to phrase them. Did the strange little man know what he was doing? At least he seemed sure of himself.

Eduardo looked over his shoulder at Cruz, who stood silent in the shadows. Possum's gaze followed. Cruz nodded his head. He, too, had confidence in Don Pedro.

The old *curandero* set aside the clay bowl and lightly slapped Pace's face, twice. When Pace didn't respond, he broke off the arrow shaft and cast it aside. He ripped open Pace's shirt, exposing the oozing wound high on Pace's left shoulder. Moving swiftly, he sliced the skin above and below the wound. Ignoring the rush of blood, he inserted two grimy fingers into the wound. With a twist of his wrist, Don Pedro removed the arrowhead.

Possum pushed Don Pedro aside and leaned over to examine the wound. Fresh blood bubbled from it.

Eduardo pulled Possum back. "*Es bueno*," he said. "Now he must heal."

"He's lost too much blood," Possum muttered.

"*Sí*, but Don Pedro can cure."

Don Pedro began stuffing powdered green herbs into the wound. When it could hold no more, he covered it with a rough bandage. Wiping his hands on his cotton trousers, he nodded to Possum.

"Señor Colorado?" he asked.

"*Sí*." How the hell did he know what to call me?

"He may live." Don Pedro spoke in halting, strangely accented English. "*Dios mediante*. It is in the hands of God."

After two feverish days, Pace opened his eyes. The girl who attended him called Possum to his side.

"How you feeling, Cap?"

"Weak as a puppy. What is this place?"

Possum grinned. "The doctor's office. Eat your soup."

"Tastes funny." Pace closed his eyes.

"He will get well." Eduardo spoke from behind Possum. "Don Pedro says God was good to him."

"I guess Don Pedro was, too."

Don Pedro's hut reminded Possum of a settler's log cabin back in Tennessee, except that it was made of different materials. The tamped dirt floor looked familiar. The walls of the hut—Eduardo said it was called a *jacal*—were of branches and wooden strips calked with a mixture of lime and clay. The *jacal's* roof consisted of branches tightly woven together. A ragged goat skin covered the only door. No windows.

The white, stone building loomed over their *jacal*. Eduardo explained that the inhabitants assembled in it when they needed protection from Indians or bandit raiders. It was constructed of limestone blocks that Eduardo referred to as *sillar*. Rifle slots flanked the heavy wooden door. A single wood-framed window on either side offered daylight to the interior. Eduardo pointed out that people could hide on the roof behind a parapet and shoot down at invaders.

Limestone blocks quarried nearby were used for such permanent buildings. *Jacals* were temporary but might persist for years.

Only two of the compound's *jacals* seemed to be occupied, one by a Tejano family and the other by several rough-looking men whom Possum concluded were Indians. All of them served Don Pedro.

A third *jacal* served as housing for Eduardo, Possum and Cruz. Never far from Eduardo, Cruz seemed to have taken Possum under his protection, too. He followed behind them, silently, at a respectful distance. Their main meal, at midday, was *frijoles* and *tortillas* which Cruz found for them. Cruz ate ravenously. Possum thought the food bland but filling.

Don Pedro received visitors during daylight hours. Possum and Eduardo squatted in the shade of their *jacal* and watched them come. Wavy images appeared in the distance across the prairie, finally recognizable as men or women walking through the haze. Eduardo pointed out some as Mexicans or Tejanos, others as Indians. One pair Eduardo identified as Apaches, which alarmed Possum, but Eduardo said they were friendly. Mission Indians, he said. Most sought Don Pedro for advice, or medicines, or charms.

"Perhaps, my friend, you should ask Don Pedro for a love charm. To make you irresistible to my sister."

Possum stared at Eduardo. Was this a jest? No, Eduardo looked quite serious.

Since Eduardo had mentioned María, Possum took the opportunity to ask him about his sister. She was Don Octavio's eldest child, Eduardo said, two years older than the twin boys. Born on their *rancho* on the Nueces River, she'd been pampered by Don Octavio's *vaqueros*. They would saddle a little pony for her and then pick her up when the pony brushed her off under the branches of a mesquite tree. When they found baby animals—rabbits or foxes—they presented them to María. Even a pet baby javelina. Her father sent María to school in Monterrey to learn the manners of the *gente bien*. Don Octavio took no such pains with his sons, Eduardo said, with a tinge of jealousy.

When Possum asked him about the Benavides *rancho*, Eduardo's mood brightened. He rose to his feet and waved his arm. "Much finer than this poor place," he said. "We have many cattle and horses, not merely goats. And many *vaqueros* to attend them. Our vaqueros sleep in fine *jacals*. And our *casa mayor* is much bigger and taller. Behind it is a large stone patio with a kitchen at the far end. The family lives there in comfort. When we are not staying in town, in Victoria. Or the Benavides *casa* in Mexico. Although I suppose we will no longer stay in Victoria," he added with a frown. "Tejanos are not welcome there."

"You have a house in Carmago? In Mexico?"

"Oh, *si*, *Casa Benavides*. It is our—our—where we come from. How do you say? Our *domicilio*. The Benavides family has been in Carmago for *cien años*. One hundred years." Eduardo's voice rang with excitement. "Yes, my friend, we were among the families brought from *España* to settle in the *frontera*. To shield Monterrey and Saltillo from the Apaches. And now from the Comanches."

Eduardo sat down again. "We have a *portion* along the *Río Bravo*. The Río Grande, you say. And were granted the large *rancho* along the *Río* Nueces. We would visit the *rancho* to manage the cattle. As did others. When the *índios* raided and attacked us, we would go back to Carmago."

"I suppose that Don Pedro did not build the stone *casa* in this compound," said Possum. "Did it belong to some family, perhaps from beyond the Rio Grande?"

Eduardo laughed. "Perhaps. Don Pedro is a—a wanderer. He travels. *Peónes* and *Indios* follow after him, seeking his favor. Here he is a—a—visitor?"

"A squatter?"

"*Sí*, yes, a squatter, that is good. One day, the owners *de veras* may return."

Possum said, "What about your family house in Victoria?"

"Yes, a fine house, as you saw. My grandfather built it. It became home to us, when we wanted to—rest—from the *rancho*. Those were happy times." Eduardo picked up a pebble and tossed it at a chicken, which squawked in agitation. "Tell me, Colorado, my friend, what will happen to us now?"

Possum picked up another pebble and made as if to toss it. The hen scurried away. "What do you mean?" he asked.

"We were Mexicans until this war came, war between Texians and Mexicans. We are always Tejanos, here in the *despoblado*. This is our home, here in South Texas. But Texas is now a separate country, separate from Mexico. Texas says the Rio Grande is the border. Mexico says the *Río Nueces* is the border. We are in between the two rivers. What are we now?"

Possum hefted the pebble, flipping it up and catching it in his palm. Finally he tossed it, striking a fence post with a thunk. He remembered Tongue's question, when they had first met. Who will you fight now, Tongue had wondered.

"You ain't any different, are you?" Possum said. "Still Tejanos. I guess I'd stay right on that *rancho*. Let the governments settle the border. Just wait for them to figger it out."

Eduardo stared intently at Possum for a long moment. "It that what you would do, Colorado? Stay on the *rancho*?"

"I would. Say, Eduardo, that's another thing. How come people here seem to know me. As 'Colorado'? Don Pedro, he called me 'Colorado'."

"Perhaps it is the color of your hair," said Eduardo, chuckling. "And your beard. Or perhaps they have heard of the *rojo*

Texas Ranger who was the honored guest of Don Octavio Benavides. Who knows?" He reached for another pebble.

They both looked up when a shadow fell over them. Micah Pace stood over them, his right hand holding onto the *jacal* for support. "Find me a goddamn horse," he demanded in a raspy voice. "Get me away from this goddamn place."

Chapter 25

They joined a caravan of traders trekking along the San Antonio River road. Guards rode on both sides of a line of oxen-drawn wagons loaded down with trade goods. Two German immigrant families brought up the rear. All were well armed, the Germans with fowling pieces. Possum bargained for horses for himself and Cruz. Micah Pace insisted that they could buy more steeds at the end of the day, when they reached one of the San Antonio mission *ranchos*.

Possum rode on one side of Pace and Eduardo on the other. Pace's face was ashen, but his jaw was set in determination. He spoke in a low, raspy tone when he spoke at all. The oxen held the caravan to a slow walk. Pace twitched impatiently, anxious to get to San Antonio and reclaim his command. Possum watched him out of the corner of his eye. Was it too soon for Pace to travel?

Don Pedro had raised no objections when a shaky Micah Pace hoisted himself onto Possum's horse. Possum saw Eduardo slip a leather pouch into Don Pedro's hand. The old man solemnly nodded to everyone from the door of his *jacal*. On the way to the river, Possum walked beside Pace's stirrup. Cruz led the way at a moderate gait, and Eduardo followed behind. Pace was trembling slightly when they reached the river but declined an offer to dismount.

The wagon master galloped back beside the caravan and reined in beside Possum. "Is the Captain doing all right? He could ride in one of the wagons if he's ill."

"I can speak for myself," croaked Pace. "I can ride a horse. But thank you."

"Suit yourself." The wagon master saluted Pace with a touch of his coiled whip to the brim of his hat.

At dusk they arrived at a little rancho protecting the pastures of the Mission San Francisco de La Espada. Possum helped Pace to dismount. He tried to steer him toward a *jacal*, but Pace said "Not that!" and slumped down beneath a live oak tree. Possum left him and went in search of supper. "Find me a good horse," Pace called after him.

Two days later, the caravan reached the outskirts of San Antonio. They passed simple houses with vegetable gardens and cornfields. At sunset, families sat in their yards, staring at the ox-drawn wagons rolling past them. A few men worked their fields. Their siesta was over.

Pace spurred his new horse to gallop ahead of the teamsters. He rode erect. His color had improved and his voice had returned to its normal deep baritone. But Possum had seen something that worried him.

Possum and Eduardo followed well behind Pace, with the faithful Cruz right behind them. "Have you noticed?" Possum asked in a low tone. "He doesn't use his left hand."

"Cruz says his left arm is paralyzed. From the arrow."

"He crooks his left arm a little. He never tries to grasp anything with his hand. But he sits that horse like nothing is bothering him."

Possum pulled the brim of his hat lower to block the setting sun from shining in his eyes. Perspiration coated his body; his shirt was stuck to his back. "Don't Pace ever sweat?" he asked.

Eduardo nodded to an *hombre* standing beside the road. "I have not been to San Antonio since I was a child. It was an exciting place." Eduardo stood in his stirrups, straining to see ahead.

"I'm hoping for a bath in that river and some warm food. And some real whiskey."

"Your wishes will be granted, Señor." Eduardo laughed and turned in his saddle to look at Cruz. "And you, Señor? What is your desire on this fine evening. *Qué queres?*"

Cruz ignored him.

Possum looked about himself as they proceeded down a narrow street. None of it looked familiar. He tried to remember more of his brief time in San Antonio with Davy Crockett. Back then, his journey had led him directly to the Alamo compound. Had he ridden down this street? He couldn't remember. Though the sun was sinking, he kept his hat brim pulled low. It was unlikely that anyone would recognize him or even remember him. He'd been a mere lad at the Alamo. Now that he was larger and stronger and sported a beard, he didn't think he was in any danger of discovery.

Well, he would have to take some chances anyway. After all, he wanted to look for Davy, and that meant asking questions. He hadn't considered how to go about doing that. Who could he talk with?

The street ended in a broad plaza. "There's the San Francisco Cathedral," exclaimed Eduardo. They stopped to stare at it. It does look somewhat familiar, Possum thought. I must have been here, in this plaza.

"*Plaza de los Islas.* Named for the Canary Islanders who were brought here as settlers." Eduardo began pointing out landmarks he recalled. "The Solís house. They hold *famoso* dances. And there, Don Colorado, a hotel with a very nice barroom. Don

Octavio would do his business there. Perhaps I can arrange to meet my *abogado* there. My lawyer."

"Red," Micah Pace called. "I am going to ride up to San Pedro Springs, just a bit farther to the north. That's where the Rangers camp. I hope to find Caleb there, and the troop, if it's not out on a patrol. You men are welcome to join me."

"Not I, Señor Captain," said Eduardo. "I have business here, which I hope to complete tomorrow. But I thank you for your offer." Eduardo doffed his hat and offered a bow from his saddle.

"It is I who must thank you, Señor Benavides. You and your friend—" Pace nodded to Cruz—"have certainly saved my life. If ever I can repay you, please call on me and the Texas Rangers."

"You have the friendship of the Benavides family, Captain."

"And please—my best *recuerdos a* Don Octavio. How about you, Red? Will you join me at San Pedro Springs?"

"Cap, I think I will try that hotel over there. If I can afford it."

"All right, but ride up to the Springs soon. You have some pay due to you. And, Red..." Pace eased his horse closer to Possum's. "You have accounted yourself as a Texas Ranger and my friend as well. I apologize for the doubts I spoke of."

"Captain Pace..."

"No, I was wrong. We all have secrets, events in our past we do not discuss with anyone. Say no more of it. Come to the Springs tomorrow, if you can." Pace turned his steed away, his right hand guiding his left to the saddle horn. "*Adiós*," he called.

They tied their horses to the hitching rail. Eduardo dismounted and stood beside his horse, arms outstretched. With a small brush, Cruz vigorously swept the trail dust from Eduardo's clothes. Cruz offered the brush to Possum who shook his head no.

The hotel lobby surprised Possum with its air of elegance. Dark wood trim was everyplace, around the walls, the doors, the desk. Brass-mounted oil lamps hung on the walls, diffusing a soft glow. An oriental rug covered the floor. Landscape paintings were displayed on the walls. One broad door opened to a barroom, another to a long corridor.

Eduardo strutted up to the desk and drew himself up to his full height. When a small, neatly-dressed clerk extended the register to him, Eduardo pushed it back. "I am Don Eduardo Benavides," he announced.

The clerk frowned at him. "Señor," he began.

"Don Eduardo Benavides. *Hijo de* Don Octavio Benavides." Eduardo rapped his knuckles on the bar. "My usual suite. If you please."

The clerk reached beneath the desk for a little bell, which he rang twice. In a moment he was joined by a heavy-set, frowning manager in his shirtsleeves. The clerk stood on tiptoes to whisper something in his ear.

"Of course," the manager exclaimed, all smiles now. "Don Octavio's family. Welcome, Señor." He glanced at Possum. "Señores, both, welcome to my hotel." The little clerk passed a key to Eduardo. "How may I assist *ustedes*?" he asked.

"We will dine presently." Eduardo beckoned to Cruz, who had appeared in the lobby with saddle bags and blanket rolls from both horses. "We require hot water for the bath." Eduardo sauntered down the corridor with Possum in his wake and Cruz after him.

"That's all you do?" Possum called from behind. "Mention your father's name?"

"Don Octavio is well known in San Antonio. In some quarters, at least."

The next morning, the rising sun splashed color across Possum's face. He rode out of the plaza, eastbound, toward the Alamo fortress.

After a restless night, he decided to begin his quest for Davy Crockett with a visit to the Alamo. He had only fragmentary, distorted recollections of San Antonio and the Alamo and the battle there. Maybe seeing the old fortress would kindle some suppressed memory, some clue about the final events there.

He reined to a stop on the river bank and sat astride his horse in the shade of a large cypress tree. Across the river, the sun rose behind the barracks. That building was Davy's assignment, he remembered. The Tennesseans were given the long barracks to defend. Was that the place that came back to him in dreams? The gunshots, the rifle barrels burning his hands, the smoke, the shouts, the screams? A wave of dizziness jolted Possum; he slipped sideways and fell from the saddle. He lay on his back, eyes closed, the screams now ringing in his ears, the acrid gun smoke burning his eyes. He squeezed them tight, forcing tears from the corners, gasping for breath.

He opened his eyes when something jarred his head. It was his horse nuzzling him, its head close to his. Possum sat up and reached for a stirrup. He tried to rise but stumbled. He felt a hand under his armpit, helping him up. A teenage Mexican boy, sober-faced, steadied Possum when he gained his feet.

"*Está usted enfermo? Tiene malo?* Sick?" asked the lad.

Possum shook his head. "Just a dizzy moment. Thank you. *Gracias*."

"I speak the English." The lad smiled up at Possum.

"So you do." Possum smiled back.

"Here is the Alamo."

Well, this is as good a place to start as any. "Tell me about it," said Possum. "Did you watch it?"

The lad launched into an animated tale of the battle, pointing out where the Mexican armies camped and where the attack took place.

"Did you see all that yourself?"

"Oh, *sí*, I watched. General Santa Anna watched from where we stand."

A chill ran up and down Possum's spine. Santa Anna stood here? He shuffled his feet.

The lad didn't take notice of Possum's uneasiness. With broad gestures of his arms, he described the assault on the Alamo from the Mexican viewpoint, pointing out where the troops breached the walls in spite of their terrible losses. Possum's mind raced in the opposite direction. He found himself recalling waves of Mexican soldiers confronting him, ever pressing at him. And Davy yelling encouragement behind him.

Enough! He interrupted the boy's story. "After the battle," he asked, "did you see the fort? Go inside?"

The boy nodded vigorously. "I did. With my uncle. Santa Anna asked to be shown the famous *Americanos*. My uncle showed him the body of Señor Bowie, a good friend. And others as well."

"Davy Crockett? Did you see his body?" Possum braced himself for the answer.

"The Crockett. Yes, we were shown his body, too."

"Did you know him? Recognize him?"

"Not I, Señor, but my uncle knew him. He pointed out the Crockett's strange hat, with the animal tail."

Anyone can wear a cap, Possum thought. Maybe someone else picked it up. If it was indeed Davy's cap. Was Davy the only one with a coonskin cap? He couldn't remember. Another wave of dizziness rocked him.

"Señor?" The lad looked anxiously at Possum.

"Were there survivors? Among those defending the fort?"

"Some women and children, yes. Santa Anna was generous. And..." He leaned close. "Two men, who hid themselves among the dead. At night they escaped."

Possum took a sharp breath. "And who were they?"

The lad pulled back, laughing. "Two Mexicans *de* San Antonio. They were ashamed, because they had acted like women. They fled the city."

It was possible. Davy, too, might have escaped the slaughter. But if he did, where would he go? Possum felt faint. He grabbed the saddle horn for support.

The lad took hold of Possum's other arm.

Possum shook free. "I am well. It is well. For your trouble." He handed the lad a silver peso. "*Gracias a usted.*"

He rode back to the main plaza, a slow walk, his thoughts churning. I must talk with an Anglo resident of San Antonio, he decided. The Mexican boy's story seemed authentic, but Possum was not convinced. There was still a chance of mistaken identity. Or that Davy had hidden himself and escaped at night, like the two men the boy described.

On the other hand. Possum reined the horse to a halt. On the other hand. If Davy truly escaped the slaughter. Where would he go? Why, he would be in the same position I am in! Possum laughed aloud. Davy couldn't go back to Tennessee, either. All the defenders died valiant deaths. There were no survivors. Susanna Dickinson had insisted that it was so; that was the story she brought to Sam Houston and spread throughout Texas.

Like me, he realized, Davy would find himself footloose in a strange land, a foreigner to most of those he met. Living with a secret he must always conceal.

It's my own fault. Possum sighed, thinking it through. I was confused. Young. Lost among strangers. Suppose I had ignored Susanna Dickinson's demand that I keep silent. If I'd told them at San Jacinto that I was an Alamo survivor, they would have believed me. After all, I was still suffering from that bayonet wound. It would be no disgrace. My problem is of my own making.

And I have survived it. Proven my manhood. Fought the Mexican army. Fought Indians. And joined the Texas Rangers. I have become a Texian, in fact and deed. This is my land now. Texas is my country.

I will not find Davy Crockett here, not in this San Antonio or elsewhere in Texas. If he still lives, he will be someplace on the frontier. Not back to Tennessee, that is certain. Like me, he would be forever exiled. A victim of his own reputation.

Possum squared his shoulders and spurred his horse toward the main plaza. He felt younger, lighter, as if a weight was lifted from his back. The search for Davy Crockett was ended. Now, he decided, I must pursue my own destiny. That's what Davy would do, isn't it?

Chapter 26

He found Micah Pace sitting on a bench beside San Pedro springs. The extensive system of bubbling waters burst from a rocky outcrop and filled a fair-sized pond, before feeding into San Pedro creek. Possum had followed the creek from San Antonio, a distance of several miles. He dismounted and looped his horse's reins over a low branch of a mesquite tree.

"My troop's out on patrol," said Pace. "Two dozen strong. Caleb took them southwest. We had a report—bandits on the Laredo road. Scoundrels, from their descriptions."

Would one of those scoundrels be Bleeker? The thought crossed Possum's mind. He remembered the dead man, Farrier, they'd found beside the San Antonio river. He had died from knife wounds. Possum thought of Bleeker right away. Had the other Rangers suspected Bleeker? No one had mentioned it at the time.

"I decided to rest up here at the Springs," Pace continued. "Still a little shaky from the journey."

"And the arrow wound," Possum added. "That's still kinda fresh." He remembered his own bayonet wound, how slowly it had healed.

Pace tugged a piece of paper from his pocket. "Here's your pay chit, Red. Take it to town. The Longhorn Saloon will give you cash for it."

"Thankee, Captain." Possum pocketed the chit without looking at it. "Come back to town with me. I had some good whiskey last night in the hotel bar. They called it *aguardiente.* Much better than that rot-gut we had in Columbia."

Pace laughed. "Anything would be better than that cactus juice. They's a pot of coffee on the coals. Get yourself a cup there."

Coffee sounded good to Possum. He felt light-hearted, relieved of his self-imposed obligation to find Davy Crockett.

"Here they come now." Pace heaved himself to his feet.

Possum looked up to see three Indians approaching on horseback. Comanches! He reached for his pistol.

"They're friends," said Pace. "San Pedro Springs is neutral territory." He raised a palm in greeting and stepped toward the Indians.

In last night's bar, Possum had heard that Comanches visited San Antonio on occasion. Such visitation often brought opportunities for trade. While Pace jabbered with them, Possum studied the Comanches, an older man and two younger ones. All three remained mounted on their steeds. Dressed in breach clouts only, with high leggings covering their shins, they exposed bare chests. Chevrons of white paint stood out against their dark upper arms. The older man's hair was twisted in a knot, and three eagle feathers were stuck in it. The other two wore their hair in braids. One of the younger Comanches held a wicked-looking war lance pointed at the sky. The older Indian chuckled softly from time to time in conversation with Pace. The other two stared at Possum, stone-faced.

Pace called to Possum, beckoning him closer. "Red, the chief says he hopes to have a horse race today. He invites you to race with him, even though his horse is tired."

Possum looked at the Comanche's little prairie pony, noting its well-defined shoulder muscles and generous hips. Could his grass-fed animal outrun the Indian's horse. Not over a short distance, he decided. "Tell the chief my horse is lame," he said with a chuckle. "It can't run."

This brought barking laughs from the Comanches when it was explained to them. Pace said, "I think you just accepted their challenge."

"Say, Cap, do you suppose they would know anything about Cassandra? The black woman that the Comanches captured? You remember, back in Columbia, I asked you about tracking her down, how I might go about it. I wanted to ransom her. Ask the chief if he knows anything about a 'buffalo woman'."

The Comanche chief jerked to attention when Possum spoke the words "buffalo woman." He beckoned to the other Indians, who pulled close and conferred in low, rapid, guttural bursts. The young Indian holding the lance pointed at Possum with it. The chief began shouting at the two braves.

"What's the matter?" asked Possum.

"I couldn't follow all that jabber. Something about you, I think. My Comanche ain't that good." Pace backed up a step or two. Flicked a glance at the rifle he'd leaned against a mesquite tree.

Possum's hand found the handle of his pistol. Three against two. The Comanches had no firearms, but the chief had a quiver on his back and the younger warrior had that lance. We could make an even fight of it, Possum decided, if Pace can reach that rifle.

Abruptly, the chief turned his horse away and galloped back toward the hills, kicking up dust. The other two Comanches followed. The lad with the lance hesitated for a moment, shaking the weapon in Possum's direction.

"What was all that about, Cap?"

"Damn if I know. Something about you musta spooked 'em. Mebbe it was your red beard. You'd think they woulda seen red hair before."

"Well, they scared me."

"Me, too," said Pace. "I thought it was gonna be a friendly visit. I believe I will accept your invitation. For a whiskey, I mean."

They found the hotel bar empty in mid-afternoon. Pace rapped on the counter with his pistol. That brought a scrawny barman out from the rear. "Whiskey," demanded Pace. "*Dos whisky.*"

Two shot glasses appeared in front of them. After the barman poured, Pace grabbed the bottle. "We'll take that table by the window," he said to Possum. "Bring them glasses."

"Cap," said Possum as they settled into chairs. "Been thinking on it. Them Comanches jumped when I said 'buffalo woman'."

"I believe you're right." Pace gulped down his shot of whiskey and poured himself another. "That's what set them off."

"You think it might be my friend Cassandra?"

Pace studied his whiskey glass. "Your Indian friend Tongue told me all about her, how she knew medicine plants and magic. And how she run off to save her boy. He thinks she's safe. Made herself valuable to the Comanches as a witch woman or something."

"The other thing—remember Willie Kinney taking an arrow in the ass? The Comanches came back to get Sandra's boy-child. I always thought she done sent them for him."

Pace refilled Possum's glass and topped off his own. "You got it right. I mean, about this whiskey. It's better than those Columbia corn-squeezings."

"Do Comanches come to San Pedro Springs very often? Cap, you could ask them about Cassandra."

Pace emptied his glass. "I could. But I ain't gonna. You seen the way they acted." He set his glass down and refilled it.

"Maybe Tongue could ask. Talk to them Indian to Indian, kinda."

"There's enough hatred between Tongue and the Comanches to fill a water trough." Page laughed and poured himself more whiskey. "Fear, too. He don't mind scouting against the Apaches, but he don't want no business with the Comanches."

"He told me, 'Bad business to shoot at a Comanche'."

"Times are changing, Red. There's more of us all the time, and fewer of them. They know it, too. What with Jack Hayes hurrahing them back in the hills, and more settlers moving in, it's just a matter of time." Pace settled back in his chair, relaxing. His eyelids drifted down.

The whiskey's working on him, Possum thought. That arrow wound likely bothers him more than he'll say. Pace had held the bottle in his right hand to pour, and then set it down to pick up his glass. He hadn't used his left arm at all. Guess Cruz is right; it's paralyzed.

"Red," Pace said suddenly, "Whatcha gonna do?"

"Do?"

"Where will you go? You could stay with the Rangers, you know. Join Jack Hayes and his company and fight Comanches. Learn their palaver. Find your colored lady friend."

"I ain't thought about it." Possum had never mentioned Davy Crockett to anyone. Now that the search had proved fruitless, and rescuing Cassandra seemed to be a remote possibility, he had no goals pressing on him.

"Or, you could join up with my troop and chase Apache raiders. We patrol the bandit trail between here and Laredo. Likely you'd meet up with that skunk Bleeker."

That idea seemed more attractive. Not so much because of Bleeker. Patrolling to the south might mean that he would see María Benavides. "Cap," Possum began.

Pace snored, a thin whistle of escaping breath. Slumped in his chair with his head tilted back, the Captain had fallen asleep.

He's earned a rest, Possum thought. He picked up the whiskey bottle. It was half empty, and most of the whiskey had gone in Pace's glass. Possum considered pouring himself another but decided against it.

He leaned back and studied the captain. What will become of you, a one-armed Texas Ranger?

Pace had asked the question, "What will you do?" Possum turned that one over in his mind. If he were to stay in Texas and not go scurrying off into the wilderness of the frontier—well, the South Texas plains appealed to him. He liked the idea of life on a Tejano *rancho.* And, of course, María sprang to mind.

María and Cassandra. Cassandra and María. His two loves. He helped himself to another glass of whiskey. Yes, he had to admit, he had been smitten with Cassandra, maybe in love with her. Her exotic nature, her forceful personality, her dark beauty, all those things enchanted him. Once, he would have taken desperate chances to rescue her from the Comanches. Now, older and wiser, he realized that such a venture would have been foolish. It could not succeed.

But María. Ah, his heart leaped at the thought of her quiet, refined beauty. He recalled the graceful dance, the fandango, so exhilarating that night in Victoria. She'd replaced Cassandra in his affections.

He downed the whiskey. A sense of betrayal, an acknowledgement of guilt surged through him. He had made no vows to Cassandra, nor had she given him encouragement. Friends, perhaps. But still...Perhaps, like settling the score with Grady Bleeker, rescuing Cassandra was an obligation that would continue to plague him. Just as he believed he must have a show-down with Bleeker, he still felt a responsibility to help Cassandra.

He downed the whiskey.

Possum started when a tap on his shoulder awakened him. Pace still slept in the chair opposite. I must have dozed off, too, he realized.

"Señor Colorado, you must join us." Eduardo laughed at him. "Ha ha, you were sleeping. That is a good thing to do. We all need the *siesta*."

"And how is my friend, the famous horse thief?"

Possum twisted his neck and saw Juan Torres staring down at him. "I am well, Señor...Torres, is it not?"

"But of course. And I have something that belongs to you." Torres opened his coat and pulled out a saddle pistol. He presented it to Possum, handle first.

"Thankee." Possum examined the weapon; it was indeed the pistol he'd secretly passed to Torres during the trial at Columbia. He stuck in into own his belt, across from its twin.

"I would have returned it to you immediately after the trial, but it seemed expedient for me to leave Columbia in all haste."

"Colorado, you must join us." Eduardo spoke with his customary enthusiasm. "Come and sit at our table."

Possum sat quietly, half awake, trying to ignore the drone of business matters that passed between Eduardo and Juan Torres. Clearly, Don Octavio's affairs were nothing new to Torres. While Torres was now a legal council in San Antonio, it soon became evident his relationship with Don Octavio went back many years. Perhaps they knew each other in Mexico, in Carmago across the Rio Grande, when Torres was known by the name of Torreón.

"This will interest you, too, Colorado." Eduardo unbuttoned his shirt and retrieved an oilskin packet. He unlaced it and removed some yellowed documents, which he placed on the table. "Our original grant of land in Texas is explained in these documents. *Aquí es* our title to a *porcion* along the *Río Bravo del Norte*. You call it the Rio Grande.

And our *rancho* on the Nueces River."

Torres shuffled the documents back and forth between himself and Possum. They were written in an archaic Spanish that Possum couldn't interpret.

"I will take them to court and have them certified." Torres carefully folded the papers and replaced them in the packet. "I will find two men to swear to their authenticity. You, Eduardo, are too young; you are not of an age. The *alcalde* of San Antonio will be one of the men. The documents will be duly recorded.

"But as I told Don Octavio last year, these originals must be carefully guarded. Texas is now governed by *americanos* who do not understand our customs. All Tejanos are in danger of losing their lands to evil speculators."

Possum said, "I recall you asking Judge Peavey which code of law he followed, that of Mexico or that of the United States. He didn't give you a satisfactory answer."

Torres nodded. "That is true. He did not know how to answer. I expect the Texas Legislature to codify the American system of jurisprudence. They may have done so by now."

"What must we do?" asked Eduardo.

"I believe you know the answer, young Señor Benavides. It sits at the table with us."

Possum looked back and forth between the two men. Their silence puzzled him for a long moment. He leaped to his feet when he grasped the import of Torres' suggestion.

"No!" exclaimed Possum. "I will not be part of such a plan!"

"But it is now happening often in south Texas, among the better families. The elder daughter becomes wed to an American. Both Mexican and American customs are thus satisfied. Satisfied in a legal way, that is." Torres struck a match and applied it to the end of one of his ever-present cigarillos.

"And Colorado, you have told me that my sister *es muy hermosa*."

"She is beautiful, and I love her. But I will not wed her in a forced marriage. No, I will not do it. No." Possum's thoughts whirled. Are these people insane? Trying to bargain a lovely girl—a lovely woman—like María into a such a marriage for a legal advantage? Anger rose in his gut. He felt sick. Using the lovely María as a poker chip?

He pointed a finger at Eduardo. "You offer to sell your own sister to a stranger. What kind of man are you?"

"Calm yourself," said Torres. He put aside the cigarro and scowled up at Possum. "And sit down. You are disrupting the barroom."

"Please," begged Eduardo. "You do not understand."

Possum sat back down. "It seems plain enough," he muttered.

"But no! You must court her. You must win her yourself." Eduardo leaned closer. "She favors you already."

"*Mita*," said Torres. "Do you think a gentleman, an aristocrat like Don Octavio, would force his only daughter, the jewel of his eye, into a loveless marriage?" He picked up the cigarillo and studied it. "María Benavides will marry a man of her own choosing. Believe it."

Possum looked to Eduardo, still wondering what was taking place.

"It is true," Eduardo said. "You wish to take my sister for a bride? You must pay court to her."

Torres waved his hand at the bartender. "This calls for the finest *aguardiente*, my friends. For today, our *amigo* Colorado begins life's most interesting journey.

"Then we go to a dance on Soledad street," said Eduardo, all smiles and excitement. "I will teach you the gentleman's part of the fandango. You will learn the courtship ways of the Spanish in the New World."

Possum bowed his head and sighed. And smiled a secret smile.

PART FOUR

Chapter 27

He reined in his horse on the ridge overlooking Rancho Benavides and swept his gaze across the moonlit plains before him. The two-story *casa mayor* gleamed white under the full moon's rays. Faggots blazed on posts along the high fence. Two torches beckoned to him from the sides of the main gate.

His horse nickered and pawed the ground.

"Patience, my friend. You know the procedure. We must always check our path before taking it. All appears clear ahead." He flipped the reins and the horse jumped into a gallop, headed for the gates of the rancho.

"*Bienvenidos*, Don Colorado!" A *vaquero* threw open the big gate, grinning broadly.

"*Gracias*, Felipe. It is good to be back. Is everything well?"

"Sí, Don Colorado. All is well here at the rancho."

Red passed the horse's reins to Felipe and hurried to the main house. He hesitated when he saw María standing in the doorway, silhouetted by lamplight from within. God, what a picture she was! Her long hair hung down on both sides of her shoulders. The outline of her tall, slender body beneath a silken gown made him catch his breath.

"My husband—is all well with you?" She started towards him.

He rushed to meet her and took her in his arms. "Now it is well, my wife. The world is right again. I am so glad to be back, to take you in my arms."

"And I have ached to have your arms about me. How did you fare with the *volantes*?"

"All will be told. But first, I would rest by the fire and look at you."

In preparation for Red's return, *vaqueros* had carried a burning mesquite log into the main room and arranged it in a corner. The great room had no chimney; smoldering coals carried from outside provided the only heat. Red and María shared a leather-covered wooden bench facing the glowing mesquite embers.

"The children are well?" he asked as he settled onto the seat.

"Very well. David tries the patience of everyone, even Lupe. He is never still. And baby Graciela grows so fast!"

"I must thank your mother again for sending Lupe to us."

"Yes, she has been a blessing. My husband, your David tried to stay awake to greet you."

"Your pardon." A fat little *Tejano* appeared behind them, bowing, a platter of food held out for their inspection. "Will Don Colorado partake of supper? And Doña María as well? I have prepared a simple meal."

"Raul, your meals are never simple. Each is a masterpiece." Red held the platter while Raul set a small table in front of them.

"And the wine? A bottle?" Raul asked.

"Very good. Thank you." The wild grapes growing along the Nueces river could be fermented into an excellent wine, one that reminded Red of his native Tennessee.

"Let us bless this meal," murmured María, bowing her head.

"And our reunion," added Red.

Raul's simple meal consisted of finely chopped *cabrito*, barbequed goat flavored with an exotic sauce. Pinto beans with cheese and onions were served with fresh tortillas. Red ate greedily; he'd had short rations while riding with the *volantes*. María matched him, bite for bite, sip for sip of the wine. Red glanced at her from time to time. Her appetite for life never waned.

Sated at last, Red poured the last of the wine and leaned back on the bench. Raul slipped quietly in to remove the little table, leaving Red and María alone by the smoldering mesquite log.

"Now, my husband, tell me of your journey."

Red settled himself more comfortably and began his story. "We met the other *volantes* at the Medina River crossing, as usual. José Angél Garza was elected leader. We received reports of bandits riding against Mexican farmers along the Laredo road."

"Were there reports of Indians? Apaches?"

"No, my *querida*, not this time. We did encounter a group of a dozen Comanches on their way to Mexico. Our numbers were equal, and no fighting took place. I tried talking signs with them, as Paco Ramirez does. He has taught me some Comanche language."

María shuddered, clasping her arms about her. "I fear the Comanches," she said softly.

"We have seen no wild *indios* here at the rancho, not for the past three years, my dear. If the fear is unbearable, we could reclaim the house in Victoria. Or you could move to Carmago for the winter. Your parents would be pleased."

"I will not leave you, my husband."

Red used his knife to lift a coal from the mesquite log and light the end of a cigarillo. He'd picked up the habit of smoking cigarillos from Torres. María deplored chewing tobacco, so he'd given that up.

"You saw no Apaches either?" María frowned.

Red reassured her. No Apaches were seen. "José Angél says the Apaches are packing up and moving to the mountains of western Mexico. The Comanches are too much for them."

"You see?" demanded María. "Even the Apaches fear the Comanches."

Red laughed. "The Comanches would rather raid in Mexico. Or along the hill country above San Antonio where the Germans settle. Or at Austin among the *americano* farmers. Our rancho is larger and stronger. And I am here to protect you," he added with a chuckle.

"Continue," she muttered. "About the *volantes*."

"As you know, this was my third patrol with them. At first they doubted me. Now, they value me because I am good at reading tracks. I have proven that I am willing to stand and fight. And, I am becoming a better horseman than I was." He'd found that horsemanship ranked high among the *Tejanos*. At fiestas, they would challenge even the Comanches to feats of horsemanship.

"As I said, we did locate a bandit gang on the Laredo road. Preying on the farmers in the area, and robbing travelers. José Angél marveled that I could track them through the chaparral, but I found it easy."

"And what did you do with the bandits?'

"They fought. We had no choice. Sadly, there were several young lads among them. Mexicans. We pleaded with them, but they were afraid to surrender."

"Ah." María shifted uneasily in her seat. "That reminds me, my husband. Cruz has something to discuss with you."

"It will wait until morning." Red took María by the hand and helped her to her feet. "Let us retire."

María favored him with a knowing smile.

Young David, bursting with energy, raced back and forth in the big room, pretending that he rode a horse.

"Lupe, please take that child out onto the patio. Perhaps the cold air will slow him down." María held the infant Graciela in her arms. "What will it be like when that boy is older?" she asked Red.

"Good morning, good morning." Emiliano doffed his hat and helped himself to a seat near the smoldering log. "Ah, we have *huevos rancheros* this morning. He reached for a plate and began helping himself to breakfast. "Colorado, how went the patrol?"

"A quiet one this time. Merely a few bandits to deal with. Perhaps, Emiliano, you are ready to replace me when another patrol is called."

"No." interjected María. "He is still too young. Emilito, you must wait for your adulthood. Papa would be furious if you joined them now."

"My *cumpleaños* is almost here," insisted Emilio.

"Who would tell Don Octavio, anyway?" asked Red.

"Any one of the *vaqueros* would tell Papa. Certainly Cruz would. Who waits to talk with you, remember." María handed her infant girl to Lupe, who had followed little David back into the house. "Cruz has been patient."

"Very well," said Red. "I must be on my rounds anyway."

"I will accompany you." Emilio grabbed a tortilla and followed.

Cruz squatted on his haunches on the patio outside, catching the morning sun. He sprang to his feet when Red approached. "Don Colorado, *buenos días*." He took Red's hand and shook it vigorously.

Red bit off the end of a cigarillo and appraised Cruz. The man wore a perpetual harsh expression on his face, but Red had learned to read the nuance of an eyebrow, a flared nostril or the twitch of a cheek.

"Cruz, my friend, something is bothering you."

Cruz cut his eyes at Emiliano and waited silently.

"*Mita*, Cruz, everyone knows about it. The *vaqueros* have seen him. Even María knows." Emiliano stomped his foot angrily.

"Knows what?" Red stopped in the act of striking a match. He stared at Emiliano. "What?" he repeated.

"Comanche," said Cruz, still watching Emiliano.

Red waited but Cruz said no more. He turned to Emiliano. "What Comanche?"

"The *vaqueros* say that a little band of Comanches is camped by the river, a good four miles upstream, in a grove of trees. Not doing any harm, just camped there."

Red struck his match and held it to the end of the cigarillo, thinking. So that's why María was worried about Comanches. A band camped close by.

Cruz and Emiliano were watching for his reaction, waiting silently.

He shook out the match. "So, did anyone talk with them?"

"Cruz scouted them," said Emiliano. When Cruz scowled at him, he added, "Well, everybody knows you did. The *vaqueros*, they all know."

Cruz spoke up. "It is true, Don Colorado. I crept up upon them. Four braves and a woman. They have been there for six days. I could have taken their horses. I waited for you to return."

Red raised his eyebrows. If Cruz could take the Comanche's horses, he was better than most Apaches. Still, nothing about Cruz surprised him. Don Octavio had complete confidence in the man. Red sometimes felt Octavio watching him through Cruz's eyes.

"They do no harm?" Red asked, puffing his cigarillo to life.

"There is more," said Emiliano. He looked at Cruz.

"The one Comanche," said Cruz. "A warrior. Each morning he rides up from the river and waits. He watches the *rancho*. He goes back to the river at sundown."

"Now that is indeed strange," said Red.

"I told you," said Emiliano to Cruz.

Cruz watched Red, waiting quietly.

What could they want? Red gazed out across the patio. A beef, a longhorn? No, they could have taken one and who would know? Medicine? Don Pablo was still in business, as far as he knew, near the San Antonio river. Well, it was a mystery.

"Have Felipe saddle a horse," Red commanded. I will see what they want. "Come with me, Cruz? Not you, Emiliano; if trouble starts, I want you here with your sister."

Red and Cruz stopped a hundred yards away from the Comanche warrior. He didn't move. Still as a statue, he simply watched them. Red had used his little telescope to examine the Comanche from a mile away. There was nothing distinguishing about him.

"What do you think?" Red asked.

Cruz gave a noncommittal grunt. He checked to see that his boot knife was in place.

The warrior slowly lowered his lance and pointed it at Red. He made a come-here gesture with the lance, not stabbing or threatening, just a beckoning motion. After repeating the gesture twice, he sat still again.

"Let's go see what he wants," said Red.

"Wait," said Cruz. "I go first."

"He meant me." Red checked his pistol. It was loaded and a cap was in place under the hammer. "Cruz, stay here unless I beckon to you. If I wave—skedaddle back to the rancho and get the *vaqueros*." He was sure that Cruz would protect María first and foremost.

When Red was within ten yards of the statuesque warrior, two additional Comanches rode out of the oak grove. Red checked his horse and drew his pistol. He started to wave to Cruz, ordering him back to the rancho.

Something about one of the Comanches caught his eye. Red froze, staring. The Comanche smiled broadly, white teeth gleaming from a black face.

Cassandra!

Could it be? Yes, it was. She wore a shapeless dress of animal skins sewn together, some with the fur on the outside, some inside. Her face was painted with white designs. Circles of white surrounded her eyes. Her hair exploded in all directions, abundant and kinky. Red could see ribbons in it. Was it adorned with animal bones, too? She was a frightening spectacle.

She raised a palm high in the air. "Possum?"

Thunderstruck, in awe of her changed appearance, he raised his own palm and nodded his head.

Cassandra kept licking her lips, searching for words. Has she lost her English? Red kneed his mount closer to her. He realized that Cruz was right behind him, contrary to orders.

"You grown. You—man now." Cassandra smiled.

"What are you?"

She frowned. "They—call me—*Bruja*. Witch."

Red walked his horse forward and reached a hand to Cassandra. She took it and held it. Red bit back a smile. Cassandra, always so meticulous in her grooming, now smelled of rancid bear grease.

The two warriors stirred nervously on their steeds. Cruz eased up behind him. Red released Cassandra's hand.

"Sandra," he said, "Come with us to the rancho. Live with us. You will be safe here." He looked toward the oak grove. "Is Marcus with you?"

"He—raid in Mexico. Comanche warrior now."

Red said, "I worried about you for a long time. I tried to find a way to rescue you but I failed."

Cassandra nodded solemnly. "I hear."

"Please, come back with me. To the *rancho*."

"No." Cassandra sat straight in her saddle. "I am Comanche now. Warrior's—wife. In your world—slave."

"I would never…."

"White Texas slave country. I—happy with Comanche."

Was she happy? At least, he knew she was safe. Comparatively safe. No Comanche would be safe for long.

"More—thing," said Cassandra. She beckoned to the warrior who rode with her.

Is this her husband, Red wondered? He was no stripling.

"He—thank you," she said. "You bury his father." She spoke to the man, a guttural speech. He nodded and held out his hand, a gesture of friendship. Red took the hand and they shook, a broad motion, three times.

Cruz spoke up in a loud voice, a language unintelligible to Red. The Comanche nodded and replied to Cruz, speaking more softly.

"You honored his father," said Cruz. "You gave him burial, by your custom. This man watched you. He came back for his dead father. You bury him."

"I remember." Red gasped. The Indian raid on the Kinney's cabin, so long ago. Red had insisted on burying the Indian he had killed. Tongue kept saying someone was watching them. Did the Comanche know that Red was the one who killed his father? Probably not. He only saw Red bury the body.

The Comanche trotted his horse back to the oak grove.

"Comanches not attack *rancho*. You safe. All safe." Cassandra spoke to Cruz, who nodded to her. "I put spell on *rancho*."

The warrior returned. Smiling broadly, he held a rope over his shoulder. The other end of the rope led to a bedraggled specter of a man, tied by his wrists. He stumbled, blubbering and moaning. The warrior handed the rope to Red and pushed the man down to the ground. "Gift," he said.

Cassandra and the Comanches kicked their horses into a gallop and sped back to the oak grove.

Red stared at the creature writhing before him in the dirt. "No, no, no..." came a whining plea. Red dismounted, an instant ahead of Cruz. What kind of gift was this? Were the Comanches returning a hostage?

The man rolled onto his back, sobbing. His nose was gone, only a burned scar remained. Both ears were missing. One eye was an empty socket. Tears poured from the other.

There was something familiar about him.

Red sat back on his heels, staring. Grady Bleeker. The Comanches had relieved South Texas of a bandit gang. The gang leader was Cassandra's gift to Red. In payment of an old debt.

Chapter 28

Autumn in South Texas brings its own delights. Red and his family gathered on the patio at *Rancho Benavides* to watch the sunset. Puffy white clouds tinged with orange floated across the sky, harbingers of cooler weather and fall rains to come. David leaped flatfooted from the yard's dry grass onto the patio's stone. Red, ever the tracker, noted the trail the boy left behind. Crushed grass stems coated with termite dirt marked his wake.

"A man comes." Cruz appeared at Red's elbow. He spoke to Red but fixed his gaze on María.

"My husband, this man worries me."

"Nothing to concern you, my dear. He is an old friend. He comes alone." Red gained his feet. "Come," he beckoned to Cruz, "let us greet him at the gate."

The lone rider approached slowly, walking his horse toward them, at least a half-mile away. Red marveled at the odd means of communication his *vaqueros* used. Information passed from *rancho* to *rancho*, *Tejanos* and mission *indios* somehow involved, but effective enough that his *vaqueros* warned him of events near his *rancho*.

Red stepped outside the gate and waved his hat. The rider nudged his steed into a rapid trot to reach the gate.

"Welcome, Micah. Step down."

Cruz took charge of the horse. Red led Micah around the big *sillar* block house to the patio behind, where his family waited.

María rose to her feet; her hands swept nervously at her skirts.

"May I present my wife, Doña María *de* Benavides *y* Castillón? My dear, this is my friend Captain Micah Pace of the Texas Rangers."

Solemn-faced, María bobbed her head, her eyes fixed on the captain.

Pace, his hat held across his chest, bowed low. "Tales of your enchanting—beauty—." His Spanish failed him and he stuttered. He'd planned a little speech, but lost track of it.

"We speak English very well, Captain," stated María in a flat tone.

"My apologies."

"Micah, these are our children," Red hastily interjected. "Our son David and daughter Graciela. Our youngest, our infant Octavio, is asleep upstairs. He's had a long day."

David stepped forward and, grinning, shook hands with Micah. Graciela buried her face in her mother's skirts. María beckoned to Lupe the nurse. "Take the children into the house," she said quietly.

"And the two young men? The twins? Your brothers?" Pace smiled at María.

"Emiliano is in Boston, learning to be a doctor," said Red. "He assisted Don Pablo for a year. Now he wants to learn how Yankees practice medicine."

"Don Pablo?"

"You should remember Don Pablo. He took the arrow from your shoulder."

Pace looked at the floor. "You know, Red, I don't remember much about that time." He shuffled his feet.

"My brother Eduardo is in San Antonio. He learns the law with Juan Torres," said María.

"I ain't seen him."

María lifted her chin. "Captain, you come armed into our home." She frowned at the large leather strap draped across Pace's shoulder.

Pace hastily pulled the strap from his shoulder. "My apologies, Doña María. I bring a gift for your husband." He handed it to Red. "Heft one of those hog-legs," he said, grinning.

The strap supported a pair of pistols, twin six-shooters in holsters.

"It's a heavy rig, ain't it?" Red drew one of the pistols and tested its weight."

"Captain Walker told Sam Colt he wanted a pistol heavy enough to use as a club when it was empty." Pace laughed. "I don't think he's clubbed anybody with it yet."

Red pointed the pistol toward the sunset and sighted along the barrel.

"Walker got tired of the damn Patterson five-shooter. It's too hard to reload, especially in a fight. Changing out the cylinders is a—." He glanced at María. "Hard to do with arrows coming at you."

"It's a fine pistol," said Red.

"Walker drew up what he wanted, and Sam Colt made it."

Red re-holstered the weapon and offered the rig to Pace. "I can't accept it. It's a fine pair of weapons, and I thank you for the offer, but I can't accept."

Pace refused to take them back. "No, they are a gift to you."

"Captain Pace." María drew herself up to her full height. Arms folded over her chest, she glared at him. "What brings you here? What is it that you want?"

Pace looked out across the patio at the darkening evening sky. "I am here to ask Red if he will—well, do some scouting for us."

María scowled at him. "What scouting?"

"Patience, *querida*," said Red, addressing her in Spanish. "Captain, what did you have in mind?"

"Mebbe we could talk in private," mumbled Pace, eyeing María uneasily.

"There are no secrets between us," said María.

Red said, "That's right. Whatever you got to say, we'll all hear it."

"Look, Red. You done a fine job with them *volantes* of yours. Keeping bandits off the Laredo road and all." He hesitated, looking at María. "Matter of fact, I'm authorized to offer Walker Colt pistols to your company of vigilantes."

"And why is that?" asked María.

Pace gazed at Red, a silent plea in his eyes.

"I think the captain is pleased by the work we've done in chasing bandits. Ain't that right, Cap?"

"Look, both of you. Your *volantes* ride as vigilantes. That's illegal now in Texas. We're part of the United States and their laws don't allow it. You will need some kind of formal recognition."

"Mexico still claims us," insisted María. "We only protect ourselves. We don't bother you. Why do you care?"

Pace eyed her for a moment. "War is coming," he said at last. "If it hasn't started already. Zachary Taylor has marched south from Corpus Christi."

"We know that," said Red.

Pace stared at Red. "Well," he said, "News gets around. Taylor will fight. President Polk wants this war, I'm told. He will invade Mexico."

"Mexico is a big country," María said. "Mexicans will defend themselves."

"Is it about the *despoblado*, this country between the Nueces and Rio Grande rivers?" Red waved his arms. "Why can't they just sit down together and work out an agreement. You can't grow cotton here. Why do the Yankees want it, anyway?"

"I don't know, Red. Mebbe it's more complicated than that."

"So you are here to stop the volantes from riding?" María unfolded her arms and pointed a finger at Pace. "Then why do you offer them these fine weapons?"

"No, no. no." Pace took off his hat and wiped his forehead on his shirtsleeve. Red was startled to see that his hair had turned stone gray.

"All right," said Pace. "I will lay my cards on the table. Red, I want you back in the Rangers. I want you to bring your *volantes* with you, as many as will come. I am forming a company of Rangers to ride with Zachary Taylor's army when he invades Mexico."

María gave in to cynical laughter.

Red stared at Pace, dumbfounded. "Do you know what you're asking of us, Cap?"

"My husband!" María burst into rapid Spanish. "Remove this old man, this dog, this crazy man from our *rancho*. Else I will have Cruz kill him!"

Cruz, who had been standing against the patio wall, took a step forward.

Red waved Cruz back. "Captain Pace," he said, "Are you aware that my wife's family has been here, in this place, for a hundred years? They have defended it against Indians. Against bandits. This has been Mexico, nothing more, nothing less, for decades."

"It's Texas now."

"It always was. We are *Tejanos*. I have become a *Tejano*. María's family has accepted me as one of them. Do you expect me to turn on them? Turn my coat?"

"Red, this is the United States now. Texas has joined the union. You stand on American soil."

"Cap, you know Mexico disputes that."

"So," said Pace. "You will not fight with us."

Red offered the weapons to Pace once more. This time, Pace accepted them.

María walked over to stand beside her husband. "I think you had better go," she said softly.

"Night has fallen, *querida*. The captain should stay until morning."

"I can find my way to the river. I will camp there tonight." Pace put on his hat and hefted the strap holding the weapons. He threw it over his shoulder. "It wasn't my intention to insult you, Doña María. Or your family."

She drew a deep breath. "I am sorry."

Pace smiled at Red and extended his right hand. After a moment, Red grasped it and shook it.

"You have come very far, my friend, from the frightened lad I first met in Columbia. Possum, you called yourself then."

"Those days—they seem like a dream now, a time of bits and pieces, broken memories. I thank you, Micah, for sheltering me in the Rangers."

"Have you caught up with that snake that gave you so much trouble? Bleeker?"

María spoke up. "That poor man is buried in our *campo santo*. The graveyard beside our little chapel."

"Ah." Pace waited, but no further explanation was forthcoming.

"Well," he said, "I wish you good fortune. You and your family. Keep a close watch, my friends. Difficult times are coming."

"We've fought off Apaches, bandits, and two Mexican armies on their way to San Antonio." Red laughed. "I expect we can take care of ourselves." He put his arm around María's waist.

Cruz had brought Pace's horse up beside the patio. Pace mounted with difficulty, his left arm dangling useless. On the third try, he managed to heave himself into the saddle. Cruz made no effort to assist him.

Pace turned one last time, and offered a salute. "*Adiós*," he cried.

"*Vaya con Dios*," Red called after him.

"My husband, do you miss the bugle call to battle?" María smiled at Red.

"*Dios*, no! I am starving. Where is that rascal Raul?"

Printed in Great Britain
by Amazon